THE CREATIONS OF BELIEF

The Lost Goddess

K. C. Morgan

PublishAmerica

Baltimore

First printing

ISBN: 1-59129-746-X
PUBLISHED BY PUBLISHAMERICA BOOK PUBLISHERS
www.publishamerica.com
Baltimore

Printed in the United States of America

This book is dedicated to

My dad
Gary Klinglesmith
(who will always be my biggest fan)
You picked me up when I fell, you loved me when I was impossible, and
you fought in my corner when I needed it the most. Thank you for
supporting my dreams.
Thank you for making them take flight in my mind to begin with.
Love you, Dad

And for the best friend anyone's ever had,
Angela Decker
You are the person I tell **everything** to, the one who I can call when I need
to cry, the one who agrees with me even when I'm wrong, and the one who
celebrates my achievements. Thank you for being even happier than me
when I succeed at something. And thank you, Angie-la, for being there
when no one else was. You **are** the best.

And to my grandparents
Faurest and Retha Klinglesmith
You've done more for me than I can ever begin to list,
and I will always love you two for giving me a real home
when no one else could.

Author Acknowledgments

The author wishes to thank her mother, Lois Noroozi, for not only being a wonderful mother but for also being a die-hard English professor at all times. Without her, this novel would surely be full of grammatical errors that would frighten anyone.

Thanks also should go out to Adam Gardner, for being such a wonderful sounding board for all the author's off-the-wall ideas.

Thank you so much to Morgan's Photography in Louisville, Kentucky for helping with the photographs of the author. Hey, guys, how about a discount next time?

A huge thank you also goes to the rest of the author's family—Blake McGowan, Brandon McGowan, Brent McGowan, and Carolyn Klinglesmith—for coming through at crunchtime. Certain deadlines would never have been met without these four perfect and wonderful people. They should be thanked not only for putting up with more drama than is necessary simply because of fault of proximity to a flighty and eccentric writer, but also for coming through in a pinch.

And, of course, to my wonderful editors and publishers, without whom no one would ever read this book. All errors in this book could never possibly be theirs, but belong solely to the author.

PROLOGUE

Every day was the same. Always the same people, always the same amusements to pass the time, always the same foods…always the same view. Every day, passing quietly like the one before it and the one before that, and on and on and on for the past six months. She could no longer remember with any clarity what life had been like before life was just this…this nothingness. She knew there had once been life, fun and parties and boyfriends and family and friends and sunshine. But she could no longer remember it. The memories were too old and faded, hazy and out of focus, as if someone had taken the pictures from her mind and clouded them.

It was only bits and pieces she remembered clearly. The feel of sand beneath her feet; the noise running bath water made when the tub was full of bubbles; the smell of her latest reckless cooking attempt burning and charring away in one of her old pots; the sound of a ringing telephone… Yes, she could remember those things. She just couldn't remember what it had been like, felt like, to actually live. It seemed that she hadn't been alive in so long, that living was no longer reality.

No, reality was death. And ending. That, too, was real to her now. Coldness, loneliness, contemplation, and too much time—yet conversely, there was too little time, and that was the problem.

So she lay here, day after day, and suffered the sameness and the monotony. There were still cards lining the walls, and flowers that came every week or so and wilted. The white roses she always kept right on the windowsill, all purity and elegance and prettiness to make her feel…something. The other flowers wilted around the rest of her small sickroom, the fragrances blending together into one to sicken her and remind her of funeral parlours. White candles lined the tabletops, so that flame and cards swayed gently in the breeze from the open window.

Young autumn air had carried a chill this morning and she knew that soon the window would have to remain closed. Leaves had started to turn blazing colours, all bright and beautiful for one last time before winter came with its

7

bleakness and its death. What a joke, she thought. She hadn't grown more beautiful, nor blazed in one last glorious flash, before death came to sweep her into oblivion. No, she'd grown paler and thinner and was wasting away here, while the trees dropped bright, lovely leaves on green grass and nature said good-bye to warmth and growth.

Good-bye, she thought. Good-bye to summer days and warm sunshine and clean, soft breezes. Good-bye movie theatres with too-salty popcorn, good-bye to late-night television, good-bye to reading novels in the bathtub, and good-bye to amusement parks with cotton candy and roller coasters.

The cancer had come without warning. It started with a few cramps in her lower belly, some abnormal bleeding. Two weeks after her twenty-fifth birthday, the doctor said the words that would eventually end her life. "We think it's ovarian cancer—very rare for someone your age, but it does happen occasionally. We're going to treat you with radiation, but first we need to perform surgery to remove the tumors," they'd said...or something to that effect, anyway. She couldn't remember. It had started with an abnormal Pap smear after her checkup, a sonogram that showed a strange mass connected to her right ovary. Soon enough, they'd removed both her ovaries. Just like that, and she would never be able to have children.

So now, she lay here, in this sickroom, every day of her remaining life. And waited. She waited for death, waited for life, waited for some kind of closure. Wishing for death, wishing for the end was a dark and secret thing that she kept hidden away in the very back of her mind. She was only twenty-six, after all, and no one should wish for death at the age of twenty-six. But the half-life she was leading now didn't seem worth it. After all, what was she waiting for? There was no cure for cancer, and after hearing "There's nothing left to do now, but wait" she knew that there wasn't any hope, either.

Her mother came in every day with her crystals and her mysticism, wiggling the prisms over her abdomen and preaching about how positive thinking can change everything. "Mind over matter!" she chanted, with tears in her eyes and regret in her voice.

In fact, everyone treated her differently now. People around her spoke in hushed tones, wore strained and smiling faces, and gazed at her with deep concern and lines at the corners of their eyes.

How she hated it. How she hated staring out this window every single day, watching the world that she would no longer be a part of. How she hated being stuck in this nothingness.

And at night, the dreams and the darkness stole even her bleak sense of reality from her. Strange images and half-formed memories that danced through her thoughts, so that every night was restless and sleepless. Some nights were just too painful, causing her to sit up in bed and chain smoke, waiting for dawn to come. Her life would dance through her head. She would remember the boys, the closeness with her friends, the joy just of existing and the freedom of youth. Other nights were filled with strange nightmares and visions. Faces flashed behind her eyes, voices speaking in guttural syllables that she didn't understand, strange images of lands and structures she'd never before seen. Those nights, she lay awake too, but would lay on her back and stare at the ceiling, her mind too rattled and confused to welcome the sleep that would bring more of the same.

Twenty-six years she'd passed, and now autumn was here again. She would not be around to see the snows come, and the branches turn bare and claw-like. Winter was a time for death and dying, the time to be rid of the old. Soon, spring would come again and the world would welcome life and growth and rebirth.

It was simply her time to leave that all behind.

Death came in the bright and sunny afternoon, while her eyes focused on the soft white rose petals. She felt feral breath against her cheek, a bony hand scrape against her jaw. She welcomed him, as one would welcome the ending to a wonderful movie, with little reluctance and a great sense of joy and completion.

Good-bye to seasons changing. Good-bye to mother's crystals. Good-bye to white roses. Good-bye, life.

CHAPTER ONE

After Life

It was the sound of scraping that caused her eyelids to flutter open, scraping coupled with a cheerful little whistle. Her eyes focused on a wide canopy ceiling of crisp white above her head, and the first thing she realized was that she didn't know where she was. The second thing that came to comprehension was that the pain was gone—that same pain that had haunted her for so long was finally gone.

So where were the angels, the trumpets, the gates of Heaven? Slowly, her eyes burning against the bright sunlight, she looked around her. From where she lay, though, there was little to see beyond thick stone walls and the high bed.

Walls? The thought seemed to echo in her head and then she knew she had to get into a sitting position, no matter how heavy and exhausted she felt. There weren't, after all, supposed to be walls in Heaven…or the other place, for that matter.

Slowly, very slowly, she pulled herself up into a sitting position. Her head ached dully, a thick thumping sensation, and she felt dizzy. Once her eyes adjusted, she could finally make out her surroundings. The room was large, someone's bedroom, she guessed from the furnishings. Herself, she lay in the center of a huge bed. How she got up on it, she couldn't hope to guess, but a small stepladder sat at one side for whoever slept here regularly. The walls were thick stone, the windows no more than chunks cut into the rock and covered over with thickly decorated tapestries, and the floor was a gleaming wood covered over with an ornate rug. The bed itself was the largest she'd even seen, four posters outfitted with sheer white bed curtains and heavier velvet draperies.

The scraping noise that she'd heard was coming from the same location as the whistling, the huge fireplace directly across from the foot of the bed. Judging from where she sat, it looked to be taller than she was, and wider even than the huge bed. A small purple chaise lounge and two elaborate armchairs sat grouped around a small antique table that was holding what looked like an even more antique oil lamp to form a cozy sitting area just between the bed and the fireplace.

An elaborate mantelpiece lorded over the wide stone hearth, where even now a small redhead was cleaning the ashes with a fire poker. As she scraped at the grate, she whistled a breezy little tune.

"Ahhh…excuse me," the woman on the bed squeaked, her voice much harsher than she had expected it to be. Her throat felt like sandpaper.

A rather loud clatter and the redhead turned around with a start, grinning from ear to ear. "Mistress, you're finally awake!" With energy like a jumping bean, she bounded over the chaise and to the side of the bed, green eyes bright with real joy.

"Uhm…yes…I guess I am." Not a very elegant way to introduce herself, she reasoned after the fact.

The little redhead—the woman decided the girl couldn't possibly be more than sixteen—was pulling back the heavy down comforters and the white furs that were piled on the bed, words tumbling out of her like an avalanche. "Everyone is waiting for you downstairs, Mistress—it took you an awful long time to wake up! But don't worry, I have everything all ready and your dress all laid out. There's water for washing over in the basin."

Now the girl had a firm grasp on the woman's upper arm and was pulling back the heavy down comforter, flinging furs and sheets across the room in her haste. "Waiting for me?" the woman repeated, moving like a somnambulist compared to the young girl's eager enthusiasm.

"Of course they are! And for a long time, too! Oh, please move a little faster, Mistress, there's just so much to do." Plaintively, the girl started tugging on a listless arm, until finally the woman took the hint and twisted around so her legs were dangling off the bed.

For less than a moment, the older woman debated arguing with the girl. After all, she hadn't been more than three feet out of bed for the past six months, but of course all that was over now. She had died—she remembered it—she had looked into Death's eyes and she felt her soul float above her body. The body, and the cancer, had now been left behind…

So why did the girl's short little nails digging into her skin hurt so badly?

With a smile that looked as though it appeared readily, the young girl helped the woman from her perch and led her to the window, where a large wooden bowl stood supported on a round table that looked as though it were made just for the task. "You go on and wash up, now, and I'll get your undergarments."

With little choice, the woman did exactly as she was told, taking too long for the young girl's patience to scrub her face and neck. With an exasperated sigh, the young girl removed the sponge from clumsy fingers and took over the job herself, clucking the whole time in soft annoyance at the older woman. Then, without even a word of warning, she grasped the flimsy fabric of a white nightgown the older woman couldn't quite remember ever putting on and yanked it up and off so fast there was nothing the woman could do but yelp.

The high-pitched sound gave the young girl some pause, and bright green eyes blinked up into a startled face with confusion. "Mistress, is something wrong?"

"W-what are you *doing*?" She demanded self-righteously, finally regaining some of her wits. Brows screwed together fiercely, she crossed her arms over her body to shield her nakedness as best she could.

"Did you…ah…want to dress yourself, Mistress?"

The poor young thing looked so utterly confused that now she just didn't know what to do. "…J-just do whatever it is you normally do, I guess." Was this how the dead were treated? Perhaps she was supposed to be served…perhaps she was going to Heaven soon, or whatever the final resting-place for souls was. She'd never been too sure there was a Heaven, anyway, but she certainly knew she wasn't expecting something quite like this.

The fireplace girl offered a tremor of a smile and went back to her chore, taking the sponge and giving the older woman a brief wash before leading her towards the bed and a pile of fabric that surely wasn't all going to go on her body.

The woman's head was buzzing with questions, and she was in the middle of trying to figure a way to ask them eloquently when her mouth was filled with coarse fabric. Yanking and tugging and moving about her in a circle, the young girl started pulling clothes on her. First, a loose-fitting garment that fell just short of her ankles. It was an ugly thing, gray in color from numerous washings, sleeveless, with a wide scooped neck.

"Mistress, stop fidgeting! What has gotten into you today?" the girl demanded even as she tugged another garment over the woman's head on top of the other, this one a white silk gown-like dress that was much tighter, still sleeveless, and slightly longer than the first.

"Why do I need two dresses?"

"Two…I'm sorry, Lady, I don't understand," the girl answered, turning her charge around bodily so that they were no longer facing each other. "Surely, your thoughts aren't as scrambled as you want me to think!"

Before the woman could think of a way to rephrase her question, she was assaulted by what could only be described as torment. Suddenly the girl had slid a thick, wide band of fabric around her midsection and started pulling it tight with lacing. "*What are you DOING?!*" Desperation. The woman tried with all her might to jump away from the thing, but the laces were all but tied now, and the thick band had her stomach and waist in a fairly painful vise.

"Lady?" Startled, the girl took a step backwards, and green eyes blinked in confusion when the woman whirled around to face her.

Well! Even if she had just woken up from the dead and all, there was no reason to torture her in this thing—whatever it was! "I am not wearing this!" Petulantly, her face screwed up into a scowl and she crossed her arms under her breasts—her "I'm doing this my way or not at all" position.

The girl looked like she might cry, her face was so confused. "B-but…you always wear a corset, Mistress! The gown won't fit right in just your shift." Pleadingly, she spread out her hands. "This is how we always do it."

The strangeness of the younger woman's statement would not sink in until much, much later—unfortunately. Presently, she was only capable of thinking of ways to get out of the bizarre device she was now trapped in. Even now, her arms were stretched halfway up her back as she futilely tried to rip the laces off her and free her ribcage up for breathing again. "Corset? I've never worn a corset in my entire life—and after this, you can count me out for the entire rest of it!"

Haltingly, the girl took a step forward. "How about I loosen it up for you a little, and then you put on the gown, and we'll see? Mistress?" The poor little thing was almost begging now. "You always say that compromise is what gets people through the rough spots—please, Lady?"

Had she said that to this girl before? Oh, well, it didn't matter. She turned around quickly, and the serving girl chased her hands away to undo the laces. With a long, low sigh, she reveled in breathing freely again as the girl slipped yet another garment over her head. This one was long-sleeved and tight—almost too tight, especially in the arms. The sleeves were tight as if tailor-made for her arms from shoulder to wrist, and tiny white pearls lined the wrists in a pattern up to her elbows. The neckline was nonexistent, dipping down to the corset-thing, and it fell in one seamless sweep down to her ankles, where more pearls decorated the hemline all the way around.

The woman took a step away, the half-formed thought in her head trying to lead herself towards a mirror to find out just what kind of trussed-up Christmas package she looked like in all these clothes when a staying hand on her shoulder stopped her. "Almost done now, Lady."

Almost done? What the heck else could this young thing manage to do to her? Before she could fathom a reply, the girl dropped a cloud of soft silk over her head. She tasted fabric, saw a flash of pink, and felt the girl tying laces and straightening her skirts. Finally, after she'd been patted down and tucked and pulled and pinched, the girl took a step back with a satisfied little sigh. "There now, Mistress. Go and sit by the fire, and I'll get your slippers and your rose so I can dress your hair."

She was going to dress up her *hair* now, too? The things they did to dead people! Resigning herself to more torture, she dutifully went to the plush chaise in front of the fireplace and seated herself.

The girl was rifling through a large wardrobe on the wall by a thick, carved door. She returned sporting a wide smile and an armful of hairpins and silver combs and one thick white rose blossom. "Oh, Milady, you for sure will be the belle of the party tonight! And I'm sure you have so much to tell everyone—aren't you even a little excited? You've done nothing but complain since the Awakening. It must just be jitters. I know how nervous you get in front of crowds." As if forgetting the outburst from the older woman only a few moments previously, the young thing was clucking and chattering happily as she moved combs through thick blonde hair.

By this point, she felt so muddled and tortured she couldn't even think up one intelligent question to ask the girl as her scalp was pulled in fifteen different directions, quick hands moving through her hair deftly. "So...are you some sort of servant? You always prepare people for the Afterlife, or something?" The little thing was obviously a fan of conversation; maybe she could get some information from her by playing along.

The hands paused for only a few seconds before they were moving in her hair again. "I don't understand, Mistress. You know that I am your girl alone."

That didn't make any sense. "Mine alone?"

"Of course, Milady... Of course, you must be pulling at my stem! Aren't you a funny one, now?" She giggled and the hands finally stilled. With a flourish, she plucked the white rose blossom from where it lay on the small table and pinned it into the coif she'd just prepared. "There now, all ready. Go and have a look in the mirror, if you want, Lady."

Finally! She quickly jumped to her feet and glanced around the room, searching for the purported mirror. She saw handmade rugs on wooden floorboards, elaborately decorated tapestries on stone walls that looked a little too thick, and expensive antique furnishings—but no mirror. "Ah…where, exactly, is the mirror?"

The girl looked up from where she busied herself straightening the bedclothes, red eyebrows raised up like question marks. "Milady? You have forgotten where your own mirror is?"

"How am I supposed to know—I only just got here!" She felt a need to defend herself all of a sudden, because this young girl had a strange way of making her feel like she was missing something very important.

"…Of course." She smiled tremulously and pointed to the huge wardrobe doors. "On the door, there, Milady." Her hand wavered slightly.

She nodded briskly and made her way over to the mirror, tripping herself up on the long skirts three times in just the few steps that she walked. "I think this is all too long," she called out over her shoulder as she pulled open one surprisingly heavy wardrobe door.

And nearly fell over in shock!

"Is that me?" The whisper came out before she could control it, and she took a hesitant hand and touched the mirror to be sure it was really a reflection of herself. The blonde hair that had lain so limp and lifeless for so long was gleaming, swept up into an impressive pile of curls and decorated with small gemstones and satin ribbons winding around a tight crown of braids at the top of her head. Soft, loose curls hung around her face to frame her rosy cheeks—rosy cheeks, she wondered, when was the last time her wan complexion had supported such loveliness?—and pouting lips. The huge white blossom was tucked up next to the curls, a bright white burst to set off big blue eyes.

And the gown! Oh, my, the gown! This was really the stuff that dreams were made of, she thought. If only she'd had a heroine that looked like this while she was growing up, playing Barbie and watching Disney. Even Shakespeare had never envisioned something like this! The layers the girl had dragged her into made her skirts look fuller, while the corset had cinched her waist into something small enough for a man's hand to span. The gown itself was almost transparent pink silk, the long white gown underneath it shining through in the light. Bell sleeves fell back when she moved her arms to reveal the elaborate embroidery of the under gown, and the front of the gown fell just short of the under gown to show more of the painstaking pearl work at her hem. A long, glittering train decorated with more gemstones dragged the floorboards behind her, and when she raised her arms she saw silken ribbons and lace lining the dangling bell sleeves. The bodice was a bit too low cut, she thought, but my, how impressive the swell of cleavage looked in that corset thing! Wonder bra, say good-bye, she thought with a tiny little giggle.

"Does it please you, Milady?" The woman turned to see the young girl perched on the foot of the bed, timid eyes watching her closely.

"It's beautiful—glorious! I'm almost ready to die all over again." She grinned. Spinning around to better admire herself, she was swishing her full skirts across the highly polished floors.

"...Milady?" The young girl shook her head, which the older woman had noticed she did whenever she was too confused to form a reply.

"Never mind...now that you have me all dolled up, what am I supposed to do next? I mean...this is some sort of holding area right? Am I going to Heaven?" As if the cobwebs over her brain had been shaken free, she suddenly bubbled over with questions and thoughts.

The girl raised her hands in front of her as though she could physically block the verbal onslaught aimed at her. "Mistress, what are you saying? You know that everyone awaits you belowstairs, in the Main Hall."

Ah, so that was where she would find the answers to all her questions. Purposefully, she spun on her heel and took off toward the door, nearly falling over in a heap when the toe of one soft silk slipper caught the long pink train of her gown.

But the girl was suddenly next to her, steadying her with a quick hand. "Milady, slow down! You know they won't leave without you." She smiled. "Just call me if you need anything."

"But what should I call you?" She'd been almost halfway to the door when she realized she didn't know the girl's name. It seemed only right they should acquaint themselves, even if she would never see the little serving girl again.

The girl was silent a moment, then she laughed. "Aren't you always one for kidding! Of course, you know my name! Go on, now, before Eury eats all your chocolates!" With a little shove at the small of her back, the girl somehow managed to send her right through the bedroom door, which the woman could have sworn was closed just a little while ago.

And with that, she was all alone for the first time since her death.

The hall she stood in was deserted and endless. It stretched off in both directions and each end turned off into another hall at a sharp ninety-degree angle. Beyond that, she could not see how far the rest of the hall went—but already she could tell the place was huge. And the funny thing was, it didn't look ethereal or Heaven-like at all. It was solid, all stone (she rapped against a wall with a knuckle just to be sure and came away sore, so she knew it was as real as her). Doors and other hallways branched off from this main one, and a few feet to her right stretched the most impressive staircase she'd ever seen. It curved and twisted downward in a spiral shape, but no matter how far she leaned over to look at it, she couldn't tell where it was leading to. But the girl had said "belowstairs," so she had no other choice but to place a steadying hand on the polished wooden banister, and make her descent.

As she carefully picked a path down the soft red carpet of the stairs, one fist firmly holding her long skirts out of the way, she saw that the staircase had a twin, and the two sets of stairs curved and spiraled around each other. They stopped at a large landing, where one wide set of stairs led straight down into what she could only assume was the "main hall," as the serving girl had called it. She wanted to pause and gather her wits by sitting in one of the plush burgundy chairs at the landing, but decided it was best to get the formalities over with first.

The Afterlife, so far, was nothing like she'd expected. Where were the choirs of angels, the thousand trumpets? Not a religious person by nature, she had never put much stock in blind faith. But then it seemed that she'd suffered some sort of illness…not that she could really remember anymore, but somewhere in the back of her mind she seemed to recall an illness of some sort that made her reevaluate the whole idea of an Afterlife. But whatever the case, she hadn't expected something as solid as rooms with doors inside huge houses and custom-built staircases that, while impressive, could be seen where she'd just come from. As she fingered the silk dress she decided she wasn't too disappointed…but she would like some explanation as to what, exactly, was going on.

So, sucking in her breath and holding her back straight, she started down the final flight of stairs.

She'd made it less than halfway down when the sounds of revelry drifted up to her ears. "A party?" she murmured. And that's what it sounded like— one huge party. She heard voices; so many voices it sounded like a thousand people talking at once, and laughing and glasses clinking. Was it Heaven? She raised her skirts more and started down the staircase at a much faster clip.

It was when the room finally came into view that she froze completely, halted on the stairs in her tracks. This was no Heaven like any she'd ever imagined, and it didn't appear to be the other place, either. It looked like…well, to be honest, she thought it looked most like a big costume ball, or Halloween party.

The room was huge—*huge*—with a soaring forty-foot ceiling that she knew for a fact extended straight up to the second floor, for she'd tried to lean over the railing and peek down at this room, only the winding staircases had blocked her view. Now she knew what a view she'd been missing. She wished she could have seen it beforehand, or else it would have taken twenty people to drag her from the quiet, peaceful bedroom!

The biggest room she'd ever laid eyes upon and it was so crowded with people it was a wonder any of them had room enough to stand. She thought she caught glimpses of expensive furnishings and rugs on par with those in the bedroom upstairs between the groups of people, but couldn't be sure.

It was the way they were dressed that made her hesitant. All manner of dress, the strangest array she had ever imagined! They wore costumes and clothing the likes of which she had never thought of. Every creed and color and race and type of person in existence (and she wasn't sure, but it looked as though there were some new breeds in the mix, as well) filled the room to overflowing. She saw one man wearing a full suit of armor, and one woman was wearing a dress that looked like clouds, it was so light and shimmering and transparent on her. But they all laughed and talked with each other in such perfect harmony…surely this couldn't be anything but Heaven!

Still, she didn't move. Her eyes remained glued on the scene below her, while her heart pounded like a parade drum. Something in the back of her mind niggled at her. She felt as though there was a big piece of a puzzle missing, just missing completely, and she felt like she should know what that piece was and fit it back into place. It troubled her, and turned her feet into lead.

Until a loud shriek rent the air. "LOVE!" A young woman, she guessed about the same age as herself, was suddenly bounding up the stairs like a shot. Thin, bare arms were wrapped around her neck in a fierce hug before she could dodge. "Oh, Love, how good it is too finally see you! And looking every bit as gorgeous as ever!" The strange woman, who was clad most oddly in a long belted white gown that fell in thin pleats to her sandaled feet and swum around her willowy figure loosely, tucked her arm through her captive's, shining a brilliant smile at her. She noticed incongruously that they were the same height.

Another woman, younger than the other two, was hopping up the stairs quickly. "Oh, Ena, do give her a chance to catch her breath. You are always so bossy!" She flashed a grin at the odd woman and turned to plant a kiss on the cheek of the center of attention. "Love, how you have been missed, my dearest!" The young woman had surprisingly muscular arms, she noted as she was crushed up in a warm hug.

The odd woman, whom the younger woman had called "Ena," snorted, "Temis, you're the chatterbox—never shutting up. You know how you go on!" Ena clucked and laughed, taking a playful swat at the younger girl, who was now flanking the woman who felt like a prisoner, arms laced in the same manner as the odd woman's on her left side.

"Temis" and "Ena." They had strange names to match their stranger attire. For the life of her, the woman didn't know quite what to make of the costume "Temis" was wearing. It was a short, sleeveless white dress that fell short of her knees. A slit went all the way up her right side, and her endowments were readily viewable in spite of the thick cord tied around her waist as a belt, but if she noticed then it didn't bother her. She had a bow full of arrows slung across her back, a wicked-looked double-headed axe tucked into her belt, and heavy fur boots that extended halfway up her calves.

But she supposed she had no right to throw stones. She was, after all, wearing a gown in a style from the Middle Ages. With a shrug, she accepted her new compatriots and turned her head to flash a smile at each, Ena on her left and Temis on her right. "So—you're Ena, and you're Temis, right?"

Both women giggled like sorority sisters, and right in her ear. "You're such a little tease, Love!" Ena chirped, while Temis guffawed, "Oh, sure, you weren't on Earth for that long!"

And before she could think up a way to stop them, they were leading her down the stairs and right into the maw that had her rooted into fear in the first place.

"Already you two have found the most beautiful woman at the party, and you're already trying to learn her secrets! I just won't have it!" The voice was so powerful and booming that she started, and would have tried to back away if the women at her sides didn't have such a firm hold on her. She was bodily turned around by the other two, who seemed to think that she was completely at ease with what was happening, and was confronted with the largest man she had ever seen. He was tall and thick like an oak tree, easily topping six feet and outweighing her by two hundred pounds (and that, she reasoned, was a rather kind estimate), with muscles that rivaled any

THE CREATIONS OF BELIEF

professional wrestler or athlete that ever lived. His longish, shaggy, sandy hair came to his broad shoulders, and his gray eyes sparkled with mirth.

As friendly and open as his expression was, his sheer size—not to mention his manner of dress—had her terrified. She thought briefly of fleeing the two women and rushing back upstairs, but a mental reminder to herself that she was already dead calmed her pounding heart a little. Before she could introduce herself properly, the man clad in furs that looked like a caveman suddenly swept her from the two women and had her up in the air, crushed against his thick chest in a powerful bear hug. Her little slippered feet swung uselessly a foot off the ground.

"Oh, Love," he whispered in a voice that seemed far too soft and gentle to be coming out of him, his face pressed close to her neck. "Things just haven't been the same." He squeezed her close for a moment before another voice broke into the group.

"Put her down, Thor, and let me get a good look at her!" Another male voice, this one lighthearted and more soft-spoken.

Her feet connected with the ground within the next instant or so, and she found herself staring up at the one called Thor's wide smile. He ran a callused finger across her cheekbone and offered her a little wink. "Glad to see you again, Love."

"Go along with you now, before you make Freyja jealous!" The other man laughed, playfully chasing him away with a long, gleaming sword that he pulled from a sheath at his waist effortlessly. He then turned an auburn head toward her, dark eyes shining with mirth. "Love!" he opened his arms to her as if expecting her to rush inside, wide smile raining down upon her.

It was all she could do not to take a step back. For, while there was nothing at all threatening about the man, she had a suddenly uneasy feeling. All of these people acted as though they knew her—when surely she would remember such a strange group, had she ever seen them before!

Here these people were calling her "Love," a title usually reserved for lovers and dear friends. Yet these people were nothing but strangers to her— and surely, she'd given them no indication that she wanted to have such close relationships! Why, they were running to her and coming to her almost like a long-lost sister!

As if sensing her discomfort, Ena stepped forward to flank her again, smiling sweetly at the auburn-haired man with the sword. "I think our Love must be ready for the feasting, so she can tell all of us about her experiences at once." Ena's voice was raised loudly enough to echo about the large room.

21

Murmurs, shouts, cheers, and cries of agreement made her ears ring, and a laughing Ena and Temis led her through a wide archway farther into the room, where a table big enough to seat even this huge crowd stood waiting. Already servers were scurrying around the wide table, piling it high with foods of every kind imaginable. She was led right to the head of the table and seated by Ena, who wore a wide smile the entire time.

With Temis at her left and Ena on her right, she took her seat at the head of the table and watched while the rest of the crowd followed suit. It was an impressive sight, all right, all those different-looking people in all their strange costumes, sitting down all at once. The shouts and calls and cries and murmurs and voices all started to quiet, slowly at first, until there wasn't even a breath of sound in that huge, huge room.

And slowly, slowly, every eye in the place turned to rest on her.

Ena looked at her with a wide smile, supporting her curly, dark head in one fisted hand, brown-gold eyes looking at her expectantly. Temis was staring at her with all the impatience of a young child, splitting her attention between staring at her with starving eyes and looking at the food with an even more ravenous expression.

…Only she had no idea what she was expected to do. Trying to draw as little attention as possible—as if that were possible—she leaned over and whispered to Ena, hiding her mouth with one upturned hand. "Ena…what do I do now?"

The dark-haired woman laughed a strange, dry sound that somehow seemed foreign coming from her expressionless face. "Don't you want to tell us all about your time on Earth?" Ena, not sensing the other woman's discomfort, made no effort to check the volume of her voice. The question echoed through the soundless room, and a round of shouts and cheers and stomping feet followed her query.

"T-tell you about my time on Earth? Do you mean…what lessons I have learned… my sins? Something like that?" She was beginning to feel hot and worried under the piercing gazes of the odd strangers…and yet still that strange feeling sat in the pit of her stomach, that niggling worry that she was missing some very important piece to this little puzzle of Afterlife.

Her faltering questions were met with a stony silence, and Ena was gazing at her in the most odd manner. Ena's mouth curled up into a strange, forced smile. "Your…sins? Did you live the life of a Catholic while you were down on Earth?"

She felt her cheeks flush red. Never in a million years would she have supposed that Heaven was denominational when it came to religions! "Catholic, no…I was…uhm…not really religious at all."

The huge brute who'd lifted her up before slammed his fist on the table with a loud belly laugh, shaking the table all the way down to where she sat. "At least you did not have to express Christian beliefs, no?" The assembled occupants, even Ena, laughed rowdily at his comment.

How odd. Perhaps she wasn't in Heaven after all, and not even destined for such. Could she really be going to…that other place? Not that she'd ever truly believed in either, but she'd hoped she wouldn't end up in a lake of fire for eternity just because she didn't go to church every Sunday and Wednesday. She took a deep breath and swallowed back some of the bile that threatened to rise up in her throat.

"What was your name?" Temis asked after the chuckles had quieted down to a dull roar, her green eyes bright and curious. They were all so inquisitive and interested…and for the life of her she couldn't figure out what any of it meant.

Finally—a question she could answer! She smiled faintly, and her mouth opened automatically to respond. Yes, she knew how to answer this! She wasn't faltering and hesitant about this—her name! Of course, she knew her own name! "K-k-k-…" Only she couldn't remember anymore. Come to think of it, she couldn't even remember where she'd lived, or how she'd died, or how old she was supposed to be…and it seemed that, even as she searched for them, the memories fled away from her grasp as the moments passed. "I don't know!" She suddenly wailed, feeling as though the weights of the world (and the afterworld) were crushing down on top of her. Death was supposed to be a resolution, a solution, and an answer to life's questions! Would she have to live again, to get the complicated answers to death's questions? "What's going on!" She wanted to run, to fight, and to get away from these people with their piercing eyes and their questions and their manner that suggested they knew her personally and deeply.

She felt Ena's hand clamp around her upper arm like a vise, and suddenly she was being pulled to her feet. "Isn't Love a card?" She smiled brightly— much too brightly compared to the strange, brittle sort of smile that she'd shown earlier. "If you don't mind, I have a personal little gift for her. We'll just go up to the front parlour. Pray, continue on with the feast. We won't be but a moment, really."

Before she could open her mouth, the one called Ena had dragged her from the table and was pushing her up the stairs. "Get up here, now, quickly before someone tries to follow," Ena hissed close to her ear, both hands pressing against the small of her back.

She could hardly catch her breath long enough to grab a fistful of her long skirts, and tripped up the stairs the entire time as Ena pushed against her, half-dragging, half-pulling up both curving flights. It wasn't until she'd been pushed inside the bedroom and the door was closed that Ena turned to look at her.

"Who am I?" One sandaled foot tapped against the wooden floors impatiently, intense gold-brown eyes boring into her blue ones so that she felt naked and transparent.

"Who...are you?" she repeated dumbly. How in the world was she supposed to know? "That woman—Temis—called you 'Ena.' Aren't you Ena?"

Ena cocked her curly head to one side, lips pressed together as if in thought. "Have you ever seen me before today?"

She couldn't help it, but the question was so absurd she started to laugh. Even with Ena's dead serious expression, it seemed such a ridiculous thing to say. "Of course not—I've never been dead before today!"

Dark brown eyebrows snapped together into a deep scowl. "Who are *you*?"

She felt a tickle of memory at the back of her mind; some secret door to her mind that she could not quite unlock, and felt tears sting at her eyes for the frustration of it all. "I don't remember! Oh, why don't I remember?" she wailed, lowering her head so this stranger wouldn't see the tears on her cheeks.

Ena was pacing now, her long white gown lapping against her ankles as she plodded back and forth quickly. She was muttering to herself and glancing at the woman seated on the bed from time to time, shaking her head and frowning.

"Do you know who I am?" Hopeful, tears under control, she lifted her head and tried to cast a pleading glance at the woman who looked even more worried than she felt.

"I know *exactly* who you are." Ena paused, turned, and assessed her with sharp eyes, then just shook her head again and went back to her pacing.

"You do? But...how is that possible?"

Ena stopped again, turning around to fully face the woman on the bed. "Because I have known you since before the beginning of time." A flat, expressionless, dry statement. Coming from this stately, severely serious woman, it seemed as though it could only be the gospel truth. Her golden-hued eyes never wavered, her face remained set as though it were stone.

Yet it was the most ludicrous thing the other woman had ever heard, and she felt her mouth turning upwards in a smirk without volition. "Oh, really?" She tried to keep the dripping sarcasm from her tone. "Then how is it that I've never seen you before in my life?"

Ena's lips quirked, but otherwise she didn't move a muscle. "You don't have a 'life.' You are Immortal...You are a Creation of Belief."

Now she was more than confused, she was angry. Instead of answers, she got riddles. Instead of clarity, she got confusion. And in her time of need, she was being mocked and ridiculed by this stranger in her bizarre clothes, with her strange eyes. She gave the woman a glare that would knock her over if looking meant anything. "And what in the Hell is *that* crap supposed to mean?"

"None of this sparks any kind of memory at all?" Ena flung her arms out, gesturing all around them to the bedroom.

"Of course not, how could it? I just woke up here today."

"What about Dite? Do you remember the name Dite?" She pronounced it Die-tee.

"Dite? No, what is that supposed to mean?"

Ena sighed, an exasperated sound. "It's your *name*, for sakes!"

Dite. She rolled it around in her mind, mentally repeated it to herself. "No...no, I'm sure that isn't my name. I think my name starts with a K. Karen...Kristen...Kristy...Something with a K."

"It *is* your name. Well, your nickname, anyway."

She shook her head. No, she'd never heard that word before. She couldn't be sure about much of anything, but she was sure that Dite wasn't her name, and that she'd never seen any of the people in the hall downstairs, including this riddle-talking woman.

Ena looked at her more closely, golden eyes turning more pleading in her somber face. "And you don't remember me? Look closely."

"No, not at all... Why? Who are you?"

The woman drew herself up straighter and let out a sigh. "My name is Athena, but you usually call me 'Ena,' just like everyone else."

She had to fight to bite back a smile. After all, there weren't many people who were named after antiquated Grecian goddesses. "Athena, huh? Well, that's pretty. Were your parents into mythology or something?"

"Parents?" She repeated the word as though it were completely foreign to her. "No..." She started to laugh that strange-sounding laugh again. "I wasn't named after Athena...I *am* Athena, first of the Nine Muses, patron Goddess of the city of Athens, Goddess of Thought and Thinkers and all Wisdom." She said it proudly, standing tall and stately in the middle of the large bedchamber that looked like something out of a movie about King Arthur.

She couldn't control it any longer, and the woman on the bed burst out into loud laughter. "Right!" she heaved, tears rolling down her cheeks. "And I'm the Queen of England."

Ena snorted and crossed the room in quick, long-legged strides. "No," she replied over her shoulder, plucking a tiny golden bell from the top of the mantelpiece and ringing it fiercely. "You're the Goddess Aphrodite."

CHAPTER TWO

Muse

It was the most ridiculous, outlandish, silly statement that she could have imagined. In fact, she was so dumbstruck by the sheer absurdity of it that she couldn't even speak. No, she could only laugh—and laugh she did. She laughed and she laughed and she laughed, rolling back on the high bed with tears of mirth streaming from her cheeks until her sides ached and her stomach whined in protest to the torture.

"Well, I don't see as how that's any way for someone of your ranking to behave." Ena's dry, monotonous voice made her laugh even harder.

"It must be a dream!" She finally concluded out loud. "I'm not here—I'm not even dead!" The thought gave her comfort. No, she hadn't died. Hadn't looked Death in the eyes and whispered, "I'm ready now." She hadn't let go of her mortal coil and looked beyond, waiting for whatever magic the Afterlife had to offer. None of those things had happened. Even now, she was dozing peacefully, probably in some heavily induced sleep because of all her pain medication. In a few hours she would wake up, safe and sound and out of this insanity. "Oh, I assure you, the mortal life you were living is indeed over." "Athena," as she called herself, had finally settled down and was perched on the edge of one of the two matching chairs in front of the fireplace, golden-brown eyes trained on the carved door.

"Fine, we'll play the game." There was nothing else to do but to go along with this prescription-drug-induced dream, anyway. "Where, ah, are we?"

Intense eyes flicked over her face for a moment before skipping back to the door, as though she could will it to open by sight alone. "Immortality, of course. Eternity. For ever. Infinity. Hereafter. Whatever you want to call it, it all means the same thing."

"Heaven."

"No—not 'Heaven' in the Christian sense of the word…not really," she amended quickly, gaze still locked on the door. She clutched the golden bell in her fist; as if letting it go would cause some catastrophe.

"But this is where people go when they die."

"No. This is where the gods and goddesses dwell—the home of the Creations of Belief."

Ena had used that phrase twice now, "Creations of Belief." With a mental shrug, Dite decided to dive in to her strange little world. "And what does that saying mean—'Creations of Belief'?"

Her round eyes widened until they looked like they might pop out of her head, attention diverted from the door finally. "You mean you don't know?"

"How could I, possibly?"

"Because you are one of them!" Frustrated, the self-named Goddess threw her hands up. "You are the Goddess of Love, a carnation of romance and feeling and love itself. A being that is made up purely of emotion, a creature that can only exist because love, itself, exists."

That didn't seem to make any sense. "If that were true, then I wouldn't have a body." She held out one arm as if to prove her own mortality.

"You don't really have one." Ena shrugged, as though Dite were silly for even supposing as much. "You aren't mortal, you aren't a human…you are a Goddess…a carnation. You are, specifically, a feeling."

The woman on the bed snorted, very unladylike. "I'm a feeling."

Ena looked at her sharply. "What did you believe in, down there?"

The answer that sprang to her lips was one she wanted to reject, but even racking her brain couldn't make it untrue. "Nothing. I don't think blind faith makes any sense."

"Nothing," Athena repeated. "Then why is it so hard to believe in this, right now?"

Before she could give her answer, a sharp rap on the door broke into their thoughts and conversation. Ena sprang to her feet as though help had finally come, and she wanted to rush to greet it. "Enter!" she barked.

Timidly, the serving girl slipped inside. Clumsily, she half-bent to perform two curtsies, picking up the edges of her plain white dress tentatively. "Athena, Milady, the messenger is here to see you." She directed her words to both women, eyes lowered to the floor.

Dite grinned at her, pleased to finally see a friendly face. All her anger at the girl from only a little while ago had faded away, because she was wonderful compared to the harsh and confusing Athena.

"Send him in, please, Rose." Athena seated herself again, patting at her hair and straightening the long folds of her gown to regain her composure.

"Aye." The serving girl curtsied again, offered a weak little smile to Dite, and fled the room quickly.

Rose, Dite mused. Now she thought about it, the little thing did look like a "Rose," what with her red curls and her bright green eyes.

The door opened this time to reveal a smiling, curly-haired youth that Dite guessed couldn't be older than fifteen. His eyes were big, bright, and blue, and his smile came with an easiness that looked natural in his young, freckled face. "Love, Thought!" he cried, grinning from ear to ear and offering a courtly bow to them both. "What can I do for the two most beautiful Goddesses?"

Dite wanted to speak up and ask the lad if he knew her, or if this was all some sick joke, but Athena's crisp words offered no room for discussion. "We have a very serious problem. I need you to get the Mother."

The lad's stiff posture slumped, shoulders turning inward, and the jaunty expression melted into one of sheer panic. "The Mother! Ena, you know she's going to ask me why!" His eyes turned pleading and his voice had now become a high-pitched whine.

"Tell her…" Athena's eyes flicked over Dite slowly before she turned fully to face the youth. "Tell her that the Goddess Aphrodite has the Affliction, and she must come at once."

"T-t-t-the A-af-ff-fff-fliction?" he stammered, taking a step back in fear. His eyes rounded out and turned huge as he looked over to Dite, who sat placidly on the edge of the bed. "You can't be serious! She looks fine!"

Ena's spine straightened like a shot and she stared at him, her expression turning dark. "You will deliver my message to her and you will go now. You have the winds at your disposal—GO!" she commanded, and Dite could see her control reaching the breaking point. The young man quickly raced from the room.

Athena sighed and sank back down into her chair as though completely drained. She rubbed her eyes a moment, then looked up. "That's what we'll do… C'mon, Dite, we're going on a little trip."

Dite shrugged and stood. She might as well be a good sport about this whole dream thing, after all. "Where to?"

Athena was already leading her out of the bedroom. As they paused near the staircase Ena managed to spare her a quick glance while she tried to lean over to see down into the main hall. "My father's."

So, Goddesses could have fathers. Now she knew this was all some weird dream. "And I guess he's a God?"

Athena looked at her with a frown, as though she'd just made some ridiculous statement. "Of course not—that's not possible. He's one of the Elementals. I think they're all gone now, let's go." Taking her hand, Athena dragged Dite back down the stairs.

Up and down. In and out. She was being thrown about the house like someone's rag doll, Dite thought angrily.

Now that she could view the large room downstairs without the crush of people, she could see just how elaborately decorated and huge it really was. Two gigantic crystal chandeliers swung from the ceiling, the rugs and tapestries depicted scenes of romance and love and looked hand-woven, and the furniture was too beautiful to touch. Dite could catch only glimpses of it, and the doorways that led into airy rooms leading off from the main room as Athena dragged her to the front doors—which looked for all the world like something out of a medieval movie.

It took both women to push one of the heavy wooden doors open, and Dite followed Athena out of the grand house.

…It was at that moment that Aphrodite realized they hadn't been in a "house" at all, but a castle. A real, live and true castle. Towers stretched upwards into the sky, pink banners snapped in the wind from their domed tops. The castle itself was made of thick, heavy stone, while ivy and pink climbing roses covered the building almost all the way up to the topmost tower. It was too huge for Dite to take in all at once, and she had to move her head from side to side, up and down, to get a full view of the place. There was even a moat—a *moat!*—with a drawbridge.

"Middle Ages Castlean architecture," Athena explained, watching Dite's awed expression. "The height of the romantic period… You don't remember it at all?"

"No, but I sure bet I would if I'd 'a seen it before." Dite nodded. "It's remarkable."

Athena's lips quirked once. "It's called 'Love's Palace,' and you've lived here for the past five hundred years. There have been extensive renovations…" The Goddess of Wisdom broke off on a sigh at Dite's expression.

"Five hundred years, huh?" Dite just laughed and walked over to a rosebush to inspect it.

Athena rolled her eyes and turned away, raising her head and letting loose a shrill, piercing whistle.

Dite flinched at the high-pitched noise and started poking her fingers into the moat. The water was cloudy and muddy. Did anything live in it? It didn't seem clear enough for fish…and she'd never believed in "moat monsters" before, but it seemed as though anything was possible in this place.

"Aphro*dite*!" Athena snapped.

"Huh?" Dite spun around too quickly and caught the hem of her gown in the toe of one silky little slipper, landing right on her bottom. It was just as well that she was sitting down for the sight that met her eyes at that moment, anyway.

Ena's whistle had been a call, and before them stood a huge horse (bigger than any Dite had ever seen, this monster was twice the size of the Clydesdale horses she'd seen on the television) and gold. And not gold as in a warm brown—but really gold! Its hair was snow white, and it pulled a gilded carriage decorated with diamonds shaped like teardrops behind it.

"Holy Mary, Mother of God!" Dite whistled, trying to rise to her feet.

Athena looked at her with a frown. "Who?"

"Uhhh…." Not quite sure how to reply, Dite only pointed to the beast standing placidly before them. "I don't guess I could convince you to *walk* to your father's house?"

"Don't be ridiculous." Athena was walking around the carriage to open the door, one impatient hand resting on her hip as she gestured for the Goddess of Love to climb inside. "It's not possible to get to Cloud Castle on foot."

Dite had one foot in the carriage when the reality of those words struck her, and she paused. "What do you mean, not *possible*?"

Athena, with an impatient grunt, pushed Love into the carriage and climbed in after her, shutting the small half-door with a firmness that matched the unbreaking set of her mouth. "You'll see soon enough. And quit acting so fidgety—you know the East Wind almost as well as I do."

"The East Wind?"

Ena rapped on the side of the carriage, rolled her eyes skyward, and looked at the other Goddess. "The East Wind—the horse that's pulling the carriage."

Love snorted. "This huge horse is the East Wind? Forgive me for being skeptical, but—" Her words stopped suddenly when the animal lifted up on its hind legs and suddenly, it, the carriage, and the two women were airborne. The scenery started flashing by so fast that Dite couldn't look out the small windows without feeling air sick, and she quickly sat back to try and calm her stomach. It would be a very unpleasant ride if she ended up getting sick all over the small, somewhat cramped space. "You've got to be kidding me."

The Goddess of Wisdom glanced at her with as much humour as Wisdom could feel. "The East Wind is a smooth ride compared to the way some choose to get around."

"Spare me the details." She was busy concentrating on keeping the contents of her stomach safely lodged inside her body.

Suddenly, the East Wind lurched and stopped with a slight shudder. Athena looked at her with a smile and opened the carriage door. "We're here."

"That was quick," Love murmured, following Thought out of the small contraption.

Her feet met with a soft, marshy, squishy surface, and she quickly picked a path across the ground, following Ena step for step, until she saw the structure that stood waiting before them. "What is *that*?"

"Cloud Castle," Athena chirped crisply, as if it were the most natural thing in the world.

Only it was the most extraordinary thing Dite could have ever imagined. The structure itself—and she could only label it as such loosely, considering— was formed of swirling, moving, gossamer clouds. Clouds! It floated on thin air, the foundation a small hill of puffy white vapor, the mists forming the walls and towers of the castle. It seemed to move and sway with the wind, and she could have sworn some of the rooms and towers changed sizes and positions even as she watched the grandiose creation. Cloud Castle stood grandly, as different dewy shades of white, blue, even light shades of violet and pink, larger than life and twice as impressive.

…It was at that moment that she realized they were in the sky. She looked down and realized with a terrified start that the marshy, squishy "ground" they stood on was not the ground at all—but clouds. With a startled shriek, Dite went hurtling back into the carriage that she'd feared only moments before.

"Oh, for sakes!" Athena heaved, chasing after her, wisps of fog dancing around her ankles. "It's completely safe, and even if it weren't you can't be physically injured!"

"I…can't?" But of course, she thought to herself, I *am* already dead.

"You're not a *human being*," Ena said the words as though the phrase "human being" were on par with "disgusting vermin." "You're Immortal, and you exist as long as love exists. Really, now, stop being ridiculous so we can go talk to Air!"

Dite stuck her head out the carriage window, eyes narrowed. "Talk to Air? We can talk to the air right here! Hello, air, how are you doing?" She waved her arms around wildly, gesturing to the atmosphere.

"Grant me strength!" Athena muttered, yanking Love's arm to pull her from the carriage. "The Elemental Air, Love, my father? Just like I said. Now, come on, I don't have all of Eternity to spend with you and your silly little human thinking!" With that, she bodily pulled Aphrodite from the carriage.

The woman landed on the clouds with a thud—what a soft fall!—and sprang to her feet as though standing could keep her safe from the haze. "Fine!" she grumped loudly, stomping on ahead of her companion. "But I'm not at all happy about it!"

Athena hissed out a sigh that would do any martyr proud and continued on after the Goddess.

The door of Cloud Castle writhed and pulsated in the mists, little droplets of dew wetting their hair and faces as they approached. "Thought and Love," Athena chirped brightly, directing her words to the door, and the mists lifted and parted to reveal a beautiful entranceway.

Dite needed no prompting to rush right inside the castle, which was somehow even more impressive on the inside than outside. The floors and walls were gauzy and seemed to go on forever and ever, making the place look even larger than it really was. Beautiful decorations and adornments lined the walls, carvings of beautiful artworks and paintings, delicate furnishings, and marble staircases gave the place an airy, light feel.

"Well, well, well." Love could have sworn that the man standing at the foot of the wide, curving staircase had appeared out of nowhere. He smiled at both women, a strange, tight grimace of a smile that was remarkably similar to Athena's. "The two most intrepid Goddesses of Immortality, already hard at work. And to think, I supposed you would be feasting and celebrating for a few days at least, beautiful Love. Surely, whatever you two are up to can't be good for the Gods!" He winked at Athena. "Should I go ahead and summon Thor now, just to keep the peace?"

"Father!" Athena stepped forward to plant a kiss on his cheek.

What was the word Athena had used to describe him—an Elemental? He certainly looked perfectly normal, Love was thinking. His hair, which he wore a bit too long, was white-blonde, and he dressed more sedately than any of the people she'd seen at the Feast…was that only a few minutes before? He wore long, bright yellow robes that seemed to ripple with his movements and flow across the ground as he walked. He stepped back to smile at his daughter. "You look to be in the midst of a grand problem, my child, surely you have come to share this riddle with me!"

He stepped forward quickly and bent to kiss Love's hand, so fast she couldn't pull away from him. "And the Goddess of Love, 'tis rare I see you in this place. Surely you have worked out some fascinating situation in which Love and Thought can finally mix well enough to do both justice, yes?"

"I…" She could think of nothing to say. Looking up at him, she was confronted with the most intense pair of eyes she had ever gazed into. In fact, they looked to be so deep and so wise that she thought he must surely know everything, and standing under such probing scrutiny made her feel naked. Not only the intensity of his eyes, but the color had stopped her cold. While Athena's were a warm golden brown, his were a bright, light yellow that was almost transparent. She shivered and wanted to step away from him.

"Father." Athena glanced over at the visibly shaken Goddess. "I fear we have something of a…situation."

"Oh?" Finally, he turned away and faced Ena. "What can I do for you?"

"Aphrodite seems to be…well, I think she suffers the Affliction."

He reared back as though the word itself were an infection. "No! Really? No!" He whirled to stare at Love again, his eyes examining her even more closely. "She does have a different light in her eyes than usual…a different way about her. Tell me, Love, what is your name?"

"What is the Affliction?" she demanded. Now she'd seen Athena tell two people the same thing, and she didn't at all appreciate being treated like something contagious. Imagine, if all the people who died were treated in such a fashion! "I don't have anything wrong with me but the cancer that killed me!" she snapped, stomping one foot on the shimmering ground for emphasis. The ripples moved all the way across the floor and shook the far walls.

"Cancer?" Air looked to his daughter for an explanation, but she only shrugged.

"She's acting like she's human, Father. I don't know what to make of it. You know, she didn't know who I was. She couldn't even tell me her own name!"

"Love." Piercing yellow eyes met hers again. "What am I?"

"She called you an Elemental." Every moment she spent in this place was like being on a quiz show, she thought sourly. She decided then and there she wasn't going to answer any more questions without first getting some answers.

"Yes, but do you know what that means?" He tried to form a smile to prompt her, but the expression looked so strange on him it only frightened her more.

"I don't know what any of this crap means." Love crossed her arms over her chest and glared. "All these strange words and things and people, and no one is taking any time to explain any of it to me. All I know is that I died and woke up here and I know—I *know*—this place ain't Heaven. Anymore I don't care if I go there or not, but I'm pretty well sick of being here and I want someone to give me some answers PDQ." She gave a nod of her head to punctuate the little speech, drawing herself up straight and trying to assume an air of authority.

The Elemental's brow creased into a frown. "Well...she is certainly not the same Love that left, that much can be made known." He directed his words at Athena, but managed to keep most of his gaze directed on the fuming young woman standing in the middle of the huge front room. "I would say she is Afflicted, yes. I will call a High Tribunal. You have summoned the Mother?"

Athena nodded. "I did that first thing, and then came here. No one knows yet but you and I, and the messenger."

The man's eyes flashed dark for a moment. "You told him?"

"I had no choice—who else was I going to send to find Her?"

Love was beginning to boil over with rage. Here they were, talking about her like she was no more significant than an animal in the corner—and they were still talking about her being diseased! "I am not going to put up—" she began.

"And she remembers nothing?" The Elemental started pacing, and the floor rippled and moved with him as he crossed from one side of the castle to the other.

"Not that I can tell."

"—treating me like I'm not even here, and—"

"Have you tried taking her to Fluidity?"

At the Elemental's suggestion, Athena visibly perked up. "That could work! So you think I should take her to Fluidity, maybe to jolt loose some memory?"

"Water should spark some emotion in her—he does everyone else. And after that, maybe Castle Flame?"

"—all this talk about Afflictions and strange names and words I've never heard before, and all I wanted was to die in peace—"

"What am I supposed to do, give her a tour of Immortality?" Athena's hands flew to her hips.

Her father shrugged in reply, glancing over his shoulder at Love, who stood haranguing an armchair in her anger. "Whatever else, we have only one Goddess of Love. There is always the possibility the Affliction will be permanent...and she must learn to leave behind all those vapid human thoughts. How can she perform her duties if she does not know what Immortality is?" His patient, kind voice served to calm Athena, who was tapping her foot now and glaring.

"Wouldn't Q or someone be a better tour guide than me? She already doesn't remember me, and you know I've never really even worked with her!" The Muse was watching Love, who stood still ranting at the chair in a corner of the room.

"You are closest to her, my First Daughter. And Q does not possess the powers of a First. You know that."

"I know," Athena visibly softened. "Well, what should I do, just start with the Elementals and try to teach her our ways? How does one go about teaching something that took millennia to form?"

Air sighed, a reedy, windy sound that seemed to fill the room. "I am unsure...for how does one teach what has never been spoken of aloud before? I suppose you should take her to as many of the Elements and the First as possible and have them try to explain themselves to her...while you, in turn, tell her as much about Immortality as you can. At least until the Mother comes, 'tis the only thing to do."

Athena nodded. "Speak to her now, then, while I dispatch the winds to tell the other Elementals we are coming." With that, the First Muse slipped out of the room to go complete whatever tasks had been laid out for her.

"Love." Air's soft voice stopped her cold.

Dite turned slowly, her long speech suddenly forgotten, all anger dissipating in the face of his vast knowledge. "I'm not some walking disease just because I'm human!"

The Elemental shook his head, his eyes kind. "Love, my dear, you will never be human. Let me explain something to you." Gallantly, he offered his arm for her to lace her own through, and they walked through the front doors together to the field of clouds outside.

The East Wind picked up his huge, shaggy head and whinnied lovingly at his master, and the Elemental answered in turn with a soft whistle that sounded for all the world just like a sweet summer breeze rifling through tree leaves.

"The life of a Goddess, or God, even the life of the Elementals, is not an extremely exciting one. We are spawned by the beliefs of man, and so we spend our existences serving man and helping the world. We are, after all, deities, and it is us who must maintain the very delicate balance that exists. You see, First Creations like yourself spend much of what is called 'time' in the Earth realm among humans. Either to further maintain the balance, or for some other reason...and you," he turned to bathe her in one of those odd smiles, which she was becoming used to in just the short moments they'd spent together, "you like to live among them. You think it helps you to perform your duties better."

"So you mean that Gods and Goddesses are walking around Earth all the time, pretending to be humans?"

He shrugged. "Sometimes pretending to be humans, sometimes they are there, but mortals cannot see us."

She quirked her mouth into a wry smile. "And you're trying to tell me that I'm the Goddess of Love and I went down to Earth to live as a human being?"

"That is exactly who you are and what you did." He smiled warmly at her, having missed the wry sarcasm in her tone.

She snorted. "Right. And I suppose Satan dances around on Earth all the time, too, right? If I'm the Goddess of Love, why don't I remember anything but my own life? Why do I have human parents?"

The Elemental sighed again, and the whistling noise seemed to circle around her head a moment before it was gone. "Satan is a rather new creation, much younger in terms of human time than you, but he has been known to spend quite a bit of time on Earth realm. And you have what is known as the Affliction, which is why you can't remember anything before your human life, which you lived for the span of twenty-six human years. Which was too long, just as everyone told you." He patted her arm and sighed again, an affectation she was beginning to think he was overly fond of.

"Forgive me if I don't believe you."

The Elemental nodded. "It is understandable. You are, after all, thinking with a human mind. Well, let us forget about that for now. I will simply tell you about who I am, yes?" He stopped and gestured around them to the hanging clouds of vapor and mist.

"You're a deity." Her words dripped with dry disbelief.

"Not exactly, no." He cupped her chin gently and looked down into her eyes. The bright yellow orbs seemed to fill her up. "I am the embodiment, if you will, of the elemental air. Four elements make up the human world, Earth, Air, Fire, and Water. I am Air. I rule the East, the powers of creativity and intelligence. It is because of this that I fathered the Muses, of which the

Goddess of Wisdom is First.

"I control the forces of travel, thought, and will. These are the aspects of humanity that fall under my domain. To control and balance these forces, to foster these aspects, I have fathered my children, the Muses. Athena is my First Daughter, but you will also meet Creativity, Serendipity, Poetry, Song, Music, Dance, Genius, and Virtuosity. I am the father of invention and all thought." He smiled. "It is hard to understand, I know...but you must learn to think less in human terms.

"These aspects of humanity that you took for granted for twenty-six years, never realizing your true potential and identity, were created by the ones on Earth realm. We in Immortality exist only by the grace of man...but at the same time, we prevent chaos. By controlling, constraining, and fostering those gifts from Earth realm, we maintain the balance."

She stared up at him with troubled eyes, trying to make sense of it all. "So for every emotion, there is another deity created in Immortality? For every aspect of all humanity, there exists an embodiment?"

He smiled slightly. "You are getting closer to understanding, but still you think like a human. No more of this, now. You and my daughter must go to Fluidity, where surely we will shake some memories loose for you!" Air hugged her gently, pulling back to look down at her once more. "Poor, dear, Love. We will make you well again!"

Athena came bounding out of the cloudy doorway, face screwed up into a frown on concentration. "I have dispatched messages to Castle Flame, Fluidity, and the Habitat," she told her father, standing up on tiptoe to kiss his cheek. "We have to get going, Father."

"I wish you the luck of Eternity, my First Daughter."

The Goddess of Wisdom hauled Aphrodite back into the carriage, and they took off instantaneously, Athena leaning out the window to wave good-bye.

"We will make you well again," the Elemental had said. Only she wasn't sick, and sooner or later she would find a way to get out of this awful place with all its strangeness. Imagine, her as a deity! She laughed at the thought and leaned back against the carriage, trying to mentally prepare herself for whatever strange game they would play next.

CHAPTER THREE

Elementals

The so-called Goddess of Love was trying her best not to look out the small carriage windows as the East Wind, in the form of a horse bigger than any that grew on Earth, carried them off to some strange new location. "Here's what I don't understand." Her tone was sharp. When she was confused, or didn't understand something, she started attacking others. She felt as though she'd been attacked since arrival, and now it was time to put someone else on their toes. She turned to Athena with a martial air, ready to battle with the one weapon she still had: words.

"Hmm?" Ena focused golden eyes on her, turning her curly head from the window.

"How could he be your father if you're a Goddess? Gods and Goddess don't have fathers…and who is your mother, if he is?"

The First Muse stared at her for so long without answering that she had given up hope of ever receiving a reply. "You are right, and deities do not procreate in the way humans do—it is impossible. He is my father because the powers of intelligence and wisdom fall under his rule. And right now, we are on our way to see your father."

"My father?" A face, long familiar, flashed behind her eyes. Yes. Her father. "But my father isn't dead…my father is a car salesman on Earth."

Thought sighed; a noise that sounded remarkably like the one Air often made. "Not the man who lived as your father while you were pretending to be human. The Elemental who created you."

Love was silent for a long moment, simply looking at Athena and saying nothing. Then: "He would be the Elemental who controls emotion, wouldn't he? Since Love is an emotion."

The Goddess looked at her with raised eyebrows. "I'm surprised, Love. You never seemed this bright before." The sting was removed from her words by the attempt at a smile she formed on her face.

Love sighed and leaned her head against the back of the carriage. "This is impossible to believe."

"What is?"

"The thought of Gods and Goddesses walking around on Earth, living human lives, all the time."

"No other First Creation has ever done it as much as you have. But twenty-six years is too long. Usually, you get pulled back after twenty or so," Ena explained.

Aphrodite laughed. The thought was just too outlandish for her. "So I, ah, have done this before, have I?"

Athena gave her an "are you joking?" look. "But of course. And every time you do so, something goes wrong—*every time!* But you never listen to reason. You're convinced it's the best way to learn about them." The Muse followed this up with a martyric sigh and a quick roll of her golden-hued eyes.

Dite smirked. "Oh, right. I go down to Earth, live as a human for twenty years, and come back, hmmm? Why don't I remember it?"

"Well, it's not like you remember anything else!" Thought snapped hotly. "And don't believe me if you don't want. It's not as though you can't just look it up."

Now she was just confused. "Look it up—where?"

The Muse, eyes glued to the passing scenery, lifted her right shoulder in a halfhearted shrug. "Any history tome, I'm sure. Go and read about the war of Troy, in fact. *That* was one of your major blunders."

"The war of…what on Earth does that have to do with me?" Love demanded. War of Troy, indeed! That happened hundreds and hundreds of years ago!

Owlish eyes turned to give her a scathing glance. "The woman, the 'face that started a war,' the one who started it all, remember? Now, who else do you think that could have been, but the Goddess of Love in her mortal form?"

For three full heartbeats Love couldn't work up enough steam even to speak. "You mean *Helen of Troy*? Are you suggesting that I was Helen of Troy?"

The Goddess shrugged one shoulder again, raising a hand to pat her neat brown curls. "I am not suggesting it—I am saying it outright. It took years and years just to clean *that* mess up, and two hundred years later you went back down to Earth as though nothing was wrong."

Love snorted. Helen of Troy, my eye, she thought, dismissing the notion completely.

Suddenly, the carriage thumped to a halt. "Fluidity," the Goddess of Thought announced, opening the door.

"Fluidity," Aphrodite repeated to herself, sensing a certain familiarity with the word, following Ena outside the carriage. As impressed as she'd been with the castle made entirely out of clouds, it was very little compared to the wonder that Fluidity was. While the Elemental of Air dwelled up in the clouds high in the sky, the Water Elemental lived in the midst of a rushing, running, crystalline lake. Marshes and water surrounded them on all sides. Nervously, the East Wind was pawing and neighing at the thin sandbar they'd alighted on. A thin bridge of multi-colored stones led the way to the castle itself, which was constructed entirely of rushing waterfalls. White foam broke at the base of the structure, and Love stared at the different hues of greens and blues for so long she almost felt mesmerized.

"Dite, for sakes!" Athena sighed and latched onto her arm. "Hold your skirts up and mind you don't slip on the rocks," the Goddess clucked like an overprotective mother, leading her across the bridge.

Love followed the Muse's instructions, stepping carefully across the slippery stones in her thin little slippers, trying to keep pace with Ena's fast clip. They finally reached the foot of Fluidity, where the noise of the waterfalls was almost deafening. "Say your name," Athena hissed, jabbing her friend in the ribs roughly.

"What? Oh—Aphrodite!" she announced to no one in particular, and a panel of water suddenly fell away to reveal the glittering interior.Athena hurriedly pulled her into the castle, and Love was greeted with the blessed quiet now that the noise of the waterfalls was left behind. Even more surprising, the inside of Fluidity was more beautiful than the watery outside. Shells and stones of all shapes and colours made up the walls, and the water that made up the outside walls rushed between and around them to create a beautiful, flowing look. The floor was completely transparent, so that the lake floor could be viewed easily. Schools of fish and other sea life darted around their feet. Tapestries that looked to be woven from varying shades of seaweed lined the walls, and starfish dangled from long ropes of pearls affixed to the high ceilings. The furnishings were sparse, consisting only of a few scattered pieces. There was a high-backed chair that was really a huge clamshell with soft cushions of sand lining the inside, a long chaise that was made up entirely of packed white sand, and assorted pieces of old shipwrecks that had been arranged carefully. Huge fish tanks were placed everywhere, much more elaborate and larger than any she'd seen in life, where water life of every kind imaginable lived. One of the tanks even contained seahorses!

"Daughter!" An archway leading off into a room Dite could not really see revealed the voice, and suddenly the man was rushing toward her with arms outstretched.

Unwittingly, she took a step back to avoid contact with the man, whom by sight only had already put a knot of nerves into her stomach. His hair was stark white and over-long, curling up about his neck and ears in soft waves, while his eyes were such a deep blue she could see their color from across the room. As he came nearer, she saw that they had an endless, deep quality to them, with many shades of white and green buried beneath the blue, blue surface. Although his features and expression were completely kind and soft, the raw emotion exposed by the set of his red lips and the worried crease of his dark eyebrows took her back.

Either not noticing her worries or not heeding them, the Elemental pulled his daughter into a warm embrace that was so tight her face was pressed up against the soft wool of his long gray robes. "Oh, my sweet Love!" he moaned, his face pressed against the top of her head. "How I grieve for my poor daughter!" His voice was terribly strange, ending and beginning in odd gurgling sounds, and in his sadness it took on a deep, resonant tone that seemed to echo around the huge castle.

Athena cleared her throat impatiently. "Elemental, you are frightening her."

"Frightening!" The word came from him shrilly; ending in a high whine that probably would have broken glass in the mortal world. Water pushed Love from him with both hands on her shoulders, holding her at arm's length to look at her. "Oh, my daughter! You stand before me, just as you have always done, yet you look at me with eyes that belong to a human girl, and not my own First Creation!" The words ended on a sob that sounded like bubbles, and he pulled her against him again for another vise-like embrace.

"Water! Control yourself long enough to let that poor child go!" The voice of Wisdom cut sharply into the room and at her command even the overly emotional Elemental obeyed, releasing Love, who stumbled away quickly.

"I take it you have already heard the news." Thought's voice was as dry as paper.

Water sniffed, managing only a small nod. "What can we do!" His cry was dramatic, and in the background Love thought she heard a wave crash against the bank outside.

"We can start by calming ourselves down. Aphrodite is quite convinced she is a mortal and incapable of thinking beyond her supposed mortal coil, but it isn't the end of Eternity."

Water looked over at his daughter, who was standing rigid and waiting to see what he would do next, and then back at the First Muse. "You mean…even her mind is still stuck to the Earth realm?"

With one of her windy sighs, Ena nodded. "I'm afraid so. She doesn't even think any of this is 'real.'"

Water gasped, a sharp sound that Dite couldn't quite find a comparison for. "Then we are truly in a spot, then, for how is she to fix the—"

"Shhh!" Athena cut him off quickly, with a tilt of her head toward Love. "I haven't even told her yet—her weak human mind can't take it."

Water nodded, his face twisted in pure pain. "I got your message on the West Wind. I suppose I am to try and explain things to her, hmm?"

Ena nodded, pulling Love forward again. "If you would, please, Elemental. We will go to the Habitat next, and Mother knows how long *that's* going to take."

Water nodded slowly, eyes affixed to his daughter. "You have not taken her to Castle Flame?"

The Muse shook her curly head, eyes darkening. "I do not know if that would be wise."

"No less wise than bringing her here to me—he will be no worse, I promise you. I have business at Castle Flame anyway, and I will go there while the two of you move on to the Habitat. I shall have a word with Fire."

Thought nodded. "Perhaps that is best, then. I must try and contact the messenger, so if you will excuse me?"

Taking the hint, Water nodded. "Of course. My daughter and I are just going for a quick stroll in the Water Park. Come, Venus." The Elemental rested his arm across the shoulders of the Goddess of Love, leading her away.

"Venus?" she echoed, following him because she really could see no alternative.

Athena slipped away silently before she had to help answer questions, because as everyone knew, Emotion was no good in thinking things through.

Water led her through the archway he'd appeared in only moments before, and she was greeted with what was surely the most amazing sight in the whole of Immortality. The Water Park, as the Elemental called it, was truly that, but also much more. Here, the walls, floor, and ceiling were transparent, so that the marsh and the lake—and even the dense forest beyond—were open to view. Small pathways made up of weathered brick, stones, shells, and sun-bleached wood wound around in small and large spirals, some even extending up into the air, where platforms rested to reveal more wonders of the Park.

Just from the brief walk-through they did, which consisted only of the ground level of the place, Aphrodite saw a frog pond complete with perfectly shaped lily pads, a lovely rock garden where turtles and other creatures peeked out at her, and wonders she could not name. There was a hidden cave entrance behind one of the waterfalls that Water told her led into an entire underground system of caves that made up other levels of the Water Park. A tall weeping willow stood growing from a tiny, tiny island where both seaweed and thick vines wrapped around the trunk. And all the while the entire ground floor of the park was nothing but different pools of water. There was even a spot where dolphins jumped back and forth across the path, and the Elemental told her that they had been known to do it for hours and hours at a time.

"Venus is another of your names," he'd explained to her as they entered the Park. "You have many, for many different cultures have recognized you as the Goddess of Love. Aphrodite is your most common name, but most of us just call you by what you are—Love."

"Uh huh." Not an eloquent response, for sure, but she was so dumbstruck at the sight of the Water Park she didn't know quite else what to say.

"Tell me about yourself. Tell me what your mortal life was like?" His voice was soft, soothing, kind. Already Dite was feeling much more at ease, and the gentle sound of the lapping water was lulling her into a sense of peace.

He was the first to ask her that question, and Dite wanted to answer him, but the memories of that life were fading fast from her consciousness. Like her name and the names of her father and mother, the small details of the life she'd lived for so long were fading, fading away so quickly. "I died of cancer," she answered. It was one of the few things she could remember, the cancer.

Water chuckled, a surprisingly rich sound. "I didn't ask how your mortal life ended—I asked what it was like. Were there friends, boyfriends?"

A young woman, the question of boys had always made her blush. "Well, no steady boyfriends. But it seemed there were always boyfriends, yes. When I got sick, the flowers never stopped coming. In fact…" As she thought about it, she remembered more about that mortal life. "In fact, I remember that I hated it. I couldn't even be friendly with a guy without him wanting more. It seemed like they always came to me and told me they had fallen in love, even if we barely knew each other. In fact, yes." Her steps stilled as the memory of it came rushing back. "I used to call it a curse, because so many of them fell in love with me, and so often, but none could ever *stay* in love with me. I always...I always knew there was something wrong with me."

Water looked at her with soft eyes, shaking his head slowly. "No, my child, there has never been anything 'wrong' with you. When the Goddess of Love takes mortal form, such things are bound to happen. It is the nature of such an experience that you cannot know who you truly are...but now that you think on it, really think on it, does it not make sense? Of course they all fell in love with you, they could do nothing less, considering who you are."

But still Aphrodite disagreed. "No, that's not right, because I didn't know— so how could they love me so?"

Water smiled at her lovingly. "Darling Love, of course you did not know, but not knowing did not change who you are. There may be a day when Athena forgets who she is, but that will not make her any less the Goddess of Wisdom. There may be a day when Mars forgets he is the God of War, but War will be no less because of it. Not knowing something does not mean it is not there...it only means you don't recognize it."

What he said did make sense, it was true...and she'd always had a problem with men falling for her. Now that the memory had come back, she could remember all their names and faces, all the declarations, all the craziness she had lived through, simply because they were convinced they had loved her.

"Think on that, a time. Now, our time grows short and I must explain things to you." Water led her to a marble bench, taking her hand in his own and staring deep into her eyes. "I am the Elemental of Water, that which rules all Emotion." He smiled slightly. "Happiness, sadness, love, hate, these are all different emotions." Water thought a moment, dark eyebrows drawing together. "I rule the West, where the sun sets on Earth at night. I govern purity, cleanliness, and all matters of emotion."

Love nodded. This was all similar to what she'd heard from Air.

"You are my First Child." He smiled softly at her. "I know that means little to you, but it is a very special thing indeed, and an honor. My other children include Sorrow, whom I'm sure you will end up meeting eventually, Joy, and sadly, Hate. But you, Love, are my First and Highest Daughter of all. There can be only one First Child from each Elemental, and so your gifts are great indeed. Hold to that, and know that Love has always been labeled the emotion that conquers all." With that, he planted a very wet kiss against her cheek and rose to his feet. "Now, if you will excuse me, I have a visit to make." Tears falling from his eyes and dripping across the floor, Water waved and suddenly vanished into thin air.

Dite sat still as stone for a few long moments before Athena came rushing through the Park to find her. "For sakes, Aphrodite, we can't just sit and do nothing! We don't have all of Eternity to do this, no matter what you might think!" Impatient as ever, the Muse pulled Love up to her feet and started marching her back through the Water Park. "We can't stay for very long when the Elemental is not here. The dwellings of the Elementals tend not to be welcoming to any but the consorts." She tossed the explanation over her shoulder as Love struggled to keep pace with her.

Finally, they broke out onto the other side of the waterfall. The levels of the water were rising, and the East Wind stood whinnying fiercely. "Was he crying?" Athena's voice was harsh as she pulled Love across the narrow bridge.

"Yes, he was. He certainly was Emotion, there was no question about that."

The Muse made a noise of anger and started running across the bridge toward the East Wind. "We have to leave, then, before the water rises too high. Come along, Love, and quit worrying about your hem!"

Even as Athena pulled Dite's arm fiercely, the Goddess of Love was trying to keep her embroidered hem clear of the breaking waves near the bridge, but finally she had to let go just to keep her arm from being pulled out of socket by the insistent Goddess of Wisdom.

"To the Habitat!" Thought barked the order out the window before they were even completely seated in the carriage, and the East Wind took off with a neigh so loud it sounded more like a roar. As they lifted into the air, Love saw the narrow sandbar get swallowed up by the rising water.

"The…Habitat?" Frowning, Love shook her head at Thought. Even the word sparked no memory, and for the life of her she couldn't think what Elemental such a word could be linked to.

"The Elemental of Earth." Wisdom nodded at her friend, voice soft and prompting.

"Uh huh," Dite grunted, watching as the carriage neared a thick stand of trees. "What's he like?"

Athena smiled slightly then, and Love thought she could see something soft creep into the Muse's eyes. "Very solid," was her only reply.

Love snorted, wondering if that was supposed to be Thought's idea of a joke. She watched as the East Wind came closer to the trees, now circling around the grove for a clearing big enough to set the carriage down. "Can't you just send me back?"

Ena muttered something, took a deep breath, and leveled her gaze steadily on Love. "Send you back *where*?"

"To Earth, of course."

"You don't belong on Earth, Love." Athena's tone came out like one talking to a small child. "You belong here, and so now I have to cart you around and 'introduce' you to everyone." She laughed, somewhat bitterly. "As though we haven't all known you for so many thousands of years. It's all just so ridiculous."

Love was glaring at her angrily. "You don't have to treat me like I'm a child, you know, or someone who is inferior to you just because I don't know what's going on. I was practically abducted, if you remember, and I would have been *perfectly* happy just to go to Heaven like all the other dead people."

Athena sighed again and leaned forward, as if to tell her more, when the East Wind set the carriage down in a small clearing. "We're here." She quickly sat back and jumped down out of the carriage, leaving her thoughts unspoken.

Dite mumbled something not so polite and followed after Ena.

The forest itself was impressive, the trees towering above their heads by at least one hundred or so feet. The ground was shadowed and covered with short grasses and dwarfed flowers. Love, who had never been much of a nature lover, was suddenly becoming very interested in all the outdoorsy things she was seeing.

It was at that point that Love noticed that there seemed to be something very important missing. She spun around in a circle to face Athena expectantly. "Where, ah, is it?"

The Goddess smirked and replied by stepping close to a large boulder. "Watch." Her voice lowered to almost a whisper, she leaned over the boulder and rapped on its surface sharply with her knuckles. After a deep rumbling that seemed to come from within the rock itself, it slid away effortlessly to reveal a deep, dark hole. "Here." Without hesitation, Ena picked up her long hem and started into the hole.

"You've got to be *kidding me*." Love planted her feet apart and crossed her arms. "I am not going in there."

"Indeed, you are!" Now only the top of Athena's head and shoulders were visible above the ground. She glowered at Dite. "This is how we get to the Habitat, don't you know."

Dite primly perched on the edge of the boulder, looking down into the hole with a grimace of disgust on her face. "I'll do no such thing! You can tell him to come out here to me."

"Aren't you suddenly Queen of the forest! Five minutes ago, you were nothing but a human, and now you think you can order the Elemental of Earth around? You get your prissy little behind off that rock.and follow me into the Habitat before I drag you there!" Threateningly, Athena started climbing back up out of the hole.

Love jumped away. "I'm not climbing and crawling into some dirt-filled hole just to satisfy your need to tell everyone that I have something wrong with me that I don't really have wrong with me in the first place! You and your friend have fun making me feel inferior without me for all I care." She sniffed and rose her chin a notch into the air.

Athena made a low growling sound and suddenly lunged out of the pit, grabbing both Dite's wrists in her hands. Without warning, she grabbed a handful of Dite's gown, ripping it, and thrust her right down into the hole!

Love shrieked and fell onto the dusty, dirty staircase that was crudely carved into the ground, bouncing down about two feet before finally bracing herself against the walls of the narrow pit. "You hateful thing!" She threw a handful of dirt out of the hole, hoping to at least get close to the Goddess of Thought.

Athena rolled her eyes expressively as she entered the hole, urging Dite along. "I can't be hateful—I don't have enough emotion in me for it."

"That doesn't make any sense." Love, already out of sorts, snapped at her meanly as she carefully eased down the stairs into the blackness below.

"Of course it does. I am Thought, and Thought usually does not rely on, or have much, emotion involved with it. Right?"

Dite groaned to herself. No matter what else, she could count on Athena to always provide a strange answer. "Right, sure, I forgot." She continued deeper into the hole.

"Is it so hard for you to think that the beliefs of mankind would mean so much?"

Love gave her a glance over her shoulder that said "you can't be serious."

"Humans have believed in a million things throughout history. Surely you don't expect me to believe that there exists a being for all faiths and all ideas when it comes to beliefs. That's just too ludicrous."

"Is it really? In the very earliest days of civilization, the Goddess of Love was worshipped far and wide. The names were always different, as were some of the perceptions and ideas, but one thing always remained concrete—the Goddess of Love was like an embodiment of the emotion itself, a beautiful, sometimes foolish thing. In Immortality, there did not exist a separate Goddess for each culture that believed, but you, as a creation spawning from them all."

"What about other religions—totally different religions? Indian mysticism, for instance—or the Hindi beliefs, or Buddha!" Love demanded, finally stepping off a stair and landing at the bottom of the hole.

Athena moved past her to rap against the wall lightly, three quick times in succession, and the rocky surface slid away. "Buddha is less a god and more of a 'perfect being,' one who has traveled through all the stages of reincarnation and reached ultimate perfection. Buddism, and Hinduism, as well as the Indian beliefs you speak of, are all religions based upon the Old Religion, wherefrom most all of us—including yourself and myself—spawned. It is the newer religions that cause all the trouble." She quickly motioned Love through the entranceway and followed close at her heels into the room.

Love's mind, so full of questions, froze when she saw what was spread out before her. "Oh, my," she whispered, awestruck by the scene before her.

"Yes, isn't it lovely?" Athena grinned.

They were in an entire underground world—or so it seemed. The high cave walls soared high above their heads to form an enormous "room" of sorts. On the far wall, directly across from where Love stood gaping in wonder, a furious waterfall poured down the entire length of the tall cave wall, crashing against the rocks and forming a small, crystalline pool. Small, gray, eyeless fish swum around near the lake bottom, their fins flashing silver in the scant light that bounced off the walls.

A wide hole at the top of the cave poured rays of sunlight into the cave. One tall tree sat surrounded by wildflowers and tall grasses on an island in the center of the lake.

"What *is* this place?"

"Welcome to the Habitat." The reply came not from Athena, but from a male voice somewhere behind her.

Love spun around to confront the stranger and knew instantly that she faced the Elemental of Earth. Just being near him was like a steadying influence; he seemed to radiate strength. He stepped forward. "Good to see you as usual, Love, though it is a rare enough occurrence to still be a surprise." He smiled tightly and bent to kiss her hand. "Thought." A swift nod to Athena.

"I suppose you ladies aren't here just to bring a little beauty to an old man, though, so come inside and we will get to whatever business is at hand."

The Elemental stepped farther away from the wall, revealing a narrow, short little door that was really no more than a crude, thick cut right into the rock face. Athena bent to go inside and Love, seeing no alternative, could only stoop down and follow behind her.

She ended up being glad she had done so. The inner space of the Habitat was no less glorious than the other Elementals' homes she'd seen so far. It was outfitted with stone work of all kinds, mostly marble and creekstone. The floors were all tiled with thick slabs of marble, while the walls were a mosaic of rocks and gemstones. It created a glorious, rainbow interior for the wide, spacious area. Small marble archways broke the inner chamber up into smaller alcoves and rooms, while some beaded curtains hung down over the walls to create an illusion of privacy for the more private areas of the caverns.

The Habitat was not much in the way of furnishings, knicknacks, and decorations, but the beauty of the place itself made up for that in Love's esteem. She quickly sat before a wide fireplace, feeling as though the dampness of the caves were sinking down into her bones.

"So, what can I do for the First Daughters?" Earth very slowly settled his rather large mass into a long chaise. He brushed a beefy hand across his brow to relieve his eyes of the shaggy dark hair that seemed to keep falling back despite his best efforts.

"I guess you did not receive my message on the North Wind?" Athena frowned, chewing anxiously at her lower lip. Instead of seating herself, she perched precariously near the edge of the fireplace, as though too full of energy to completely settle.

The Elemental chuckled, a low rumble that seemed to shake the walls. "I have not traveled above for many Earth months now, dearest child of Air. The Winds cannot go this deep underground. The messenger can always reach me, though."

"He is…tied up with some more business of mine." Ena fidgeted slightly, and Love thought how incongruous it was that Athena had been so calm and smooth before, but now she seemed a bundle of nerves. "There is a bit of a problem."

Earth smiled, the expression cutting soft lines near his cheeks and eyes. Green eyes flashed brightly. "Surely it isn't anything that we can't take care of, Wisdom, so soothe your nerves and tell me what the matter is."

"Love is Afflicted." The words burst forth from her as though she could keep them locked in no longer, and she sat back with a long sigh after the phrase was completed.

Earth's eyes widened slightly, and he cocked his head toward Dite. "Truly? Well now, that is something of a dilemma," he said stoically.

Athena snorted, obviously thinking his words were a bit understated. "I've been taking her to all the Elementals, trying to…explain, I guess."

He rose an eyebrow at the Goddess of Wisdom, face blank. "Oh? Explain what, exactly?"

The Muse lifted her hands in an "I don't know" manner. "What you are, basically…what Immortality is…so on and so forth."

Earth nodded slowly, his eyes sliding over to look at Love. "A momentous task, indeed. You are assuming, then, that her condition cannot be reversed?"

"Well, I'm actually hoping that something on the 'tour' will spark her memory."

The Elemental rose his eyebrows, which Love would discover was about as surprised-looking as Earth could be. "And what could you possibly hope to achieve by bringing her here, then? Love has traveled down here less times than I can count on both hands."

"All I need from you is to explain yourself to her, really."

"Ah." Earth stood, bowing slightly to the Muse. "I see. Sort of an insurance, just in case she is slow to improve, then?"

Athena's smile of relief looked pained on her wan face. "That's it exactly."

"Very well, then. Come along, Love. We shall walk back to the lake and I will…*explain myself* to you." His words carried just a hint of humor as he gestured for Love to rise.

Dite quickly scrambled to her feet, following the being back out of the inner caverns.

They walked in silence for a moment, traveling near the perimeter of the underground lake. The waterfall was so quiet, she hardly believed it was a natural occurrence.

"As you know, I am the Elemental of Earth. I rule the North, the powers of strength and solidarity. Earth is a very unmoving, unchanging thing, as you know from the nature of the place itself. I am most commonly associated with living things, and rocks and caves. Growth, rebirth, and death all fall under my domain." His voice was low and deep, without inflection, but resonant and strong. It seemed to travel right through Love with its strong reverberations. She felt oddly at ease, walking next to this solid, calm man.

"My 'children,' if you will, include Hades, Will, and Renewal." He shrugged his shoulders. "Forgive me; I am not used to explaining things like this. It is rather difficult for me to do. I am not inclined to learn new things or experiences." He tried to give her a small, apologetic smile.

Love felt like laughing. "Don't worry; I'm not exactly used to this, either."

Earth did laugh then, a deep, rumbling sound that filled the far corners of the caves. He dropped an arm around her shoulders warmly and pulled her into a tight, sideways sort of hug. He sobered then, standing straighter. "I am sorry. I suppose this must all be very rough on you. Why, you must think we are all strangers. And with your human thoughts, you're probably quite topsy-turvy."

Topsy-turvy. That seemed to describe her feelings, all right. "Yes, that's it exactly."

"Well," he patted her hand, "do not fret over it. Whatever happens, that is what is meant to be. You must learn to not fight against the Fates."

Dite smirked. "I never believed in Fate, myself."

The Elemental shrugged. "No bother, you will meet her soon enough."

Love had to bite back a laugh when she realized he was serious, and once again she found herself hoping that this dream, or vision, or strange after-death trance would soon end. Meet Fate soon, indeed! This place was growing more absurd by the moment, and she was beginning to feel like Alice traveling through the looking glass into an upside-down world.

"Love? Earth?" Ena was calling from the entrance into the Elemental's inner cavern. "It's time to go."

As calming and soothing as the presence of the Earth Elemental had been, Dite was glad to be out of his dark, cavernous world.

CHAPTER FOUR

Flame

"That was strange." Dite shivered as they both piled into the carriage, glad to be above ground again. She soaked up the sunlight and heaved great lungfuls of crisp, clean air. Though her time with the Earth Elemental had not been unpleasant, the life of an underground being was not for her.

"All the Elementals are confusing beings…they know much more than we could ever imagine." The Muse's face was pensive. "But, you never worked much with Earth in any capacity, which is probably why you find him so unsettling now."

"Oh, he isn't unsettling, exactly," Love quickly corrected. "He's very…almost soothing, really. But being so deep underground makes me nervous."

Wisdom nodded, glancing out of the carriage. "It does, most."

"There's only one left, isn't there? Fire." She smiled proudly at the Goddess, amazed with herself for remembering.

But the Muse's eyes were dark, and Ena wouldn't quite meet Dite's eyes. "You remember Fire?"

Dite shook her head. "Not at all. Should I?"

Athena looked away, a golden eye trained on the carriage window. "If you were going to remember anything, it would be Fire," was her only reply.

In fact, Athena said nothing else until they approached the dwelling of this last Elemental on their whirlwind tour, and that was only when Dite shrieked so loudly the East Wind reared back slightly.

"Aphrodite!" Athena's head spun around sharply, but when she saw the true fear in Dite's eyes her tone softened. "This is Castle Flame."

"It sure is," Love whispered, face pressed up against the window to get a better view. Now that her nerves had settled, she saw just what an amazing thing it was. The East Wind, a little spooked by what was below, was circling around and around, enough to give her a wonderful view of what was beneath them.

And now she knew that the East Wind was scared, not because of her loud shriek, but because there was a lake of lava beneath them. Not just a lake of lava, either, but a lake that seemed alive with the element they were now going to visit the master of. Flames spurt from the moving lake sporadically, while narrow cliffs jut out from the red, boiling liquid to provide the only landing areas available to the horse and gilded carriage.

In the center of this lake of fire stood Castle Flame itself, a true asset to its name and the most glorious of all the homes of the Elementals, in Dite's opinion. Built entirely of shifting, scintillating flames, the castle was a wonder of golds, reds, oranges, and blues. From a distance, it would look as unstructured and wild as a roaring fire, but from their vantage point Dite could see that the apex of each flame served as a high tower. The inner portions of the castle remained solid even as the flames it was constructed of licked and lapped at each other.

"We're going to have to walk," Athena explained as the East Wind set himself and his riders down precariously on one of the high, jutting rocks in the midst of the lava pool. "Keep your skirts pulled up and don't stand in one place for too long." The Muse barked out instructions even as she pulled her long tunic up in both hands, cooed comfortingly at the East Wind, and began at a fast clip across a narrow bridge stretching out to the castle.

Love tripped behind her clumsily, kicking her skirts up and half-bouncing across the swaying rope bridge. "This is the most impressive thing I think I've ever seen," she murmured, dawdling a moment to look over the edge of the bridge at the spurting firewater below.

Athena roughly grabbed her wrist and started yanking her across the bridge. "And anything that stands still for more than a minute straight will get a flame spurt right up the nose!" Her dark head titled upwards. "See how the wind is going around and around, high up in a circle? If the wind alights for more than a minute, the flames will shoot up and snuff it out. Fire consumes Air, remember?"

Dite sensed a strange new undercurrent to Athena's tone and suddenly realized why. "You're a child of Air, aren't you?"

"That's why we have to hurry!" The Muse spit back, still dragging Love across the small bridge. "You can spend as much time looking and gaping as you want when I'm not with you," she added diplomatically.

"It's beautiful," Love replied simply, because she truly found it to be so.

Wisdom's eyes bore into her a moment, the Goddess of Thought pausing for just a moment. "You remember it?"

Love shrugged indifferently. "No, not really."

The Muse narrowed her eyes, but said nothing and pressed on.

The walk was actually a good piece, and Athena explained that the East Wind could not dare to get too close, or else it would be consumed by the fire anyway, no matter if it didn't stop moving. Finally, they reached the towering columns of flame that made up the Elemental's dwelling, and Athena pinched Dite's arm. "Your name!"

"Love!" she bit out, smarting from the pinch, casting a sidelong glare at her companion.

Suddenly, it was like a coal in a fireplace inexplicably died, for one lick of flame just fell away. Athena ushered them both inside with a quickness, and before she could even blink Love found herself standing inside Fire's domain.

Love was shocked into immobility, looking around with wide eyes at the place, when a young man came rushing down a set of spiraling stairs made of orange-red sandstone. His hair was dark auburn, his eyes looked black, and his face was dark with intensity. Personally, Dite thought he was far too young to have such an expression of worry. He stepped straight off the stairs and went to her without pause, stopping just short of her so that she could see the color of his eyes well enough to know that they weren't really black, but rather a dark, deep gray.

"My Love." It came out in a low, soft hiss, his dark eyes so intense on her face she wanted to look away. Only she couldn't look away. He stepped closer to her and she smelled the scent of sulfur and woodsmoke, and without being told Love suddenly knew that this was the Elemental Fire.

"F-fire?" she stammered, gazing up at him with a knot of fear clawing through her insides.

"My Love," he whispered again, raising one hand to touch her cheek with such tenderness that she shuddered all over. His touch was hot; it felt as though he could almost sear her skin if he was so inclined.

His appearance alone told her he was the Fire Elemental. Though much younger in appearance than the other three, his being seemed to radiate heat and knowledge that knew no end. Love stood completely still, without even breathing, trapped by the dark intensity of his gaze. "Tell me it isn't true. Tell me that seeing me right now has cured you from this horrible mess." His hands now found their way to hers, and he pressed both her palms against his heart.

"Do you remember Fire?" Athena whispered softly, prompting Love, who couldn't seem to speak or even breathe.

"I—" She stared up at him a moment longer, then forcibly broke the contact by turning to Athena. The Goddess took a deep, steadying breath, relieved to be free from the Elemental's smoldering eyes. "I don't remember."

"No, it cannot be!" Roughly, the Elemental spun Love around and stared down at her. "Your eyes," he whispered, and every word came out slow and measured. "Your eyes are that of a child's. There is no depth there, there is no spark...You are not her." He pushed her away so suddenly that she stumbled, almost tripped on her long gown, and righted herself with only a little of the Muse's help.

"Fire, we are here for a reason, and it is not so that you can act like this." The voice of Wisdom was sharp, trite.

"Do not attempt to command me, Muse," Fire snapped, glaring at her. "You and I have rarely had cause to work together, but if I do recall your greatest project was the only one you could not complete without my help. I told you then that I would request a favor from you, and that day has come. Take yourself away to Cloud Castle or TROM or the woodlands—but go now and do not return until I have sent for you."

"I cannot leave her here with you! She doesn't even know you right now!"

Love was too terrified of the Elemental to speak, but down to her slippered feet she hoped Athena would not leave her alone in his presence. He robbed her of her ability to think and speak. All the Elementals had seemed frightening to her, but this last encounter left her knees rubbery and her heart pounding in terror...and something more.

Fire's gaze was hot and full of anger when he looked to Thought next. "She knows me far better than she will ever know you. You know, Muse, that I will let no harm come to her. The being that tries to harm her I will see eternally suffer in the pits of flame. Now, begone, for you know children of Air cannot linger here, but My Love may stay as long as she wishes."

The Goddess of Wisdom drew herself up as though ready for a new round of debates, but glanced over her shoulder at the lava outside and Love could see her visibly change her mind. "Aye then, Elemental. But I will return if I think you linger too long, whether you send for me or not. We have much to do."

The Elemental waved his hand impatiently and Athena disappeared out of Castle Flame.

Love gasped at this obvious display of power and took a step backwards.

Fire smiled at her, a surprisingly tender expression on his face, and took a step closer. While the other Elementals dressed themselves in long, flowing robes, Fire chose completely different attire. Like Love herself, he dressed in a style more befitting Middle Ages fashions, wearing what Dite guessed would have been what young soldiers not dressed for the battlefield wore during those long-ago times. The Elemental sported a long red tunic with elaborate gold embroidery on the front, a long-sleeved white shirt with thick leather cuffs gracing the ends, a wide belt that held his full-sized sword, tan-colored well-fitting breeches, and high shining leather boots. The Elemental walked towards her slowly, and Love matched him step for step. Every step he took that brought him closer to her, she backed up one step. Finally, she had reached a flaming wall at her back and could go no farther without setting herself aflame, and watched helplessly as he walked straight up to her, brining his face so close to hers that their noses were almost touching.

"My Love, where should I begin? I am supposed to act as though I do not know you, but I know you so very well. You look at me with eyes I have never before seen, and fear written on your face. Surely you know that I would never, could never, hurt you."

"I have never seen you before!" Love asserted, trying to shrink back into herself to be away from this man with his intense eyes that made her feel so utterly exposed.

"Come," he spun away suddenly, throwing one arm out wide to gesture, "let us take a walk in Love's gardens, and I will speak to you on the relationship between Fire and Love." He lifted her hand delicately and slipped it inside his own, giving her a slight tug to propel her forward.

Dutifully, she fell into step beside him. He talked as they moved through the scintillating castle, pointing out the furnishings and paintings. It was actually tastefully and beautifully decorated. Murals on the ceilings showed beautiful romantic scenes, many from popular fairy tales, and the ornate tapestries and rugs seemed to be depicting abstract views of fire and flames.

"Five hundred years ago, you helped me to build these gardens," he told her as they stood paused before a heavy red velvet curtain.

She laughed. "Five hundred years ago, huh?"

"Well," he smiled at her boyishly, "give or take," and lifted the curtain, urging her through with a little shooing motion.

"Love's gardens," as he'd called them, were glorious indeed. They were entirely enclosed in glass like a greenhouse, and the Elemental explained that the air outside was too dry and hot for the plants to grow otherwise. A cool, beautiful oasis, the view of the lava lake outside was truly spectacular, and the sun broke and refracted into thousands of rainbows all through the large space. "It's gorgeous!" she whispered, bending to touch one huge white rose.

In fact, as she was to learn, all the flowers were roses. Every rose that had ever grown on Earth realm was here, from sterling roses to sweetheart roses to roses she'd never before heard of. Fountains, small marble benches built for two, and statues of lovers lined the walkways and sat tucked back into the rose trees.

"Why roses?" she asked him after they had walked for a moment, pausing to press her face against an open pink rose blossom.

"They are your favorite," the Elemental replied, taking her hand again so that she was at his side once more. "Let us sit a moment, my Love, for I have a duty I must fulfill to Athena." He led her to one of the small, cozy benches.

She had a little trouble sitting on the bench without having to press either her hip or her leg against his, and ended up hanging halfway off of it while he spoke. As he talked, the Elemental stared off into the distance instead of at her, and she had the opportunity to look at him closely for the first time. His was a masculine face, with no hint of softness to lessen the effect of intensity. His chin and jaw were square-lined and stiff, his dark brown eyebrows heavy and prone to draw together over his dark, brooding eyes. His jaw was inclined to jut out, she saw, for he grit his teeth a lot. His nose was fine and straight, being just a little too thick as though carved straight from stone, but it was almost a perfect Roman nose otherwise. His lips were a little too full, but he could press them together so they appeared a cruel, tight slash across his bronzed skin.

"I won't insult your intelligence by going through all the 'I am the Elemental of Fire' stuff that you already know," he began. "What you perhaps don't know right now is that I am the Elemental which controls Passion."

Here Love couldn't help but to interrupt him. "Isn't passion an emotion?"

He smiled slightly. "You are clever. Passion sort of falls into both categories, but passion is so strong and uncontrollable that it falls into my domain. Like fire, passion is often uncontrollable and uncontainable and it burns."

That made more sense to her. She nodded, and he continued.

"My 'child' is the God of War, whom you are not very good friends with, but nonetheless he is my First son—sort of."

She looked at him in surprise. "You created war?"

The Elemental smiled and shook his head. "Man created War. That, My Love, is a long story that you will remember soon enough. While Fire is out of control by nature, there must be fire for there to be many other things, and so there must be war as well."

Love nodded. It was beginning to make sense to her in a way. She felt as though some big picture was coming into slow focus.

"I am that which rules South, and the feeling passion and all other aspects of the flame which I rule." He turned to look at her finally, and his eyes seemed darker than ever. "You and I usually work very closely together—in fact, we have known each other longer and better than any of the other Elementals and goddesses, excluding those Elementals and their First Daughters." He smiled slightly, but his eyes still remained shadowed.

But Love was still having trouble digesting all of this. "Oh, really."

He nodded slowly. "Love and Passion," he stated simply. "Our first project didn't work so well, and it took us a good two hundred years before we could figure out how to construct the perfect romance, but we finally did it." He smiled softly. "You remember, hmm?"

She frowned. "Of course not! How could I?"

The Elemental laughed harshly, looking away. "You look the same. For a moment I forgot that you think with a little human mind now. Leave me now. I no longer require you." He lifted his hand and in a thick voice said, "Spark!"

A freckle-faced redhead came sliding into the room so fast that he passed them up and had to jog back. A cursory bow and a quick "Yes, Master?" left the lad panting for breath and almost doubled over with the exertion of running thorough the fiery castle from wherever he'd been beforehand.

"Summon Athena. Tell her to take the human out of here." The Elemental stood, looking down on Love darkly. "You will excuse me, Aphrodite, but I must be off and about to other things now." He bowed slightly, his lips pressed together in such a way that she thought perhaps his gesture was a mocking one, and disappeared into thin air.

"Milady Love." The lad bowed to her before running back through the gardens, presumably to follow Fire's instruction.

Shakily, Love stood and began to try and retrace her steps to head back inside the castle, feeling somehow that she had done something irrevocably wrong.

Before she could even finish passing the beds of pink roses, Athena was striding towards her quickly, her tunic flapping behind her in the breeze she created. "Well, come on, Love, the lava's bubbling up. What did you say to

59

him, anyway!" Before the Goddess could answer, Thought was yanking her back down the garden paths with an impatient snort. "I'm tired of having to run out of every place because of you, you know! Upsetting Elementals is a dangerous business!"

Love didn't bother defending herself against the rampaging Athena; she was too preoccupied trying to keep pace with the Muse as she fairly flew down the garden trails and then through Castle Flame, out the door, and across the rickety rope bridge.

In fact, it wasn't until they were back in the carriage and up in the air that Love turned to Athena with curiosity in her eyes. "I'm confused."

The Muse nodded as though it were expected. "Of course you are. You think like a human."

Love frowned at her but decided to press on. After all, there was no one to talk to, save the Muse. If she wanted answers, she was going to have to get them out of Wisdom. "Assuming that you're right about all this, assuming that I really am the Goddess of Love and I know this place and I just have some weird deity amnesia or whatever…tell me about Fire."

Wisdom sucked in a sharp breath and raised one perfectly sculpted eyebrow at the woman across from her. "What?"

"I…I don't know, maybe it's just my imagination but I sensed…or maybe I remembered…something." She looked at Athena shyly, fearful of being ridiculed for her ambiguity. Maybe the Goddess would call her a "human" again as though it was the most awful thing for anyone to be.

But the Muse only nodded slowly and sighed breezily. "I thought as much would happen. The relationship between Love and Passion is a very strained one, indeed." Wisdom's eyes took on a dark, shadowed look much like Fire's had been.

Love frowned, not understanding what all the entendres and secrets meant, but knowing that she was tired of being kept in the dark. "Start explaining," she demanded, crossing her arms over her chest and leaning back. It was her unmovable, untouchable position, and it nearly always worked.

The Muse only gazed at her for long, long moments and then she, too, leaned back in her seat. "Name the most romantic couple you can think of."

"What?" She wanted answers, not questions, and here Athena was quizzing her on romance!

"Do it."

"Ahhh… Guenivere and Lancelot, I guess. Or, Romeo and Juliet. Sleeping Beauty and her Prince, maybe…Anna and the King of Siam…but those were all fairy tales. I don't know any truly romantic couples."

"They may be fairy tales now, but they were once living, breathing beings on Earth realm."

Love snorted. "Sleeping Beauty was real? And I know Romeo and Juliet weren't real—Shakespeare wrote that play."

"You were the Sleeping Beauty, Aphrodite. You were also Guenivere. And Juliet. And dozens and dozens of others that you can't name now because their stories were never told. All those times, Fire was Lancelot, or Romeo, or the King of Siam. Your match."

Dite wanted to laugh it off as silliness. "But those were all stories!"

"But you lived their real, true lives!" Athena cried, sitting forward in her seat. Her eyes were bright. "Stop denying everything, Love, quit being such a jaded human being! You are not now, and never have been, human! You've gone to Earth realm to live countless lives, all the time, and always you cause trouble of some sort."

Love fairly growled at her. "We were talking about Fire, remember?"

Athena gave her a "don't push it" look and leaned back again, brows furrowed. "The two things that all humans crave in their lives are love and passion. All the greatest romances are full of both these aspects," Wisdom explained carefully, her words even. "You are the embodiment of Love, and he Passion."

"So it's only natural that he and I would feel...drawn to each other," Dite concluded.

"You really have gotten brighter since your Affliction, Dite," Athena half-teased, smirking. "But yes, that's right."

Love frowned. "I see...were Love and Passion an 'item' before I came here?" she asked.

"Sadly, no." The Muse turned her dark head out the window. "An Elemental and a Goddess cannot be an 'item.'"

"Why not?"

It took Ena so long to reply that Love had reached the conclusion she simply wasn't going to when the Muse turned sad eyes toward her. "An Elemental is not the same sort of being as a Goddess. We are old, Aphrodite, and we have been here since man existed. I've heard tell that you have been here even before that. But the Elementals, well the Elementals have been here since before Time itself existed. They are the second oldest intelligent beings in the known Universe, and they are made up of different things than we are."

"So it would be almost like a human and a Goddess getting together, right?"

The Muse thought on that notion a moment and sighed. "Well, in a way, I suppose. But it's always been a very sad, sad, thing, the sorrows of Love and Passion. All the great storytellers speak of you and he, and it is a sad tale even on Earth realm. Or, it was, when people still cared for fairy tales."

Dite was moved by the sad dilemma it presented. "Is that why he and I went down to Earth realm so much as humans?"

Athena nodded. "It is the only way to 'bend the rules,' so to speak. But you've not done so for a very long time, not since the Romantic Era on Earth realm. There have been new troubles that are unrelated to that," she spit out the explanation quickly.

"That's not the only reason, is it?"

"What isn't?" Athena glared at her as though exhausted with endless questions, but Love sensed she liked showing off her vast knowledge.

"Just so Love and Passion can be together. That isn't the only reason for going down to Earth realm, is it? That's not the only reason Gods and Goddesses do it."

Athena focused her eyes out the window. "Rest yourself, now, and stop plying me with your endless questions. Your poor human head will explode if you absorb too much information. Sit quiet, now, and leave me alone."

Dite sensed that she shouldn't ask Athena more questions, but she felt as though she were getting close to whatever hidden explanation seemed to be just out of her reach. The itching in her hands was back, and she knew that there was something still being hidden from her…something big.

CHAPTER FIVE

TROM

Love snapped herself out of her deep reverie when the East Wind came to a shuddering halt. Dite received a jolt that saw her pressed up against the carriage door, and Athena was already hopping out of the carriage into whatever strangeness awaited them beyond.

"Where, ah, are we now?"

The dark head poked into the carriage window for a split second. "TROM," it replied.

"Trom?" Love mumbled, pulling her skirts up to tumble out of the carriage.

"Thousand Room Mansion," the Muse replied, helping Dite down onto the ground.

At least the landscape was more normal this time. They stood at the end of what looked like a worn country road, the dirt and gravel both hard-packed from continuous use. The house itself sat nestled in tall oak trees, and a huge wraparound porch sat overflowing with furnishings and potted plants of all shapes and sizes. "It's *big*," Love whispered, tilting her head backward to look up at the place.

"It doesn't have exactly a thousand rooms." Wisdom tried to be helpful. "Actually, it originally only had nine hundred twenty-six, but with the new additions nowadays TROM has nine hundred eighty-four."

Nine hundred and eighty-four. Love whistled appreciatively, still staring open-mouthed at the structure. Unlike the other homes she'd seen here, TROM was not beautiful or opulent. It was as utilitarian as it could possibly be, with only that huge porch to give some aesthetic effect. TROM sat like a huge rectangle, with perfectly spaced windows and one huge set of double doors. The only break in the tall, wide outside walls were the small, slitted windows that dotted the house in five neat rows. Made of brick that had faded to an uninspiring shade, TROM looked as plain as a prison.

"Who lives here?"

Athena laughed lightly, already making her way up a broken cobbled path to the large front doors. "The question is: Who *doesn't* live here?"

Love, frowning and tired of Ena's endless riddles, tripped up the path precariously in her dragging pink skirts. "Fine. Who doesn't live here, then?"

"All the Elementals and First Creations," Ena chirped, raising her hand to rap sharply on the door. "TROM is where all the second and lesser creations live, as well as all the consorts who don't live with their Masters or Mistresses. Even so, the consorts all come here to visit. TROM is a vile place," she added wrinkling her pert nose as if smelling something distasteful.

As soon as the thick door opened, the noise spilled out from TROM onto that huge porch, and both Goddesses took an involuntary step backwards. "What in the realm?" Recovering more quickly, Thought stepped forward with a vicious scowl on her face.

Inside the thousand-room mansion, it sounded as though a thousand voices were raised and merry. Loud laughter and shouted greetings and general sounds of a large gathering became deafening in the still sunlight. The door closed almost immediately after Athena's barked question, but she quickly stepped forward and planted a shoulder firmly against the oak. "You open this door instantly! Goddess of Thought and Goddess of Love arriving!"

The door swung open quickly, and Ena reached out a lightning hand to grab the youth that was trying to scurry back into the safety inside. "Oh, no, you don't." Like a mother with her kittens, Athena picked the lad up by the scruff of his neck and brought her sharp eyes close to his. "Is TROM celebrating something? I certainly hope all the merry-making is because the Goddess of Love has returned to Immortality safely."

"O-o-of c-course, Milady Thought. Good to see you, Lady Love." The boy gave them both a sickly smile, his legs still dangling mid-air.

Athena, with one dark eyebrow quirked up into a questioning arc, set him down on his feet again. "If I hear any different, I'll personally see you serving Hades for the next two hundred years." With that, she released him and he took off like a shot inside TROM.

Ena turned to look at Love, swinging open the doors. "Welcome to TROM, Aphrodite."

Warily, Love stepped inside the thousand-room mansion. Quickly, Athena tucked Love's arm through hers and started leading her deeper inside TROM. "Stay next to me, don't get lost, and if any one asks you a question—don't answer. I'll answer for you." The whispered instructions were delivered right next to Love's ear, and hearing Ena's furtiveness she moved closer and fell perfectly into step with the Goddess.

TROM wasn't any more splendid on the inside than the outside, but according to Athena it had more to do with lazy occupants than anything else. The murals and tapestries looked old and faded, and there was no harmony to the furnishings or the décor. It seemed pieces from all time periods and places had been haphazardly thrown here and there, and everything had stayed unmoving ever since. It looked more like a museum of furniture history than a home.

They crossed the front foyer quickly, and Athena pushed them on to the ballroom, where the center of activity was. Love gripped her friend tighter, already steeling herself for whatever strangeness she was about to encounter.

The ballroom was pretty enough, gold wallpaper and a tiled marble floor. There was even a very, very old, very, very dusty chandelier suspended from the ceiling. It was old enough to have real candles in it, instead of tiny lightbulbs, and Dite privately thought it lent a certain Victorian loveliness to the room.

Athena, always one to make her presence felt, moved quickly through the room with Love in tow. Most simply got out of the way when they saw her coming, but at every few people she had to stop and say, "Excuse me," in a very short-tempered voice.

As they tore through the ballroom of TROM, Athena's lips were close to Love's ear again, reporting. "See the dark-haired girl over there in the corner? That's your sister Sorrow. That creature next to her with the orange hair and the strange body markings is Fear. Remember that big Viking gentleman from your party—the one with the hammer? That's Thor, protector to all the Gods, and he's standing next to your biggest rival in all of Immortality, Eurynome."

Here Love was able to ask a question, as Athena was sucking up another quick breath so she could rush on. "Rival?"

"Eury is the Goddess of Sensuality, and the only one who gets as many Gods as you do."

"Oh." The woman in question was beautiful enough, with rich chestnut curls that fell to her waist and a certain quality about her that seemed to throw signals of sexuality through the air.

"See that devil in the red velvet jacket, the one staring at us as though we are lunch? That's Loki. Now, he's trouble, so once he hears about your condition he's sure to come around. Avoid him. And that old, old woman with the three-headed dog, that's Hecate. She's very wise. If I get the chance,

I'll introduce you later. Hecate should be able to help. And—oh!—there he is, Q!" With that happy cry, Athena started rushing forward more quickly. Love had to hang onto her for dear life just to keep up.

Almost instantly they were on the other side of the ballroom, and Athena was pushing Love and a curly-headed youth through the doors to the corridor outside. "Q, am I happy to see you!" Athena was actually grinning for once, an expression that didn't look so out of place on her porcelain skin after all. "Come, take us somewhere more private."

The boy blinked twice at the Goddess of Wisdom, looked at Love questioningly, nodded, and started leading them down the long, plain halls of TROM. After an endless maze of twists and turns that Dite knew she had no hope of remembering, the boy pushed open a heavy door and led them into a small, sweet little parlor.

"Ahhh." Athena plopped herself down on a deep purple chaise, rubbing her hands together. "How I hate coming to TROM."

Love quickly seated herself in a high-backed lady's chair, trying to sneak covert glances at the young boy, wondering what Athena could possibly need him for.

The boy, however, was staring open-mouthed at the Goddess of Love. He frowned at her, golden eyebrows screwed together over bright baby blue eyes. Then, in a gesture that surprised Dite almost out of her chair, he kneeled before her. Bowing his golden head full of curls, he waited on one knee for her to...do something.

Helplessly, Dite looked up at Athena. Wisdom must have seen the sheer panic in her friend's eyes. "Q," Ena said softly. "Rise, and sit next to me. We must talk."

The boy called "Q" pretended not to hear her, keeping his bright yellow curls bowed low, waiting for some response from Love. "What did I do?" she cried, throwing up her hands. "Rise, boy, and sit with Ena already!"

At that, the lad quickly popped to his feet and planted himself next to Ena.

Dite frowned over the situation, looking at the boy with questions in her eyes. He kept his eyes lowered.

"Q, there have been some problems—have you heard?"

"I try not to pay attention to the rumors around TROM." The lad shrugged, but cast a quick glance at Love.

"Aphrodite has the Affliction."

The boy, chin to chest, nodded slowly. "Those are the rumors, all right."

"But you see that this sort of thing cannot become common knowledge. We must be very careful."

Q looked up at her, eyes wide. "What do you need me to do?"

"I have my own matters to attend to. First, I have to deal with TROM. I have to find the messenger…well, I have affairs that I must deal with. Would you take Dite back to Love's Palace for me? Perhaps you can even help her, answer questions for her. In fact, why don't you explain the relationship of consorts to her. And tell her about the people in TROM. Just talk to her, Q."

Love, however, was terrified. Athena couldn't leave her! She couldn't go off with this young boy she'd never seen before! To no avail, Dite kept trying to catch the Muse's eye. Athena, however, wasn't paying any attention.

Q nodded and rose, giving the Muse a curt bow. "As you wish, Lady Thought." He turned to Love with a slight smile. "Milady?"

"Excuse me." She gave him a quick smile and ran to catch up to Athena, who was just now making her way out the door—without a goodbye, no less! "Ena!" Love grabbed the Muse's arm quickly. "You can't leave me with him—I don't even know him!"

Athena, pulling her arm away, shot Love a fierce glare. "Of course you do, Aphrodite. Q is your consort, for sakes!" Impatiently, Ena started away.

Love, jogging to catch up, panted alongside her. "My what?"

"Consort!" Exasperated, Ena turned to look at her. "Q is your consort, and has been for the past few millennia. If I can't leave you with him, then you aren't safe with anyone. Besides, everyone with half some cognizant skills knows that Q is your consort. You should even know that, just from your time on Earth realm."

"I've never heard of him before!" Love protested.

The Must rose an eyebrow, and Love knew that the Goddess of Wisdom was about to score a point. "You have never heard that Cupid is the servant to the Goddess of Love? Perhaps your mortal life was spent under a rock, yes?" And with that, Thought sauntered away without a backward glance.

"CUPID?" Love demanded at her retreating back, the name echoing loudly through the hallway. "Cupid," she repeated in a quieter tone, laughter bubbling up in her throat. Of course, "Q" stood for "Cupid." How this place was getting on her nerves already!

"Milady? You called for me?" The boy—Cupid—was suddenly at her side.

"I, ah…yes, yes, I did. We should be on our way to Love's Palace, I guess."

"Yes, Milady." The lad nodded smartly, even giving her the slightest hint of a smile.

And then he stood there. Love looked at him a long moment, waiting for him to start moving, but he seemed to be waiting for her. "Well I can't bleeding well find my way there myself!" she finally snapped, voice raising on a high, shrill note.

The youth seemed to shrink back, then he nodded. "Aye, Mistress, I shall lead the way, but it will be awful slow going on foot." He started off down the hallway, checking over his shoulder every few seconds to be sure she was still behind him. Dite was beginning to feel like a child, or maybe a pet that's prone to wandering off.

"Well, how else would we get there?"

Cupid was leading her down the long, dimly lit hallways quickly, glancing around periodically as if he were spooked about running into other people. "Love's Tunnel, of course."

"I'm afraid I'm not quite sure what that is, but if it's safe then I'll try anything."

"Mistress, this one cannot take you to Love's Tunnel…only Love can enter, and anyone Love takes with her."

Oh, this was ridiculous. Talking with Cupid was worse than Athena's riddles. "Fine. Take me to the door, or something, and I'll get us in." Now, how was she supposed to get in if he wasn't even sure how to?

Cupid looked at her a moment blankly, as though he wanted to say more, but simply shrugged and continued on through the long corridors of TROM. Finally, he led them to a side door and they were outside. Love had never felt so relieved to be away from any place before. The way Ena acted, the residents of the thousand-room mansion would rise up against her.

"Here we are." Cupid finally stopped moving away from TROM, somewhere near the thick stand of trees outside. He turned and looked at her with those wide eyes, waiting as usual.

She carefully spun around in a wide circle, looking for the reason Cupid had stopped. "There's nothing *here*."

The youth shrugged. "We can always walk."

"Where is the entrance to this tunnel you spoke of?"

He grinned, cheeks suddenly dimpling up at her. "There is an entrance wherever you decide there should be one. It is your Tunnel, after all…and you are one of the First." He looked like he wanted to laugh at her.

Love sighed. This boy talked even crazier than Ena did. How was she going to make an entrance to something she wasn't even sure was there. "How, ah, do I usually go about doing it?"

Cupid scratched his head, tilting it sideways to look at her oddly. "You don't know?"

She shook her head.

Cupid, with a sigh of sadness, moved to stand next to her. "Usually you raise your left hand and draw an entrance in the air."

What? Shrugging, she lifted her left arm and made a short archway in the thin air. "Like this?"

As soon as she took her fingers away, the world seemed to split and suddenly, a little wooden door exactly to the proportions of her air drawing stood before them. Unthinkingly, Love let out a whoop of joy. "Would you look at that! Just take a look at that, now! Ha ha!"

"Yes, Milady, it is the entrance to Love's Tunnel." Cupid only nodded sedately.

His mundane reaction to what Dite was convinced was the greatest thing in the world put something of a damper on her high spirits, but she tried not to let it get to her. "What's inside?" Nervously, she tapped the doorknob with uncertain fingers.

"Love's Tunnel, Milady." Of course, Cupid probably felt like he was repeating himself, but Love thought to herself that he wouldn't have that problem if he would just answer her questions properly.

"Yes," she snapped impatiently, fingers still twitching on the doorknob, "But *what?*"

The lad seemed to think on that for a long moment, because he was silent for the span of several heartbeats. "Your underground waterway. It spans everything in Immortality. You use it to travel from place to place."

Underground waterway! That was intriguing enough to send her through the short, narrow doorway. She hunched herself up, bent double, and quickly stepped through. Cupid followed fast on her heels. The door disappeared behind them, but Dite was too awestruck to notice that bit of magic. They were in Love's Tunnel, the private method of transportation that only she used. It was interesting, indeed. They climbed down, down, down underground by way of a long spiraling staircase, finally breaking out into the area after a rather long trek underground.

A dark, cavernous place, Love's Tunnel was not all that drab and dreary. Surely, it couldn't be, for it was a belonging of the Goddess of Love. It was all constructed of stone, with torches burning in the walls in their own little niches. The stones gleamed with water and a soft, steady lapping noise echoed against the walls.

"It's like Venice!" Dite cried, and that just about summed it up. Narrow streams of water cut into the thick stone foundation, but so many waterways crisscrossed around that the stone flooring was all but useless. Beautiful hanging mosses and vines grew up and over the walls, while water-loving flowering weeds sprang up through cracks in the ground.

The surface of the water was completely covered with rose petals, and moored at a little dock right next to the staircase they'd traveled down was the boat.

"Oh!" With a squeal, Dite went rushing forward to examine it. Shaped like a huge swan, the white boat was tall and elegant. Its tall neck served as a mast for the craft, while the proud tailfeathers in back worked like a rudder. The wingtips cupped the boat where people were to sit, and Dite climbed aboard with no fear. It was the bravest she had been since waking up, so long ago, but somehow she felt completely safe here.

The boat was fairly comfortable sitting, too, for the interior was outfitted with soft silk cushions, and the long row benches had small backs to lean against while riding. "This is marvelous! Cupid, hop in."

Q, at that moment, was pacing back and forth on the dock, looking down at Dite. She had settled herself quite comfortably in the vessel and sat grinning up at him. "This one is afeared of the water, Milady. You never bring me down here. Only when it's necessary."

"Well, it is, and water isn't going to hurt you. Now, sit in here and keep still!" Her voice came out a little harsher than she'd intended, and she flinched at her own words after saying them.

Cupid nodded and ever so carefully placed one foot in the boat. As if knowing his fear then, the water suddenly rose up and jolted the swan boat lightly. It was enough to send Cupid jumping back onto the dock, blue eyes wide as saucers.

"Cupid!" Love had to bite back a giggle at his antics. Imagine, being scared of such a thing!

The consort saw the laughter in her eyes and quickly seated himself. He still looked absolutely terrified, but at least he was sitting still.

…Yet there was still a problem. "Cupid." She leaned forward, lowering her voice as though someone might overhear. "Now what?"

The youth grinned, chuckling slightly. "Tell it where you want to go."

"I want to go to Love's Palace, do I not?"

Cupid never needed to answer her question, because as soon as the words left her mouth the craft started to move with no visible means of operation. It began to wend its way slowly down a watercourse, and they were on their way.

Love was fascinated with the scenery of the place as they moved along docilely in the large swan-boat. The natural mosses and vines sprouted small colorful wildflowers along with dark green leaves, and it gave the entire place a natural beauty it would not have had if decorated purposefully. "It's actually very pretty," she murmured, turning her head every which way to see it all.

"Yes, Milady. It took you a long time to construct the Tunnel. Nowadays, it's a rather popular attraction on Earth realm."

"What do you mean?"

"The, ah 'Tunnel of Love,' I believe it's called."

After the reality of his words sunk in, she spent a few moments staring at him. "You're saying amusement park owners got the idea from me?"

The boy shrugged. "Of course. Athena herself inspired the first one who created a 'Tunnel of Love,' and you loved it then."

"Uh huh," she muttered. Some of the things she heard in this place really were just too much. "Were you going to tell me about TROM?"

Cupid gave a little shudder, obviously not keen on the idea. "Of course, Mistress, it is my duty to serve you always. What is it you want to know?"

Love's mind was working in so many different directions she was afraid to choose just one. "Your duty to serve me? What do you mean by that? And why do all those people live in TROM—who are they? Is it a bad place? You and Ena both act like it is."

Q laughed. "Slow down, Mistress, I can only answer one thing at a time. It is my duty to serve you because I am your consort, and always have been. I was your first," he added with a touch of indignation and more than a little pride. "The residents of TROM are the consorts who do not live with their Masters and Mistresses, and the lesser creations."

"What is a 'consort'? And what is a 'lesser creation'?"

Cupid sighed. Obviously, he hadn't expected that he would have to explain so much to her. "A consort, Mistress, is something like a personal servant to the Gods or Goddesses. First Creations and one of the Elementals currently have consorts. The First Creations, like you and Lady Thought, use consorts to help with their business on Earth realm. Your jobs are otherwise too much for you to handle by yourselves. You usually need someone to take care of

the smaller tasks. That's where consorts come in. You created me yourself."
He flashed another prideful smile. "Lesser creations are those deities who
are not First Creations—like your brother, Hate. Eury, Loki, Thor, these are
all lesser creations. It simply means they are here to aid you and the First
Creations, and the Elementals."

"I...see." Sort of. Maybe. She thought on what he'd said for a moment,
then, "What 'business' do I have on Earth realm?"

He gaped at her, open mouthed. "Has Lady Thought not explained to you
your purpose? Have you forgotten even the reason why you are here?"

She felt itchy all over, that feeling she'd had when she had first awakened
here, that feeling that she was missing something very, very important.
"I...suppose I have."

He swallowed, nodded, and refused to look at her as he spoke. "Well,
Mistress, as the Goddess of Love it is your duty to take care of all love on
Earth realm. You create it, foster it, and direct it. It would be a very bad
mistake indeed, for instance, if a mother did not love her children. You breathe
love into all mothers, and into all children. You create romantic love...things
of this nature."

So, the deities had a duty to the people of Earth. That was why they spent
so much time there. That was, apparently, why she had gone in the first
place. "I'm beginning to understand. Cupid, you are the one who shoots your
arrows of love into people's hearts, yes?"

"Yes."

"And I tell you where to aim them?"

"Always, Mistress."

"Ah." She leaned back, nibbling on her lower lip in thought. "And the
lesser creations, we need them for the balance, yes? Hate and Sorrow and
Fear...they must exist because goodness exists, but they are not as
predominant as Thought, Love, War, things of this nature."

Cupid was nodding furiously, grinning from ear to ear. "Mistress! You
will be your old self again in no time at all!"

"Now, the consorts...the consorts are created to aid the First in their
workings. But what are consorts? They are not deities...are they immortal?
Where do they come from? Are they saints who have died?"

"The messenger was a boy who died long, long ago, but he is a rare case.
The other consorts, like me, were woven from the Aspects. And nothing is
immortal, not even the Mother Herself."

Now, she was lost. "Aspects? Mother? Woven?"

Q sighed. "I am sorry, Mistress, I keep forgetting that you are limited to human thinking." He situated himself in his seat so that he was as far away from the water on all sides as possible, and leaned forward. "The Aspects are possibly the most powerful of all things in Immortality. The weavings of the Aspects are found only in Chaos, which is impossible to go through. The Elementals, or the Mother, or the First Creations, take these weavings and weave them together to make a being—a consort, or a First Creation. I'm afraid that I don't know much about it, being only a consort myself, but the way you explained it to me is that the weavings of the Aspects are long, thin lines like spider webs. Each one represents a different trait or gift. You weave certain Aspects together to create a consort, or First Creation. But only the Elementals and the Mother know how to make First Creations, and it is difficult even so to make consorts."

"And these weavings are found where?"

"In Chaos, Mistress, but don't ask me to explain Chaos to you because I can't."

"Can you tell me why you can't, at least?"

The boy looked down, his cheeks turning pink. "We are not supposed to speak on the subject."

"Oh, well, I certainly wouldn't want to get you into trouble. Can you tell me about the Mother?"

His head popped up and one wary blue eye looked at her. "You mean you really don't know who the Mother is?"

She shook her head.

Cupid gave such a sigh, surely such a thing would break a human heart on Earth realm. "The Mother is...the Mother. She is the Mother of All. She is the Mother of the Elementals, she is the Mother of the First, and she is the Mother to the Earth realm. Once upon a time, she was worshipped by every culture of man. She was revered and the moon was looked upon as her face, the Earth as her body. But then, the rise of the Fathergod."

"The...oh, I think I'm getting this now. The Mother is the old pagan Goddess who was worshipped before Christianity rose in Rome, yes? She had so many names...lessee...she was called the 'Triple Goddess,' wasn't she? Demeter? Wasn't that one of her names?"

"You remember!" Cupid gave a little excited jump, causing the boat to roll slightly, and he let out a little yelp.

"Nooo...." She replied slowly, "I read about it once, I think. So the Mother is the true Creator, is that what you are saying?"

"She is not a 'Creator' in the religious sense, Mistress. Man is the 'Creator.'"

"*Man* is the Creator?"

The youth nodded and looked at her as though he pitied her simplistic mind. "It is because of man that there is love. It is because of man that there is thought, war, creativity, poetry, and music. You have seen their embodiments, the deities of these things…they exist only because man still recognizes them. I told you that nothing is Immortal. Well, nothing is. Should man decide one day to never feel love again, you would cease to exist, and so would I. If, one day, there is complete and total peace on Earth realm with no battles or warring at all, that will mean the end of Mars. Man chose to see the Mother, and so was the Mother named."

It all sounded far too esoteric for Aphrodite, however. It was not tangible, concrete. She had never believed in anything she couldn't see and feel and touch and taste. "Faith" was a foreign concept to her. She could not simply blindly believe in anything, and what Cupid was saying was still too far out of her comprehension.

"Perhaps we should talk on simpler subjects," she suggested kindly.

"Let us do, Mistress. This one is very bad at discussions like these. Mistress, maybe you should summon Lady Thought's consort, if she does not need him. That one is very good at philosophy and explaining things."

He sounded so disappointed that Love couldn't work up the heart to make him feel any worse. Unthinkingly, she reached out to ruffle his blonde curls affectionately. "Not to worry, Q, you are doing splendidly. What do you know about Fire?"

Cupid shrunk away quickly, when only moments before he'd been basking in her attention. Now he looked at her with eyes that were frightened and as big as saucers. "What of him?"

"Cupid…? What is the matter?"

Before the boy could answer her, the boat bounced against a small docking platform.

"Here we are, Mistress. The secret entrance to Love's Palace." And without further delay, he jumped out of the boat and the water he hated so much.

CHAPTER SIX

Love's Palace

The dock led to a small alcove, where a door stood hidden by hanging moss and thick vines. "You always keep it this overgrown, Mistress, it is for protection," Cupid explained patiently when she muttered an angry remark about "How is anyone supposed to find the silly handle?" Of course, she felt as though she could go all day long without Cupid pleasantly telling her about how it was for protection in that calm, childlike voice of his that made her feel so utterly out of touch.

She finally managed to get the creaking door open and stumbled inside the beautiful castle that everyone told her was her own.

...And found herself smack in the middle of a very busy kitchen. A handful of young maids stared at her, and she knew she looked a sight. Her hair had been falling down all day and she kept pushing it back up, so much that by now it was sure to look like a bird's nest. Her dress was ripped and tattered at the ends, and her dainty little slippers were mud- and lava-stained. What she couldn't know was that she also had dirt smudges on her cheeks, some of the latches on her gown had come undone in the back, and one of her sleeves was ripped above the elbow.

"I was in the Tunnel," she mumbled inadequately. The housemaids continued to stare. "Go along now, back to whatever you were doing." She lifted her chin up, trying to muster some dignity, and began to walk regally through the kitchen.

"Wrong way," Cupid hissed behind her, carefully taking her elbow and steering her in the right direction.

"Thank you," Dite finally told him once they were in the upstairs bedroom where this whole mess had began. "Let me guess," she said, really looking carefully around the room for the first time. "This is my room."

"They are all your rooms in a sense, Mistress, but yes, this is what is known as 'Love's Boudoir.'" And then he grinned.

"'Love's Boudoir'?" she repeated.

"You have a liking for the dramatic, Mistress."

She was too tired to even argue. "Oh, I do, do I?"

The boy shrugged. "Well, since I've known you."

"And how long has that been?" She was busy pulling off her soiled, torn slippers.

"Ohhh…." He looked upward, thinking. "Since the twelfth century. Give or take fifty years."

The twelfth *century*? "That's nine hundred years."

He smiled proudly.

This was beginning to get out of hand, she was thinking. Dite was now trying to pull the pins and tangles out of her hair at once, ripping impatient fingers through the mass.

"Mistress, you will soon be bald if you keep doing that. This one can get Rose if you wish it."

"Rose? Oh, the little redhead? She's not my consort too, is she?"

"Oh, no, you only have one consort and that's me. Rose is your maid."

"My *maid*?"

He nodded. "All the First and the Elementals have non-consort servants. Some of the consorts are just too important to waste on menial tasks."

"Menial tasks?"

"Cleaning, for instance."

She raised up an eyebrow and gazed at him through a tangle of blonde that was now in her face. "You'd think in Immortality there wouldn't be any dirt."

"Immortality most closely resembles Earth realm, Mistress. Dirt and all."

"I see. So, where do the servants come from? Did I weave Rose, too?"

"They are those who have died."

Now she was starting to get answers to those questions that truly bothered at her. "Ah ha! So this *is* where the dead go!"

"No, no." He held up his hands. "Only some of them. Most First pick their own house staff from those on Earth realm. And when they end that lifecycle, they immediately come here."

"Explain to me what happens to mortals in death, then. Slowly, please." She had managed to get one of the pins out and went to work on another, sitting herself down in the chaise near the fireplace to hear Cupid talk.

"All those on Earth realm are reincarnated. But there are exceptions. Rose, for instance, was a Lady's maid in the court of Queen Eleanor of England,

and so you picked her to become your maid upon her mortal death. Now she will dwell here, until she expresses some desire to be reincarnated back into the Earth realm, or until one millenium has passed. It's all very strict." He nodded for emphasis. "Other souls go to the Underworld to be reformed before they can be reincarnated into the Earth realm."

"So, there is a Hell...but no Heaven. I always thought that perhaps it would be the other way around." She sighed helplessly. "So the good souls just keep reincarnating and reincarnating, over and over?"

"Until they have solved their problem. Every soul is born with one large problem, or difficulty. This problem stays with that soul until it is finally solved during one of their lifecycles."

"And then..."

"We don't know."

She'd expected some sort of ludicrous reply, and she wasn't disappointed. "You don't know."

"Not the consorts, no, none of us know. Maybe the First know, but you never told me, Mistress, so I can't be sure. Or the Elementals. The Elementals know of many things they cannot or will not speak of."

She was dumbstruck. Here she was, in the land of the deities, and they couldn't even tell her what happened to human beings when they died! "What's Hell like?"

"It's called 'The Underworld,' Mistress, and you should know that Hades is very touchy about that. And this one has never been there. You have."

"Great. Maybe later I'll ask myself just how it was," Love snapped sarcastically, throwing one of the pins she'd just raked out for emphasis.

"Cupid is sorry, Mistress, but this one does not have the answers you want. This one is only a consort."

She felt her anger fade away at the plaintive sorrow in his young voice. "I am terribly sorry, Q, please forgive me. Maybe you should get the little redhead for me now. I think I need this all cut out." She pulled at a loose strand of hair and watched the whole mass move.

"Say her name, Mistress."

"What?"

"Her name, Mistress. Call her."

She had no other alternative. "Rose. Oh, Rose." It sounded strange to say the name in her normal speaking voice, but Cupid was looking at her with those confident blue eyes.

And suddenly, the little red-haired girl was standing in the doorway.

"Mistress, your hair!" She bustled over, clucking. "Hello there, Q." She threw a saucy little smile at him over her shoulder even as she rushed over to where Love was seated.

Cupid actually blushed. He ducked his head slightly to hide his pink cheeks and managed a hasty, "Greetings, Rose."

He couldn't look up again until Rose was busy combing through Dite's hair, which had turned into a haven for tangles. She even found a few broken twigs in it, probably from the quick flight through Castle Flame that Athena had led Love on.

Dite had a hard time sitting still while Rose fiddled with her hair; she'd always been wildly independent. She squirmed and moved around and kept reaching her hands up to try and help, but Rose was having none of it.

"If you don't sit still, Mistress, it can't be finished!" The girl went on to mutter things about how impatient her Mistress was, all to the sheer delight of Cupid who was laughing uproariously.

As soon as her hair was brushed down, Dite scrambled out of the chair to be away from Rose, who was fussing over the rips and stains on the special pink gown she'd picked for her Mistress.

"Oh, it's *fine*, Rose, for goodness sake! Go have a snack or something. Just, go do something and quit worrying about my clothes."

The redhead blinked at her. "Go have a snack, Mistress?"

"Please, do. And while you're at it, make me one, too. Anything that's lying around, I'm not too picky."

"You want a snack, Mistress?"

Well, for all her wizardry with clothing and hair, Rose certainly wasn't the sharpest knife in the drawer, if you asked Dite. "Yesssss," she said very slowly. "Something to eat. And drink. No milk and no water. I don't guess there's any soda, but anything but milk or water will be just fine."

Cupid was looking back and forth between the two with a strange expression twisting his mouth, but he kept silent throughout the exchange.

Rose cast a worried glance at Cupid, then sank into a tight curtsy. "Of course, Mistress. This one shall return shortly."

"Is that not part of her job description or something? I didn't offend her when I asked for a snack, did I? I'd be happy to do it myself, and all, but I don't know where anything is. I hope I didn't do something awful." This was half-directed at Cupid. Love kept glancing at him as she delivered the little speech, pacing back and forth in front of the fireplace.

"No, Mistress, seeing to all your needs is Rose's job, yes. But, the nature of your request surprised her."

Dite laughed. "But why? I haven't had anything to eat since I got here, and since then I've seen four Elementals, half of TROM, and Love's Tunnel. Now, that's a lot."

Cupid smiled faintly. "Of that there is no doubt, Mistress, but Goddesses don't eat. Nor do the dead, and if you remember, you originally told Rose to get a snack, too."

"Oh." She sat down heavily on the foot of the bed. "Well, that does make a little more sense. I can see now why she would be confused but…there was a feast, when I woke up…everyone was eating, and I know now that they were Gods and Goddesses."

The boy chuckled. "Oh, of course. There is always a grand feast as part of celebration—it is the only way to get the Vikings to come down from Valhalla, after all. But such celebrations take place only once every fifty Earth years or so, and that time passes rather slowly here."

She nodded. "I see. It won't hurt me, will it, to eat?"

He shook his head. "It shouldn't, Mistress, not at all."

"Then I guess Rose is just going to have to get over it." She grinned and shrugged. "I am, after all, a human, and I'm starving."

Cupid didn't reply, only stared at her.

Love rose from the bed to pace again while she waited for Rose to return with the snack. "Why do the First Creations and the Elementals have such extravagant homes, while all the consorts and lesser creations must exist in one shared home? This palace alone is almost as big as TROM if you include the gardens and everything outside—I know because I saw it from above in the East Wind—and Castle Flame is almost twice the size if you figure in the lava pool."

"You ask the same thing that many lesser creations ask, but the truth is that they could all have their own homes. Immortality's space is endless and infinite. The lesser creations that do not have their own homes *choose* to dwell in TROM. It is no punishment."

Her mind was tumbling over a million questions, and there was so much she wanted to know it seemed that even here, in Immortality, she wouldn't have time for it all.

"Where did I get this?" For emphasis she hit one fist against a thick stone wall.

Cupid grinned brightly. "Yours is one of the most interesting homes in all of Immortality, Mistress, and you are rightly envied. All the furnishings, tapestries, paintings, and even the small decorations were taken from the European castles. Most things you got during the Middle Ages, but you have a few pieces that you acquired from Napoleon's castle and you have a few artworks from the Renaissance period. You have nothing Victorian, though, because you aren't fond of their architecture and design. You know, you and Creativity had a huge fight during that period. All the Muses stopped speaking to you, except for Athena."

"I meant the castle itself." If there was one thing Cupid seemed to like to do, it was talk about her.

"Oh," he chuckled at himself, "it was the Castle of Prince Rhodri of Gwynnedd in the year 1350 AD. Originally, it was named *Powmarys*, for the region and for Prince Rhodri. You love Welsh architecture, but most of this design was borrowed from Normandy."

"I took an entire *castle* off of the Earth realm? What happened to the people who lived there?"

"Oh, it wasn't moved until the 1500s, Mistress, and by that time King Henry Tudor had swallowed most of Wales. An English lord who was friend to Henry claimed *Powmarys*, and Ares had the whole of the land Powys scheduled for battle. You pulled the castle out of Earth realm just before that battle. Otherwise, it would have been destroyed."

"I see. It still seems wrong, just taking things out of the Earth realm. These things could be in museums."

Cupid smiled. "They are not safe, even there. Besides, Mistress, they are only 'things.' Humans have a tendency to place such great importance on material possessions, but they are only pieces of furniture or silver. You always say that if humans spent as much time worrying about each other as they do worrying about their possessions, the entire race will be better off."

She nodded. It did make a strange sort of sense, and the items she'd seen gracing the walls and floors of Love's Palace were not immaculate or wonderful works of art. It wasn't as though, for instance, she'd taken the Sistine Chapel or anything. But it seemed strange, to be surrounded by mortal things, in this immortal place.

Love, a bundle of nervous energy, was walking circles around the room. She'd already rifled through the large wardrobe and looked inside the large chest that sat at the foot of the bed.

"Milady?" Cupid's voice was timid. "Are you searching for something in particular?"

"There's nothing personal here. Don't even deities have personal things?

Supposedly I have lived in this palace for—what?—five hundred years or so. Yet there is nothing personal I can see. Just, gowns and slippers and extra blankets."

"You want to look at mementos, things like that?"

"I guess Goddesses don't hang on to such silly things." She sighed and sat, again, on the bed.

"Oh, yes, Milady, they do. At least, you do. Cupid cannot speak for the others."

She sprang to her feet. "Then where?"

"The topmost tower room, of course, Milady." He grinned. "Where all the greatest secrets are kept."

"Well, come on!" She was already halfway to the door.

"Oh, no, Milady, only Love is allowed to enter."

"Well, it should be fine if you are with me."

Cupid continued to shake his head. "Mistress, you do not understand. No one is allowed, no matter if they are with you or not. The Goddess of Love, and only the Goddess of Love, is the only being who can enter the room."

She cocked an eyebrow. "Seems awful silly if the only thing up there is mementos."

He smiled. "The secrets of a woman's heart run deep, Milady, as you always say."

"Uh huh," she grunted.

Rose chose that moment to arrive with her mistress's snack, which turned out to be a silver platter piled so high with eatables that Dite had to ask herself if Rose understood the difference between "snack" and "ten course meal."

"Goodness, Rose," laughter bubbled up from her throat, "if I eat all that, I'll blow up like a balloon!" Instead, she leaned over the tray and picked out a wedge of cheese and a hunk of bread. "You two, please feel free to hang out and eat all you like. I'll be in the tower room if anyone needs me." She gave them both an airy wave and shot out the door. The promise of an entire room full of clues was too much to pass up.

…Only there was one major problem she hadn't accounted for. Once she stepped out into the hall, she realized she had absolutely no idea just where the Tower room was. It was up, sure, but she didn't even know where the staircase was.

Well, she decided, she was just going to have to find the thing, that was all. Purposefully, she started a search of the second floor, opening all the doors she walked past and looking carefully into every room.

The palace was beautiful and opulent, that was for sure. In every room, she found furnishings and decorations that fit with the general time period of the place. On the second floor alone, she found three more bedrooms that were almost as grand as her own, a huge sitting room with a fireplace bigger even than the one in her chambers, and a private office outfitted with the oldest desk she'd ever seen in her life.

The exploration of the house itself was so fascinating that she almost passed up the staircase, which was tucked back into an alcove on the opposite side of the house that the staircase leading downstairs was, which didn't seem to make much sense.

It was a wide, lush staircase carpeted in a deep wine red. She was able to follow it all the way up to the fourth floor, after a cursory glance at the wonders of the third floor, which seemed to be full of smaller bedrooms and one huge library in the very center. Love made a mental note to return to the library later on and continued on upwards.

On the fourth floor, she found herself stuck. She had wandered the entire length of the place, following it all the way around until she was back where she started from. As pretty as the palace looked on the outside, she'd discovered that the upper floors were laid out in a very simple square shape. The middle sections of the square seemed to be reserved for larger space, such as the library on the third floor. The second floor was empty in the middle, providing a sweeping view down into the Great Hall of the first floor. The fourth floor wasn't all that interesting. She'd run into small parlour rooms, a sewing room, a few small, scattered bedrooms, and even a small room that looked something like a chapel, but no staircase.

It took her even longer to find her way to the fourth floor's middle room, where she was convinced she would also find the stairway. The door itself turned out to be somewhat hidden behind a thick handmade tapestry (it depicted Romeo and Juliet, the balcony scene), but she was relieved to find it unlocked.

The fourth floor, towers excluded, was obviously the topmost to the castle. Above her head was a soaring high ceiling of stained glass, and the floor was highly polished wood and unadorned with rugs. The room itself seemed to be a large gathering room, much more informal and cozy than the large hall downstairs, and she could only guess this room was used for a similar purpose, or had been at one time.

But no staircase. Now, exasperated, she had to perform another lengthy search of the fourth floor to find the way up to the tallest tower. Love, at this point, was convinced that with her luck she would end up in one of the other towers. Or lost forever in this monstrosity of a house.

She found a tall, slender door half hidden behind a long chaise in the sewing room. Not exactly Hercules (was he here somewhere, too, she wondered?), it took a lot of grunting and sweating before she could move the chaise enough to open the door.

Crossing her fingers, she poked her head inside, through a thick mass of dust she'd just scared up, and saw a tall, narrow staircase leading upwards. "Whoop!" she yelped, and quickly began her journey upwards.

Apparently no one was at all interested in the mementos before this moment, because the staircase was covered in dust and cobwebs. It was quite obvious, in fact, that it hadn't been used much at all.

Holding a tattered sleeve against her mouth and coughing spasmodically, she made her way up the stairs slowly. They were rickety and wooden, and creaked and swayed against her weight. Though her shoulders brushed the walls on either side, she found herself more than a little leery of the stairs, what with all the racket they were making.

Finally, she'd reached the top of the staircase and stood facing another narrow door. The thick brass lock on the thing seemed to be no joke, either, and she reached out one hesitant finger to poke at it.

"Only Love." The door sang back at her, and she jumped back so quickly she almost went toppling down the staircase.

"Oh, shit," Dite replied.

"Only Love." It chorused again.

"Love here." Is that the sort of thing she should say?

The door swung open in reply to her silent question, and Dite found herself facing the answers to all her mysteries. It took her a long moment to work up the courage to enter, even so, and even then she did so with hesitant footsteps.

It was a much larger room than what she would have expected, completely lacking walls and containing a ceiling that consisted only of rafters. One small, round window looked out over the grounds of the palace, and she pressed her face against it to see the vantage view she had from this spot. There was little to see—the moat, a walled garden that she could only just barely see into, a few more garden beds, and a small lake nestled in a grove of trees.

The room was dusty, but not nearly so dusty as the staircase—which didn't seem to make much sense, either—and covered in trunks. There were brass trunks, wooden trunks, trunks tooled in leather, so many of different sizes and colours. She just didn't know where to begin.

Time didn't pass normally in Immortality, or at least as far as Love could tell, because surely night would have come by now if they had such a thing in this realm. Judging by Earth's time, she would have guessed—if forced to make a guess—that hours and hours went by with her rifling through the various trunks.

She found so many things. It seemed that the Goddess of Love was a true packrat. Gowns, slippers, jewelry, wine goblets, pictures, old newspaper clippings, even very old books, were all tucked away and wrapped in paper. It gave her a strange sort of feeling, picking up and examining each item, almost as though she were an intruder into someone else's world.

Only it wasn't "someone else's" world. It was, supposedly, *her* world. Some of the things she touched, an old book of Shakespeare's works, a volume of poetry by Edgar Allen Poe signed by the author, a pewter goblet with green stones, had elicited a small spark somewhere inside her. The gowns and slippers carried with them a faint sense of familiarity; she could see herself wearing them. But the feelings were so faint, so vague, that she was unsure if her imagination was playing with her or not.

By now she was covered from top to toe in dust, and her gown had found new rips in it. She was crawling all over the floor, digging trunks out from under each other and moving them around so much. The dust motes were dancing in the air, happy to be free in the still air that hadn't stirred them for so long.

It was while she was digging through a dark blue trunk with silver handles that she spotted it—way over in the corner and surrounded by other trunks. It was bright red, shining metal, and the brass handles caught the light at just the right moment to signal her eyes.

Love's heart was thumping wildly even before she opened it. Finding it unlocked, the same as the others, made her pulse pick up even faster. With trembling fingers, she lifted the lid, and was suddenly thrown back into a time no living human would still remember.

"It's beautiful, but I can't take this."

"But, My Love, you must. You must take it and keep it locked in your box of secrets."

"But where did you get it?"

He smiled so tenderly then, leaning closer to her as if to kiss her—only she knew he couldn't. "It is Lancelot's medallion. He wore this every day of the hunt for the Holy Grail, and wore it in the battle over Camelot. Sir Lancelot gave this token to Queen Guenivere before he left to find the red dragon. Let me give it to you, now, in the wish that I could make a similar vow."

Her eyes teared up, and she turned her bright blue eyes to see that his deep gray ones were as teary as her own. "I will accept it, then, and keep it close to my heart forever."

A tear splashed on her hand, and she tucked the tiny silver cross back into the trunk, reaching to pick up another item.

"Oh, Aramis." She giggled up at him, and her voice was heavily accented French.

"Christine, I do not jest with you, my love. I smell revolution on the winds, and I beg you hie away from Versailles until the activity has died down." He wore a wide-brimmed hat topped jauntily with a thick black feather.

"You are crazy if you think I shall leave you! Come with me, then, and we shall leave all of France together. Come, sweet darling, and we shall see what the rest of the world has to offer."

"I am pledged to my King, fairest, and it would not be meet to leave him in this time of need. But I will not rest until I know you are safe." He took both her hands and lovingly kissed each fingertip, spreading one fist to press a small round object inside. "Go now, my love, before the daybreak." He pressed a sweet kiss to her lips, and their wet cheeks touched for a brief instant.

"Come to me, when you have done here." And she fled, crying and clutching a fist to her breast.

Even now, her fingers had tightened around the object, and she stretched out her palm to gaze down at the small circle of silver.

It was a very small fleur-de-lis, the French symbol. There was a small hole through it, as if to wear the object on a chain, and Love caught her breath. Of course. All the Musketeers had carried the fleur-de-lis. It was a symbol of honour that only the Musketeers were allowed during the reign of Louis XIV and the two generations after him.

Now she was wracking her brain on French history. Aramis, Aramis. Wasn't Aramis the Musketeer that eventually joined the clergy? And now that she thought about it, the old story went that Aramis joined the clergy after the unfortunate death of his fiancée, Christine, who was killed by a mercenary in England.

She had been Christine. Quickly, she dropped the small thing back into the trunk, and reached for another item, and another memory.

She watched him carefully; breath sucked in, as he took a long sip from the black goblet. He held it so carefully, as though it was made of delicate porcelain. Every move was slow, calculated. Just looking at him made her blood rush hot in her ears.

He turned then, and their eyes met across the table. Pleasantly, he smiled to reveal sharp, even white teeth. "Love," he said, bowing his head in greeting. "So nice to meet you." He stood then, and offered her a formal bow.

"Fire." She curtsied politely. "I have heard many good things. I do hope we have the opportunity to work together in the future."

He reached to set the black goblet down, and his fingers brushed across the back of her hand. Her entire body seemed to go up in flames. "I am sure we will have countless opportunities. After all," he grinned at the few others assembled around the room, "the world is still very young."

The very first time she met the Elemental Fire. She clutched the goblet to her a moment, feeling tears prick the back of her eyes. Memories were rushing over her now, so fast she could hardly tell one from the other. Now she could remember that day clearly, everything about it. She'd only just been created by Emotion, and in Immortality terms she'd been young then, only alive for as long as fifty Earth years.

They'd been celebrating the creation of Thought, Air's First Daughter, and Fire had come out of Castle Flame to be present. In those days, Fire was even more standoffish than he was now, and he rarely ventured out of his home to see others.

She had loved him then. The goblet she'd taken as a reminder, and now she knew she'd never forget again.

"Oh, I can't." Tears streaming down her cheeks, she shoved the trunk away so fiercely that the lid slammed back down. "I can't," she whispered. The red trunk was nothing but memories of Fire, and she didn't need it anymore. So many memories of him were flooding her now. She remembered long walks in the gardens, trips to Earth realm together, long discussions about crafting perfect romances. Any excuse, just so they could be together. It had taken them both a millennia to learn that it only caused more pain.

In fact, they hadn't worked together for almost two hundred years. It caused the two of them such horrible anguish.

But only the memories of Fire were in her mind, now. She could remember nothing about herself—and that was what she most wanted to know. Now she knew, irrevocably, that what Athena had told her was true. She *was* the Goddess of Love, and always had been…but who was that person?

It was while she was rooting through a gold and white trunk that it came to her all of a sudden, like a tidal wave.

"Kylie!" She jumped to her feet. "My name is Kylie!" As if the memories of Fire had cleared her mind for more revelations, the name she'd lived by for the past twenty-six Earth years leapt into her mind. She was Kylie.

Forgetting the tower room and all its trunks of secrets, she went tearing down the staircase and through the small room, down the long hallways and skidding straight into her bedchamber.

"Rose! Rose! Rose!" She threw open the door to find both Rose and Cupid staring at her, both wearing the same wide-eyed expressions of surprise. "I've gone to Earth hundreds of times…but no one ever told me how to do it." She bent over double, panting, trying to catch her breath.

"Mistress? You look ill." Rose was checking her for fever.

"How do I get to Earth realm?"

Cupid rose to his feet, uncertainty darkening his eyes. "Mistress? Cupid shall run whatever errand you have in mind."

"Cupid." She broke away from Rose and grabbed both his hands, looking into his blue eyes. "I remember creating you. I remember breathing life into you, to forever seal you as my consort. Now you are widely recognized as my helper, but you know that I have never treated you as anything but an equal. I am remembering even now! All I need is to know how to return to Earth in human form."

He frowned, though his face ran through a gamut of emotions throughout her little speech. "Only the Mother herself can grant such, Mistress."

"Then I must speak with her!"

"Oh, no, Milady!" Rose cried, horrified. "You can't do that!"

"Where can I find her, Cupid?"

"Milady, if I may?" Rose stepped forward, jabbing a sharp elbow at Cupid. "Elementals have the power, Milady, I think. You said so. That's how you and Fire got into trouble when—"

"Shh—Rose!" Cupid cut her off.

But Love wasn't paying attention, anyway. The Elementals could send her to Earth realm. She felt a plan begin to form in her mind, and she turned a brilliant smile on Rose. "Rose, my flower, will you help me to dress? I have an important visit to make." And, humming to herself, she went to sit by the fireplace and wait for Rose to work her magic.

CHAPTER SEVEN

Fire

It didn't take long for her to find herself standing at the entrance of Castle Flame. Thankfully, Athena hadn't returned while she and Rose were bustling around, Love directing Rose and the serving girl scrambling to obey.

Dite had planned it all meticulously, though. Her gown was red satin, and it shimmered as she walked. With her golden hair down, coupled with the gold embroidery of her gown, she looked absolutely beautiful. Rose had placed little red rubies in her hair to match the dress, and all over she was shiny and red and gold…like flames.

After a much too slow trip to Castle Flame through Love's Tunnel, she found herself at the front entrance. Of course, she'd had to walk less than half the distance as before when she'd arrived on the East Wind, but that was of no consequence to her.

As she walked, Love collected her thoughts. Whatever she said to Fire, she had to be careful. Even just thinking about him roused half-formed remembrances and she had to prepare herself for the shock of coming face to face with him again. There was no telling, really, what her reaction would be. If their last meeting was any indication, he would lose patience with her and she, she would be too frightened even to form a coherent thought. The presence of Passion stole her senses and made it difficult for her even to breathe.

Yet she had to steel herself for this encounter. If it was an Elemental she needed to get back to humanity, it was an Elemental she would get. Love— or Kylie, as she now felt she should be called—could think of nothing but her own need to return to Earth. A certain desperation was forcing her towards Fire, who before in this quest had made her feel powerless and scared.

It was worse now, with the memories of their personal history together filling her mind, but she had to press on and remember her task. She had to concentrate on becoming human again—had to! Becoming a human being again could be the only thing she focused on. Setting her jaw firmly, she pressed on. Though Love couldn't explain why, she knew that Fire was the one Elemental she could turn to. Remembering their shared love, painful and strange as it made her feel, roused other memories of the Elemental. Passion and Love were also friends, and she trusted him above all other beings in Immortality. "Love," she chirped crisply at the door now, and the flames fell away for her.

"Fire?" Carefully lifting her skirts, she stepped across the flame-colored floor, looking around for him. "Fire, are you home?"

Castle Flame looked darker, somehow, more dreary than it had before. Even the hissing and popping of the castle had quieted a bit. Love worried that perhaps Fire wasn't home, and for a moment she privately debated with herself. She would not be able to stay if the Elemental was not present, she knew, but she didn't know Castle Flame well enough to go looking for him inside the massive structure, either.

"Fire?" Another hesitant step forward.

"Love?" Fire's voice was raspy.

She turned toward the staircase, where she'd heard him from, and flashed a bright smile up the stairs. "Fire." Hesitantly, Love took another step forward.

"My Love! Have you been cured?" Passion came rushing down the stairs to her then, arms wide. He swept her up in his arms, lifting her right off the ground, pressing close to her. "Oh, my Love. How worried I was that you would never return to me the same as before."

"Sweet Fire. I have gained back many memories." She touched his cheek, softly. "But I have pressing business in Earth realm I must attend to."

Now, here she had to be very careful. Love didn't want to lie, or trick him, in any way. Yet she knew—Love had no idea *how* she knew—that Fire wouldn't allow her to leave Immortality if he knew the reason for her departure.

Though she was unsure how it would be important to him, something inside of her prompted her to keep her lips sealed and her answers short. All the beings in Immortality seemed to believe that she belonged here for some reason. But, Dite thought, that simply wasn't true. She was human—she even remembered her name—and she had to return. All this immortal Goddess of Love nonsense wasn't as real to her as the memory of being human. Fire would be no different from the others in trying to keep her here, of that much she was sure.

"Oh." His face fell at her mention of going to Earth realm. "I guess you

89

found out about it, hmm? Well, what do you think we should do?"

"What?" The question came out without thinking.

He frowned at her, pulling back a step to gaze at her. "You said you had to take care of things on Earth realm, yes?"

"Well…these matters I'm thinking of are more…personal." She smiled at him sweetly. "I need your assistance."

"You know that I am always here to help you, my Love." He grinned. "Just tell me what I can do for you this day."

"Fire." She touched his arm softly, looking up into his eyes. "I need to return to Earth realm in human form. Preferably the same form that I just recently had."

He pulled back so suddenly that she ended up stumbling forward a few steps. "You return to Earth realm *now*, when we have so many problems to attend to? What reason can you possibly have?"

His questions were not something she'd bargained for. Imagine, the idea of questioning the motives of a Goddess! With that thought in mind, she assumed a haughty air and lifted her nose slightly. "I told you; these matters are quite personal."

Fire snorted and his eyes turned dark so quickly, Love knew she'd made a terrible mistake. "Our relationship aside, Venus, there is still a 'chain of command,' lax though it may be."

Dite could sense his anger by the strong scent of sulfur that ticked her nose, and she tried to gather her wits quickly to summon some reply. "You know I mean no disrespect, Elemental, it is just something I find hard to speak of."

Fire, only mildly placated, rose one dark eyebrow at her. "I cannot grant something, not even to you, unless I know the details." He stepped forward to place a hot hand against her cheek, and in one moment Dite saw the love he held within him for her.

And then her resolve began to crumble; she just didn't know what direction to go in next. Faced with his love, and knowing in her heart that she had once shared in that love, she could not trick him into granting her a favor he would never agree to give outright. "Please." Her voice broke on a sob as she took a halting step backward. "My name. I remember my name! I'm Kylie. I have to return. I want to see my mother. I remember her now. After I woke up here, I couldn't remember anything, but I'm remembering more and more. Please, oh, please help me get back to Earth realm!" There, now she'd told him the truth. The weight of having to lie now longer plagued her.

She'd tried to trick him, to win him over, and suddenly a sick feeling of self-contempt filled her. She was not on Earth, she was in another plane of being entirely, and human ways and thoughts had no place here. Dite knew then that she'd come here purposefully trying to use his love for her against him, and the reality struck her with forceful loathing of herself.

Fire looked at her with contempt shining in his eyes. Ashamed, she wanted to turn her head away, but could not break the hold his dark eyes held over her. He picked up her long skirts, fingering the material. "You dressed yourself this way for me, didn't you?" Passion lifted one long, golden curl and twined it around his finger. "To beguile me, trick me, manipulate me, perhaps?" He turned away, eyes shining with disgust. "How very *human* of you, Aphrodite, to try and use your feminine wiles to get something you want from a man. How very *human* of you to think that you are the only person that matters. How very *human* to suppose that everything around you will bend to your whims, instead of the other way around."

How she wanted to deny those words! Yet she could not, and the shame that welled up inside her was a tangible thing. She could almost smell it seeping out of her skin. "F-fire—" Her voice, so timid now, quivered.

Passion spun to face her then, and his face was a mask of rage and hate. "How dare you presume to come here and try to weasel something out of me? Get away from me, you vile creature. You speak to me in her voice, and look at me with her eyes, smile with her mouth, and touch me with her softness—but you are not my Love. You are a pathetic, selfish, human creature who can think no larger than her own silly wishes. You remember your *name*, do you? Well, isn't that sweet? Do you remember that you are not a human, but a deity who must protect the entire world? What of that duty—or is that less important than what you think you want at this particular moment?"

She couldn't speak. Her throat closed up, and tears threatened against the backs of her eyes. He took a step forward then, and she took one backwards. With each sentence, he took another step forward, and she followed suit by taking a step back. In some gruesome mockery of the dance they'd performed earlier in this very castle, she was still trying to back away from him. Now his smoldering eyes were alight with rage, and the heat waves around him began to spark and shimmer. Each word fell upon her like a physical blow, and Dite had to bite her lip to keep the tears from escaping her eyes.

"If you want to return so badly, then return, and I shall not mourn you. But I will not help you, because I remember who you once were. If it is your decision to abolish all love, then you may do so only with the Mother's permission. Leave my home now!" With a thunderous roar, he grabbed her arms as if ready to throw her right through the flame wall to the lava lake outside.

"FIRE!" she screamed and clung to his wrists, feet kicking in the air as he lifted her up. "You know not what you do!" A tear spilled off her cheek and hit his arm. "I do not mean to abolish Love—it is not what I want!" And it wasn't. Surely, that wouldn't happen if she returned to the realm of humanity! Her actions alone could not hold so much weight!

And with that small tear that escaped her eye, everything suddenly froze. Fire stopped and stared at that wet spot, and Love could only watch him. Then, as though everything was moving much slower than it should, he set her down on her feet. "Fire," she whispered, moving closer to him, her tears falling freely now. "Fire, I am so sorry." Love dropped down to her knees, bowing her head low in shame. "I had forgotten. I remembered one mortal thing, and it made me forget all the rest."

She looked up, eyes bright with tears, to see his face. "I cannot help what I do, Fire, for it feels there is so much confusion within me. I have only part of my memories back—and even those small memories are only fragmented pieces. There is so much, still, to figure out and to learn. I know almost nothing, when before I had acquired vast knowledge, and vast memories. Please do not hate me," she whispered. "The only thing I remember with utter clarity is my absolute love for you."

They were the forbidden words; the words that, after thousands and thousands and thousands of years, they were never allowed to speak to each other. Love, her mind muddled now, could not know the problems she was creating through her very human actions; but she no longer cared, anyway. Her pain and confusion were starting to overwhelm her.

The hate in his eyes, the thought that he would stop loving her, seemed to rip straight through her body and into her soul. The only memories she could completely recall were those of him, and their love for each other.

Now Love no longer knew what she was feeling or thinking. Her own mind was suddenly a mystery to her, and it was a terrifying, disjointed feeling. The emotions were rising up inside of her, stronger than any she'd ever before imagined. Love just didn't know how to handle her own feelings.

"Noooooooooooo." Passion bent over double at her words, tears falling from his eyes too now. "You cannot say that to me. It is forbidden to say such."

"Forgive me for speaking what is only truth!" she sobbed in reply. "I am still hindered with many human thoughts, and my memory is full of holes even still. But I do love you, Fire, and I loved you from the moment I set eyes on you. You were drinking from a black goblet. I saved it, my sweet Fire, I saved it and have it still, hidden away with all my other memories of you." Love buried her head low, surprised at the power of her outburst.

He looked at her, and for the longest moment they both felt as though a great distance separated them. "Did you keep Lancelot's token?" His voice broke as he struggled with the feelings warring within him.

She smiled at him through her tears. "I hold it close to me still, my darling."

Not so long ago, after her Awakening, saying these words to him that spilled from her now would have seemed utterly ridiculous. Now, they flowed from her without conscious thought, all the things that Love had held as a secret in her heart for centuries. Most humans know less restraint than Goddesses. But Dite's control had shattered in her mind, because her humanity was controlling her now.

Passion sobbed and suddenly had her in his arms, clutching her to him so tightly that she felt she couldn't breathe. Still, she didn't want his grip on her to loosen. They sank to the floor, which was starting to grow much hotter than usual.

"Why?" Love whispered, tears falling fast on the floor, cheek buried against Fire's chest. "Why, oh why?"

They rocked back and forth on the floor while Passion's embrace seared Love's skin. Outside, the lake began to bubble up and over its boundaries, while Castle Flame itself grew brighter and hotter. Flames taller than the castle itself started to shoot up out of the lava and in the next few moments the castle was too bright even to look at.

The flame walls were crackling and popping now, the interior of Castle Flame growing ever smaller, and still the couple on the floor remained unaware. Love's tears flowed fast and hot now, while Passion remained motionless but for rocking her back and forth in his arms.

The emotions were too overwhelming for Dite, who had only just realized she wasn't human after all, but still did not know how to deal with the awesome emotions she was capable of. Now that the floodgates had been opened, she realized just what a great capacity she had for loving. Admitting, after all these thousands of years, just how much she loved Fire was breaking her heart. The pain ripped through her physically, so much so that her heart was actually hurting.

Passion, feeling the love and heartbreak flow through her, was in as much pain as the Goddess he held. Love was often called the most powerful of all emotions on Earth realm, and that truth was evident with the feelings that ripped through the Elemental now.

Athena, riding the East Wind on her way to Love's Palace, saw the lights from Castle Flame and knew instantly what was wrong. Radically changing direction, she headed straight for the maw.

Love was now in Fire's lap because the floor was too hot for her skin to touch. But wrapped safely in his arms, the searing air could not hurt her. They huddled together, on the floor that was now nothing more than a blanket of flames, and for the first time each one had to deal with a pain they had both avoided for so many, many years.

The East Wind could no longer get even as close to Castle Flame as the exit of Love's Tunnel, and Athena was running now wildly towards the castle, which looked more like one huge column of flame that a discernable structure. As Thought neared, she realized there was no way she could get inside, because now the rope bridge had been swallowed by the flames.

"Earth! Air! Water!" Wisdom tilted her head back, shrilly screaming the words out into the wind. She repeated the incantation over and over, until suddenly a chill breeze swept over her skin.

"Daughter!" The Elemental of Air had Thought in his arms as soon as he materialized next to her. "What in all of Immortality…" The usually sedate tones of Intelligence were shocked as Air took in the state of the raging Castle Flame.

The ground trembled slightly as Earth appeared, with Water in tow. Upon seeing Fire's domain, all three Elementals began to talk at once.

"Is Love in there?" Water demanded hotly to no one in particular, and the Elemental was having a hard enough time being so close to Castle Flame.

"I believe so." Athena was headed for the flames again. "We have to get her out."

Fire's power was all around them now, and the atmosphere itself began to sizzle.

"We can't go on foot!" Earth snatched Athena off her feet just as the narrow ledge she tried to cross was swallowed by the lake of fire.

The three Elementals surrounded the Goddess of Thought, and Air lifted them up above the madness, straight to the heart of the hell that Castle Flame had become.

Inside, a circle of flames now surrounded the couple on the floor. The entire castle, in fact, was filled with fire. Flames shot up from the floor and down from the ceiling, but the couple in the center seemed almost protected. They clung together desperately, while Love's tears still fell rapidly from her cheeks, and now Passion was wailing in a high, keening noise.

"FIRE!" Athena was screaming from just beyond the door. "Fire, let us in!" Other voices joined with hers, until they all sounded deafening inside the roar of the flames.

Water was having none of it, and he quickly wrapped his arms around Athena and threw them both through the fire door of Castle Flame.

Thought's screams filled the air when the pair tumbled inside the castle, and now the flames were so high that it was impossible to see the couple on the floor. "LOVE! FIRE!" Athena tried to struggle to her feet, but the soles of her sandals were melting to the floor in the extreme heat of the place.

"Get back!" Water mumbled something and threw a gulf of water across the flames, banking them for a moment only. It was enough, however, to spot Love and Passion together on the floor.

"LOVE!" Athena, one arm thrown across her face, stumbled towards them even as the flames rose up again.

Air picked her up in his arms, protecting her sore feet from the interminable heat of the floor, and the three Elementals and the Goddess of Wisdom all converged on the same spot.

"Earth!"

"Air!"

"Water!"

"Thought!"

The four circled around the couple, chanting to raise their strengths. Here, in Fire's own domain, it was going to be almost impossible to combat his powers, especially now, while he was combined with Love's powerful emotion. The powers of Emotion, Intelligence, and Life were almost not enough against the raging, wild glory that is unchecked Love and Passion.

Goaded now, the out of control fury of the Element of Fire hissed and swayed around them all. Wild sparks flew across the room, while the floor and walls shifted and swayed in an awesome display of what fire could do. Holding hands, the three Elementals and the Goddess Athena continued their chant, though at times it seemed Castle Flame itself would rip right apart. The flames licked at their clothes and skin, and Air especially was struggling to remain in the dry, searing heat of Fire's region.

Finally, the flames seemed to soften, and it was the only prompting Athena needed. Without warning, she sprang forward into the inner circle of flames, trying to pull Love free from Passion's embrace. Air joined her, and Water worked his arms around his Elemental brother, trying to calm him.

With all their efforts combined, Air and Thought were finally able to pry Love free from Fire, and immediately Water, Thought, and Air fled from Castle Flame to take Dite safely away.

"I will stay," Earth told them, "I will summon his son, Thor. Tend to her now, and Water, be sure to take it easy when you can. You do not look good." The strength of Earth was always a welcome thing, especially during this chaotic moment.

Athena gave Earth a bright smile, and the two Elementals and two Goddesses were spirited away in a cloud of mist, Air and Water combined.

And once they were gone, Earth bent to hold his brother Elemental. "I hope you realize the damage you've caused, Fire."

Passion was sobbing wildly, still trying to get all his raging feelings under control. "We're lucky it didn't rip her right apart."

"We're lucky it didn't rip Immortality right apart," Earth replied, still in that same calm voice.

"Immortality is safe; it is Love we must concern ourselves with. She thinks like a human but feels like only the First Daughter of Water can—and her mind cannot take that."

"Of course it can. She only *thinks* she is human, but she is not. She is capable of dealing with her emotions."

"You saw her!" Fire raged, and in the corner of Castle Flame a little spark went up. "Her heart must surely be breaking."

"No thanks to you," Earth replied, evenly. "But I think, yes, her heart is definitely breaking. We will have to take care of that."

Fire sobbed, burying his head in his hands. "I don't know what to do."

"The best thing you can do is to stay away from her, until her memories have returned in full. Then she will better be able to control her feelings and emotions."

"I will not!"

"You must." Earth smiled at him placidly, a strange enough expression on one so incapable of emotions. "Or else Immortality will cease to exist, because Earth realm will cease to exist."

"Earth realm won't cease to exist, even if there is no Love." Fire hissed. "But I will."

"And with no Love and no Passion, there will be no War. There will be no Creativity. There will be no Hate. There will be no Joy, no sensuality, and no procreation. The world that is Earth realm will cease to exist, and with it, Immortality shall fall as well." As usual, Earth's voice was perfectly flat, logical, and without inflection or feeling. But his words were felt, nonetheless.

Fire sighed, and the last angry sparks in the lava pool finally settled down. "You are right, of course. I must go to her."

Earth held him down, shaking his head. "Are you crazy? You cannot go to her—you saw what she just went through! Let her rest, now. She will have to repair the damage to Earth realm."

"She can't repair the damage—she doesn't even really know what she is!" Passion protested.

"She has no choice. Now, I cannot remain here. I shall call Thor and leave you in peace." Earth bowed his head in mutual respect to his brother Elemental, and stepped out of Castle Flame.

Passion buried his head against the floor and cried his heart out, again.

CHAPTER EIGHT

Chaos

Back at Love's Palace, an entire entourage had filled out the large front parlour room. In the center, laid out on the chaise, was Love herself. On either side of her were Air and Water, with Athena perched nervously on a chair nearby. Cupid and Rose were crouched on the ground near her, holding hands and looking terrified.

"The damage to Earth realm will be considerable." Thought looked at both Air and Water, her mouth twisting into a frown.

Air nodded. "We cannot, however, send her into Earth realm to fix things. So we reach a conundrum."

"We can't 'send her' anywhere in this state, at any rate," Water pointed out. Love hadn't stirred, and her tears still hadn't stopped flowing. She was in a daze of some sort, murmuring to herself and sobbing.

"But if we do not take care of the problems on Earth realm soon, Loki and the rest will have a field day with Love's heartbreak." Athena pointed out, and the two on the floor shuddered at the mention of Loki's name.

"Oh? And what, exactly, do you want to do to get her out of this state?" Water demanded. "I will go to Earth realm to repair the damage. Allow my daughter to rest."

"You cannot repair damage if she continues to create more with her tears, Emotion!" Air snapped. "For sakes, think for a moment and quit basing every decision on your weak little feelings!" His eyes turned fierce. "Each of Love's tears causes one more heartbreak on Earth realm, and already she has shed more than enough tears to cause pain over the whole of the land. There is no way for you to fix this—only she can!"

Athena stood slowly. "You two, stop." Pleadingly, she held up both her hands. "I have an idea."

Air glanced at Water and nodded. "Tell us, Daughter."

The Goddess of Wisdom stood a little straighter, looking Water right in his eyes. "I will embrace her."

"NO!" Both Elementals denied the notion simultaneously.

"It's too dangerous." Air gave his First Daughter a look that allowed no argument.

"Both of you could be lost in the void," Water interjected. "And without Love and Thought, Earth realm will shatter. The balance will no longer exist."

"That won't happen—we won't be lost. It is the only way to save her from heart break. If Love's heart breaks, there will never be love on Earth realm again, and the balance will be lost anyway—don't you see that? This is the only way."

"It can't be the only way," Air snapped, and he'd started pacing back and forth. "Blast it all, Water, your weak daughter can't even control herself to save humanity!"

"My daughter is not weak!" Water rose up, a sheen of anger in his eyes. "It might do Thought good, every so often, to learn a few emotions. It might make her less cold and hard—no wonder no one pays attention to thinking anymore!" he raged. "And we will not lose humanity—and what of Fire's role in this damnable business?"

The two were almost at each other's throats, but thankfully it was the sort of distraction Athena needed. Before either could react, Thought had thrown her body on top of Love's and wrapped her limbs tight around the Goddess's form. "I embrace thee," she whispered.

"DAUGHTER!" Air tried to step forward, but Water reached out a staying hand.

"It is too late," he whispered. "I'll summon Thor to watch over them." He yanked on a whistle around his neck and started to blow on it, sending tinkling notes into the air.

"Thought...embraces...Love," Athena whispered, sinking deeper against Love's form. After a moment, her eyes closed.

Thor appeared in the doorway and quickly moved to stand over the two Goddesses; it was all he could do.

"YOU!" Water rose to his feet, ice in his eyes. "Begone from here! Go back to your castle."

Fire dipped his head silently, acknowledging both his brother Elementals. "I will stay for as long as my son stays, Water, and you cannot change my mind."

"You will leave when Love awakens," Air told him, casting the offering mostly to Emotion, and Fire nodded silent agreement.

Water, placated, went back to staring at his daughter's face. No being in Immortality could help them now.

"*Where...what...*" *The words were felt, not spoken aloud. She could not see or hear, in fact. There was nothing but blackness, and she could not even feel her own body. It was a strange, disembodied feeling.*

"*This is the realm called Chaos.*"

Where are you, Ena?"

"*There is no 'where' here, Dite. There is nothingness.*"

"*Why are we here?*"

"*I embraced you.*"

"*What does that mean?*"

"*It means that Thought and Love are mixed together now, in Chaos. We have to sort ourselves out and get back to Immortality.*"

"*What is the point of this?*"

"*To save you from heartbreak.*"

"*Too late.*"

"*Not yet, it's not. You must overcome this, Dite. You must overcome this and help me to save Earth realm.*"

"*I cannot.*"

"*What you cannot do is allow this to destroy Love. Imagine a world with no Love, Dite, and tell me it is what you want.*"

"*If there were no Love, then I would not have this pain.*"

"*There can be no pain in Chaos.*"

"*Yet it is here with me still.*"

Athena gave the equivalent of a mental sigh in the darkness. "You only perceive the pain, but Chaos is the realm of nothing and pain cannot travel here."

"*The pain is inside me, it travels with me.*"

"*Then let it go.*"

"*I cannot—it is now a part of my own being. To let it go would make less of me. This pain has always been here, since almost fifty years after my weaving. To let it go now would undo all that Love is.*"

"*Your pain has never before affected Earth realm so.*"

"*I never before let it, but now I no longer know how to control it from doing such.*"

"*You must come with me. We must find the way out of Chaos.*"

"*Chaos is infinite.*"

"*So is Love.*"

"No, for Love needs a vessel, a home. There cannot be Love if there is no one to feel such. And I can no longer love, so I can no longer be that being which you seek."

"You must be, for there is no other solution. Without you, there will be no Love in Immortality and in Earth realm. Imagine what will happen to humanity if the Mother cannot love them."

"She will still love them."

"She will not know how, without you."

"What of Fire?"

"You must not think of him now. You must only think of the humanity which you are pledged and bound to save. There is no selfishness in your weavings; that is simply a shadow of your human thoughts. Love is a selfless thing. Remember who you are."

"I do not."

"You must. It is the only way out of this."

"Then I do not want out." And she felt herself giving it all up.

"What's happening to her?" Water's voice rose in pure fear.

Air reached out his hand, but Thor slapped it back. "Disturb them, lose them," he grunted in his usual blunt way. "Love has lost her fight, but Thought still struggles to prevail."

"It is a battle of Emotion against Intelligence." Air rose his eyes to look at Water, his brother Elemental.

"May the Mother help us," Fire whispered.

"Pull yourself together! You must think of humanity, of Immortality. You must remember that you are not a human, but a deity, and as such you have an obligation to those you swore always to love! You cannot put your own pain before them."

"But even if I do save them, no one will save me. I will still be in the same predicament that I have been for so long—nothing will ever change it."

"I will help you think on a way to change it."

"Now? After all this time? Before, you have always refused to help me."

"You remember?"

"I am...starting to remember you. It must be because you are here with me."

"But I will help you. I promise to you now that the other eight Muses and I will all help you think on this problem. If I have to, I will even enlist the aid of my father. Please, Dite, please help us get out of here."

"Tell me how."

"You must name yourself."

"I…cannot…who am I?"

"You know who you are! Name yourself now and for evermore. You must."

"I am…"

"DO IT!"

"I am LOVE!"

"I am THOUGHT!"

Together: "Now, and for evermore!"

Love, screaming, bolted upright on the chaise, eyes wide.

"Daughter!" Water pulled her into his embrace, tears falling from his eyes. "Daughter?" He pulled back to look at her.

At that moment, Athena rose up screaming as well, and Air quickly pulled her into his embrace. Both women were shaking violently, staring wide-eyed around them as if in a daze.

Thor stepped forward to look them both over, placing warm hands on each of their cheeks. "Who are you?"

"Goddess of Wisdom."

"Goddess of Love."

"Is she…still Afflicted?" This from Fire, who was trying to remain out of everyone's way, but still couldn't stop himself from asking.

"Yes," Athena answered for Love, pulling herself to her feet and holding out a hand to help Love follow suit. "But that is the least of our concerns now."

"Fire." Love's eyes locked with his, and she took a step away from Athena as if to go to him.

"Didn't I tell you to leave!" Water roared, spinning to glare harshly at his brother Elemental.

"Father, no." Dite smiled softly at him. "'Tis against your nature to behave suchly." She waved him off, then, and stepped forward to Fire again. "Fire, I think Athena will be making me leave shortly, but would you walk me up the stairs at least?"

"I am here only to assist you, my Love." He offered her his arm, and the two walked out of the parlor smiling into each other's eyes.

Water growled, the sound coming out like bubbles, and Air shot him a warning glance. Athena sighed and bowed her head respectfully to the three gentlemen in the parlor room. "I will accompany Aphrodite to Earth realm, and we will put this all to rights. In the meantime, Water, call out Sorrow, Hate and Fear back from Earth realm and do what you can to keep them here in Immortality. Love isn't up to dealing with them now. Trick them, if you have to. I will speak to Fire about calling Loki back."

"Loki hasn't left yet." The voice came from the doorway, and in reply four loud gasps filled the space after the announcement.

"You have not been invited inside Love's Palace! You cannot be here." Athena pointed out the door as though she could force the visitor to leave by will alone.

The young man leaned casually against the doorframe, a smirk gracing his full lips. He smoothed one manicured hand over slick black hair and yawned. "Dearest darling Thought, don't you know that I am allowed to go—even uninvited—wherever my Father goes? I just wanted to be sure everything was fine with Love. Has something happened?" He blinked his eyes.

"Your feigned innocence doesn't fool anyone here," Air told him coolly.

Loki grinned and shrugged his right shoulder nonchalantly. "How is the intrepid Goddess of Love?"

Athena's eyes narrowed. "Marvelous. She and Fire are taking a short walk right now, but if you care to wait I am sure they will both be returning shortly."

Loki smiled at Athena, giving her a look that said her gracious tone wasn't fooling him. "Pity about Earth realm."

Air made a noise that was the closest sound to anger he could mimic, shooting a heated glare at the troublemaker. "Earth realm is fine."

"Weeeelll." Loki grinned at all of them, moving into the room and seating himself regally. "I think I'll just wait for my Father and Love."

In the cupola at the top of the stairs, Love and Fire were holding hands and staring at each other without speaking. Finally, Fire reached out one hand to touch her cheek. "How was Chaos?" For lack of something better to say.

She smiled lightly. "Empty."

He laughed, bringing her hands up to kiss her fingertips. "I know your memories still aren't completely filled in."

"No; I feel even more scattered than I did before."

Fire nodded slowly. "Chaos does have that effect, yes. But what you must do next is the most difficult challenge of all."

"I have to travel to Earth realm."

"Yes, but you will not be a human. You will be a Goddess, and while there you have to fix everything that we made go wrong. And you have only a very short period of time. Our time flow is different than that of Earth realm, and things will be happening very quickly each moment you are there."

"I will have Athena to guide me."

"Thought knows very little about the matters of Love, my sweet, remember that. Thought and Love rarely work together in harmony. So you will be, essentially, alone."

Love nodded; she'd expected as much. "What should I do to fix it?"

"You must create new Love. With each of your tears, another human heart was broken. You may not be able to repair that damage, and fix their broken hearts, but you can create new Love. Call Cupid down to you once you are there; I will give him something that will help." Fire leaned close to her a moment, and they both felt a pang of what could never be. "Time to go now, my Love, and good luck."

"You will be here, when I return?"

"I will wait for you."

She pressed against him for a moment, tightening her arms around him for a long hug, then scurried down the stairs and back into the parlor.

"Loki!" The name came to her lips automatically, though she wasn't quite sure just when or where she'd seen the man before.

"Ah, Love." He rose quickly, with a catlike grace, striding towards her with outstretched fingers. "You're looking glorious, as usual." Before she could ward him off, he'd taken her hand in his and planted a sticky kiss against her skin.

She pulled her fingers away quickly, still trying to place him in her memories. Everything around him seemed a shadow, but she was feeling something very unpleasant that seemed to be related to him, and she didn't quite like it. "I do not recall telling you that you could come into my home."

He smiled. "But you did invite my father and my brother. I just thought we were holding our reunion at Love's Palace this year, so I ran on over."

"Well, consider yourself uninvited," she snapped. "I have things to attend to, and everyone will be leaving shortly."

Loki placed a hand against his heart in mock offense. "Why, Love, and usually you are so very sweet and polite to me!"

She stepped closer, eyeing him. Just being in his presence was making her feel strange, somehow. "I may not know much about you right now, but I know that you are not someone I want to have in my home. Leave, and take Thor with you. I'm sure he'll be willing to see that you don't run into any unforeseen trouble along the way." She flashed him a sickeningly sweet smile to mask the threat.

But she didn't trick Loki. "I think I shall go it alone, thank you."

"Loki, we wouldn't dream of it." Air stepped forward, placing a hand on Love's shoulder. "Thor will be more than happy to escort you back into whatever hole you crawled out of."

Loki looked at them, opened his mouth, thought better of it, and nodded stiffly. "Let's go, Viking. Time for a trip into Hell."

Thor grunted, gave Athena a long-suffering look, and the two saw themselves to the front door.

Ena squeezed Love warmly. "You sounded almost like your old self for a minute, there."

Dite shrugged. "I wouldn't know."

"Don't worry," Ena whispered for Love's ears alone. "You're coming back—I can see it in you." She raised her voice to address everyone else. "We will be going now."

"If you don't mind, I think I'll be joining this little party." Water took a step forward.

"Don't be silly, old man, you haven't gone to Earth since before the Hebrew texts!" Air slapped him on the back. "Come with me to Cloud Castle and we'll stew over their safety together." His words carried an undercurrent of an order.

Emotion looked as though he wanted to protest, but looked at his daughter and finally nodded his agreement. Each Elemental imparted words of warning to the First Creations, and then they left together in a cloud of mist.

"Where did Fire go?" Athena looked around the empty parlor.

"He's around." Love shrugged. "I'm ready."

"No, not yet." Athena sat on the chaise and patted the spot next to her. "Sit down."

The two sat next to each other, and Athena warmly wrapped an arm around Dite's shoulders. "This is going to be different. Do you have any memories yet, of Earth realm that are not human?"

Dite shook her head sadly. "I wish I did, really I do."

"No matter, because I still have all my memories." Athena managed a bright smile. "So you'll be okay. But we have to repair the damage you've done."

Love took Wisdom's hand. "I know, Ena, believe me I know. I'm ready."

Something about the way Love's eyes looked and the resolve in her expression convinced Athena, and she nodded. "Let's go, then."

Dite grinned, nodding.

Athena grasped Love's hand, whispered, "Get ready" to her, and threw her head back. "Thought and Love to Earth realm from Immortality."

And everything around her became black and heavy.

CHAPTER NINE

Humanity

Dite felt a pulling at her being from all sides, as though some unseen force was trying to rip her apart. Then, finally, the pressure stopped and she felt herself being pulled back together again.

"Love?" Ena's voice was far away, but as the word was repeated, over and over, she felt herself being pulled towards it.

And when she finally opened her eyes, she found herself standing next to Athena on a busy street corner. And, after what felt like such a long time, she was back in the realm of humanity. "I thought I wasn't going to make it."

"You almost didn't! Love, you have to learn how to focus on your goal and hone into Earth realm. You can't just float there without trying." Athena's anger was really just a mask for the worry she'd experienced, and Love gave her a bright smile of understanding.

"Don't worry, Wise One, I won't let it happen again." She offered Ena a wink and looked around. "Where are we?"

"Earth realm."

"No, kidding. I mean *where*?"

"Oh." Athena looked around and shrugged. "Somewhere in England. The names of the cities now confuse me. They change too much. This one used to be called *Brittany*, a long time ago."

"Uh huh," Dite grunted in reply. "I have to create new love."

"Yes, I know. I am going to repair some of your heartbreaks while you do that." And then, without warning, Athena picked up the hem of her gown and started out across the street without glancing to the right or left.

"ENA!" Shrieking, Dite ran after her, dodging and running back and forth in between cars rushing down the road, watching in helpless fear as Ena continued across the street just as calmly as possible—but paid no attention to the cars and buses roaring past! "What in the name of—" Finally, Athena had stopped and Love gasped for breath, one hand clutched to her chest.

Ena nodded her head. "Ahead lies Hyde Park. I suggest you go there. I will be going to repair some of your heartbreaks with cold logic—that works sometimes."

"We can't split up! I don't know what I'm *doing*."

The Muse turned to smile at her softly. "You'll figure it out, I am quite sure. Meet me back here in two Earth hours. Can you do that?"

Love nodded. "I can do that."

"Good. See you then." Athena pressed a quick kiss against her cheek and took off across the street again without looking.

"No! Wait! ENA! The truck!" Love ran forward, but it was too late. Athena had stepped clear into the path of a rather large truck, and already Dite felt the tears forming in her eyes when she realized that the truck passed through Athena as though she were made of air itself.

Love laughed, and took a few moments to catch her breath. Of course, she thought. Goddesses don't get run over by trucks. With that, she was able to turn to Hyde Park. Well, she told herself, I always did want to travel. Purposefully, she started off across the park, looking for an opportunity to "create love," whatever that meant.

"Cupid, Cupid, Cupid," she sang to herself as she strolled across the park. She felt so strange and out of place, wearing her medieval red gown and walking amongst all these 21st-century beings.

"Just for Love," Cupid sang, appearing at her side. He fell behind quickly, since Love was still on the move, and started jogging to catch up. "Mistress?"

She tossed a smile over her shoulder. "Don't sound so unsure, Cupid, I'm feeling more like myself every moment. We have a job to do, or did you forget?"

Cupid, beaming more brightly than ever before, gave her a smart salute. "Not at all, Mistress, let's get to work!"

Love finally reached the center of the park and stopped. "Now…I just need to find a candidate, right? And you take it from there?"

Cupid nodded, grinning. "You were right, Mistress, you are coming back to your old self!" His smile grew even wider and he held up one fist over his head. "Fire gave me sparks of passion just before you summoned me, as well, to make our work easier."

"Good old Fire." She patted his head sweetly. "He mentioned that he would give you something." Distracted, her eyes tore over the scenery of the park. How strange to look at human beings through the eyes of a Goddess, she thought. Every person whose eyes she saw, it was as if she could suddenly tell very intimate, personal things about their lives and personalities. Almost like a weird psychic ability. She shuddered and tried to turn her thoughts back to the task at hand.

"But it has to be someone who isn't married or otherwise involved," Love murmured, more to herself than anyone. "There!" She pointed to the fountain near the edge of the park. "See her? She's lovely."

Cupid eyed the young, dark-haired girl, squinting his eyes against the noon sunlight.

"What's that she's reading?" Dite mumbled, walking closer to the girl. She was young, maybe twenty-two or twenty-three, and casually dressed in tan-colored slacks and a white button-down blouse. Her dark hair was pulled back into a neat bun. Dite bent close to read the title of the book she was reading—"Charles Dickens," she announced for Cupid's benefit. "I adore her. She must be English—see how reserved and calm she looks?" Love took a poke at the girl's shoulder. "And sturdy. Do you see a ring?"

"I don't see any jewelry," Cupid was standing on the fountain lip next to her, reading over her shoulder. "I think it's *Great Expectations*."

"How very apropos." Love grinned, already looking around. "Now, we just need an eligible man. Oh—Cupid, go grab that one!" She bounced to her feet, pointing all the way across the park.

Cupid shielded his eyes and swayed forward. "Which one?"

"The American one, with the black lab. That's the one." She quickly picked up her skirts and started jogging across the path. "Q, hurry *up*," she tossed over her shoulder.

Cupid grunted something and started hopping after her.

As she neared the man, Dite felt a surge of victory. Her Goddess instincts were either coming back, or her eyesight had turned into something remarkable. He was tall, blonde, American, and just the right age. "Check for a ring!" she hissed at Cupid, already nearing the man.

"Mistress—wait!" Cupid sprinted forward as Dite stepped up close to the man.

The black lab, which the man was holding on a leash, lunged forward at her. Love let loose a shrill scream and fell backwards.

"Cocoa!" the man cried, as the dog took off towards Dite.

Love screeched, cried out something not very Goddess-like, and took off running towards the young woman seated at the fountain. She turned her head to scream at Cupid, hiking up her long skirts to hop over a hedge. "Is there a ring?"

"No ring!" Cupid called back.

"Arrows away, then, and I'll meet you in Paris!"

"As you wish, Mistress!"

Love stayed long enough to lead the dog right to the fountain, watched Cupid cock his bow, and then cried out, "Paris!" to no one in particular while giving herself a mental picture of what—she thought—Paris looked like.

…And then she vanished into thin air. The poor black lab, Cocoa, stood barking at the fountain for a few minutes before he walked up to the young woman, wagging his tail. When the dog's owner finally found the dog at the fountain, the lab and the young woman had made fantastic friends. Cupid planted his arrows, blew a kiss at the new couple, and whispered, "To Love I go," into the air.

"How many couples are we going to have to make, to fix what I did?" They were standing in the middle of the River Seine, which ran through the center of the city.

"Realistically?" Cupid was fixing his bow and arrows back into place.

Dite nodded, sharp eyes scanning the busy crowd on both the Left and Right Banks.

"Four hundred sixty-three."

"You've *got* to be joking. I only have two hours! Less, now!"

Cupid smiled reassuringly. "Rome wasn't built in a day, Mistress, and not to worry. Thought will be using cold logic on those whose hearts you broke, and they will continue on. If Air, Fire, and Water were able to keep some of the Lessers away—Loki, in particular—then it should be okay."

Love shook her head. "It is not okay. Come, Cupid, we have to hurry."

They stepped across the river and onto the crowded Paris streets. In her mortal life, she had never traveled outside the United States. Now, the romance and enchantment of Paris, city of Love, surrounded her.

The city itself had an old affluence to it, a real history, that the United States could not have. The beautiful, flowing French language was all around her, and she saw smartly dressed young men and women rushing across streets packed with traffic. Small outdoor cafés seemed to be everywhere she looked, and the aromas of coffee and bread filled the air.

"That one and that one." Love hurriedly selected a café waitress and a chef, who was already looking her way with lovesick eyes. The waitress, however, was staring dreamily into space, and Dite picked up an image of a smooth-talking Frenchman who worked mostly as a handyman and jack of all trades in her visions. "The one she wants isn't worthy of her, and that chef will eventually become one of Paris's top-notch pastry kings," she told Cupid quickly. "And you never doubted me before." Dite scolded him with that quick reminder at his look of doubt as she continued on through the streets of Paris.

Cupid shot his arrows quickly, running to keep pace with Love. "Forgive Q, Mistress, this one still is unsure if you are completely cured."

"I am not 'cured' in any sense of the word, but my instincts are coming back. And you shouldn't be worrying about me—you should be focusing on the task at hand!" she snapped, catching sight of a young blonde woman working behind the counter at a small, out-of-the-way boutique.

Love stopped and stared at her for a moment. "I know her."

"Mistress?" Cupid had to run to catch up to Love, who was already entering the shop.

He found Dite perched right on the counter of the boutique, sitting almost on top of the woman behind the counter. She seemed to be examining her, looking closely into her eyes and studying her. "I broke her heart." Love's voice was husky with the tears she was trying to hold back.

"Well, don't cry!" Cupid rushed forward. "We'll find her new love."

Love sniffed and nodded. "I hurt so many people," she whispered, still looking into the woman's eyes.

Cupid was pulling on her hand. "Mistress, time, remember! We have to worry about time while on Earth realm."

"I know, I know." Love scooted off the counter and allowed Cupid to lead her out, glancing back at the woman only once as she was pushed out of the boutique.

"I hurt so many people," she repeated, leaning on Cupid's arm as he led her through the streets of Paris.

"Mistress, all that can be put to rights if only you don't let your own emotion overwhelm you!" Cupid told her. "You managed to get it under control after the first two thousand years or so, but I guess since the Affliction you've forgotten. But you must remember, Mistress." His eyes were passionate.

Love smiled softly, ruffling his blonde curls. "Did I borrow Passion's weavings to make you?" The youth carried a fire to his words that could only have come from the Elemental.

Cupid blushed. "Of course, Mistress…since you care for Fire so."

She nodded, took a deep breath, and focused once more on the task at hand. "The old man on the bench across the etoile—see him? He's a widower,

111

has been for the past fifteen years. There is an old woman who does seamstress work for the boutique on that corner, there. Her beau was killed in a tragic accident when she was twenty-one, and she never married. They belong together."

Love's keen eyes scanned the area once more. "The woman dressed in the severe gray suit, walking across the street with the briefcase. She's a divorcee, very bitter. Pair her with that slightly graying man reading the paper at that café. He's incredibly gentle and understanding."

Cupid was taking notes, readying arrows, and struggling to follow Love even as he made shots of love through the air.

"There he is." Love stopped so quickly, Cupid collided right into her.

"Forgive Q, Mistress." He quickly poked his head around her to see what all the excitement was about and grinned. "He's for the boutique lady, isn't he?"

Love was grinning brightly. "Perfect, isn't he? He's a poet, struggling still, but in twelve years he will be well-known throughout France." She turned to give Cupid a wink. "I'm feeling it all come back to me now, Q. Go take care of all that, I'm off to America. Look for me in the South." She bent to plant a kiss on his cheek and disappeared.

She found herself somewhere in Mississippi in a semi-large metropolitan area. Her last mortal life, she'd been raised in the South, and she had affection for their polite ways and their sleepy speech.

Love was casually strolling through the Jacksonville streets, peeking into shop windows and waving at passersby that could not see her. It seemed the more time she spent on Earth realm, the more of her Goddess instincts and senses came back to her. Now, just looking at a person she could tell everything about their romantic life. I suppose that is one of the gifts of the Goddess of Love, she thought to herself. Were there more traits she was not even aware of yet?

Spring had finally come to the United States. For a few moments, she just walked along, enjoying the sights and smells of the season. The dogwood and magnolia trees were blooming, the leaves were cloaked in fresh new green leaves, and she soaked in the scents of flowers and new life on the warm breeze.

People scurrying past her wore the smiles of eternal warmth, and she was reminded again of just how much she loved these warm, wonderful southern states. Love had seated herself at a park bench, watching a little league baseball game—mostly the young coach, whose son was the pitcher and whose wife had died three years before in a car accident—when she felt a tap on her shoulder.

"Cupid, what on Earth realm *took* you so long? I hope you managed to get the arrows shot correctly, though, and if you did then I won't be at all angry." She turned to give him a smile over her shoulder.

…Only it wasn't Cupid who stood there.

"What are *you* doing here?" She jumped to her feet, as if ready for combat.

Loki smiled easily and moved to take a seat on the bench, patting the spot next to him invitingly. "Just coming to see how you are doing, dear Love."

She screwed her eyebrows up into a scowl. "Lesser creations can't go into Earth realm unless it is approved by a First." Where that piece of information came from, she couldn't guess, but she knew in saying it that it was true.

Loki shrugged and smiled. "But I am special in that I was Fire's First Son. Even you should know that, my dear Afflicted Goddess."

Now she wasn't sure what to do. Calling Cupid to her might mean him not finishing the tasks she'd laid out for him in France—but could she deal with Loki alone? The memories were coming back to her at infrequent intervals. She would catch glimpses, fragments of things that happened, names and faces and voices she couldn't quite place. Now that the God of Mischief was near her, memories of Loki's nonstop interference into all her work was flashing through her Swiss-cheese mind.

"You're half of the devil!" she suddenly announced, and it was a good thing that mortals could not hear or see the deities.

Loki grinned in that sly way he had, lifting a shoulder in a careless shrug. "Why bother with semantics?"

Dite narrowed her eyes at him. "Why are you here?"

"I told you," he casually brushed at the sleeve of his black suit. "Just to see how you were doing."

"I don't believe it. You must have some interest in my dealings for a good reason or you wouldn't waste your time. And quite frankly, I don't really have the time to deal with you. I have to be somewhere."

"Ah, yes." The smile of predator rarely left Loki's face, she'd noticed. "England, Hyde Park."

The Goddess lifted her nose in the air imperiously. "I am not impressed that you seem to be keeping close tabs on my whereabouts, Loki."

Once, the Goddess of Love had known Loki better than almost any other Creation of Belief. It was her close relationship with both Fire and Hades that made it possible. Now, her memories were gone completely or only half-formed, but there was one thing that she knew about Loki that she hoped she'd never forget: he hated being condescended to. Loki, with his awesome sense of self-worth, could not bring himself to believe that anything was more important than Loki.

Her tone made him turn red with anger, and he jumped to his feet. "I have been waiting for this for the past three thousand years, and I will not let some weakling emotion have the best of me!"

She laughed, leaning forward to be sure he caught the full effect of her amusement. "Begone from here, Loki, for I am busy and you cannot interfere in my workings."

Loki, however, had nothing but guile and deception inside him. He smirked and moved a hand over his hair, quickly regaining his composure. For centuries, the Goddess of Love had managed to smite him at every turn. He would not allow her the pleasure this time. It was his very last chance to be rid of her completely—and he would not miss it.

"As you wish, dearest darling Love." He bowed elegantly and faded into nothingness.

Love shivered. She knew, without a doubt, that she had not yet seen the last of Loki.

Cupid was suddenly beside her. "Loki was here," he complained.

Love reached out to tousle his hair. "I know; he's gone now. See the coach, over there? The woman on the bleachers on the far side is the mother of the shortstop—cute kid, right?—anyway, they're perfect for each other."

Cupid was nodding, taking it all down.

"The woman who works in the bridal shop across the square is the daughter of the man who owns the bakery. She's terribly sad. Now, the young man who works in the bank right across the street—you'll know him because he's the youngest loan officer there—he has the biggest crush on her, but he's terrible shy. Can you take care of it?"

"You've done all this just in the time Q took to get here?"

She grinned and shrugged. "Well, we are working on a time limit."

Cupid was already shooting the arrows at the couple in the park, struggling to hurry as Dite started off away from the park and down the street.

Dite led Cupid through the warm spring streets, pointing out different people and issuing directions.

"I have to get back to Hyde Park and then on to Immortality. You will finish up here and join me there?"

Cupid nodded, coming quickly to attention before her. "As soon as Cupid can finish, Mistress."

"Very good." She smiled and gave him a little wave as she disappeared into the air.

"Athena!" Dite ended up having to run through Hyde Park, waving furiously to get her attention. "Sorry I'm a few minutes late," she panted.

The Muse's eyes were dark and heavy with sadness. "It is of no consequence. Are you ready to return?"

"Athena?" Love placed a staying hand on her friend's arm. "Is something wrong?"

Thought worked up a small smile and shook her head. "No, dear friend. It is just that this is the hardest part of my duties. This is the only way you and I ever work together. You go around and create love, spreading it and fostering it, while I...I try to fix heartbreak with logic, thinking." She laughed, and it was a surprisingly strange sound from the daughter of Air.

Dite saw Athena in a new light, then. "You don't feel any emotion, do you?"

Ena shrugged. "Some, in small amounts. Air took a few weavings from Water to help balance the wisdom and thought that is ingrained into me. But I don't feel anything even close to what you can feel without being provoked."

Dite smiled. "None of us are very balanced, are we? That is the nature of being carnations of human conditions."

"You are getting through the Affliction quite well." Ena gave her a slight smile.

Love tucked her arm through her friend's. "To Immortality!" she declared, and together the two First Daughters were pulled into a realm of blackness.

CHAPTER TEN

Fathergod

Automatically, they were each thrown into their own dwellings in Immortality. Love found herself standing in the middle of the Great Hall of Love's Palace, while Athena was sent to the Temple, her Immortal home.

"Love!" A young, curly-haired youth jumped up when she appeared. "Where is Thought?"

She looked at him closely, studying his bright blue eyes, upturned nose, and fair freckled face. "Where have I seen you before? Oh—yes. Athena sent for you right after the feasting…what was your name? I feel like I should know who you are." The trip back to Immortality had made her lose memories, and now she felt confused and tangled up again in the fragmented pieces of them.

The lad gaped at her in open-mouthed surprise. "Hermes, Love, the messenger? Athena sent for me—where is she? I thought she was with you!"

"We have only just now returned from Earth realm, Hermes, and I am sure Thought is…well, wherever Thought is when she isn't babysitting Love."

"The, ah, Temple," he prompted. "Right—the Temple. Aren't *you* the messenger? If you want her, go and find her."

Hermes frowned in confusion, bowed his head respectfully to her, and was turning towards the door when Athena came bursting through it.

"Hermes!"

"Athena!"

Both laughed; and Hermes stepped forward, bowing his head low. "Mistress Thought, I have not managed to find the Mother."

Athena's mouth opened to speak, but Hermes held up a staying hand.

"But I managed to find Fathergod."

The word, for some reason, sent a chill down Love's spine, and she felt as though the name should have some strong meaning to her.

Love saw the Muse's jaw clench for a moment, and she gave Hermes a

116

stiff nod. "Where can I find him?"

"He is waiting to come here now."

"*Now*?" Athena repeated the word too loud, and it echoed throughout the grand, empty Great Hall.

Hermes took an involuntary step back, nodding slowly. "I think he wants to call a High Tribunal, Mistress Thought. He hinted at it to me."

"Of *course* he does," Ena muttered, rubbing her eyes in what Love thought was a very human gesture. "Very well, Hermes. Thank you. Now, please go and get the Mother."

"But—" Hermes was ready to form a protest, but one look from Athena's sharp eyes and he quickly stopped himself. "As you wish, Mistress Thought." Hermes saluted to both Goddesses and vanished—literally—from the Great Hall.

"Ena?" Seeing Thought looking so angry was not something Love was used to, and her voice came out more timid than usual.

The Goddess of Wisdom was staring out one of the large windows, looking out blankly at the moat. "Hmm?"

"Who is Fathergod?"

Athena turned slowly...very, very slowly...and looked at Love for a long moment before speaking. Dite kept reminding herself to breathe throughout the long wait. "You...don't know?"

"I think I lost some memories on my way back from Earth realm. I sort of jumped around a lot while I was there." Love tried to form an apologetic smile. "But I think I did a good job."

Athena nodded slowly, then turned back to stare out the window. "You have heard of the new religion?"

"The, ah, new religion?"

"Yes, Christianity?"

Christianity! Love bit back a laugh. "It's hardly 'new,' Ena. Christianity has been the major worldwide religion since...well, since the Roman Empire."

Thought turned sharply, and Love saw a strange light flashing in her eyes. "Believe me, I know—I was there. So were you." Athena rose an eyebrow, letting out a long sigh. "Fathergod is the Christian God. He hasn't been around as long as most of us...but that is who he is." The explanation was dry, flat, and emotionless.

Love was in a state of shock. "You mean...God? As in, swarms of locusts and ten commandments—*GOD*?"

Athena nodded without looking at her.

"He's not…" Love paused, feeling a few missing puzzle pieces coming together in her mind. "He's not the Creator, is he? God is just…God is just a Creation of Belief, like you and me and the other deities…isn't he?"

Wisdom nodded. "He is."

Dite felt like she had to sit down—this was all coming to her too quickly. "Wow," she whispered. "So, the Bible—"

"Originally a storybook."

Storybook. "A bit gruesome for bedtime."

"Not originally. Your English King…what was his name?"

"James." Love quickly supplied her the name of the King who'd originally made the Bible available for everyday folk to read.

Athena nodded and continued on as though she'd never been interrupted. "King James added all of that nonsense. Like I said, my sisters had a bit of a hand in the writing of the Bible. Creativity played the biggest role—she was so proud. But your English King changed much of it around, made it into something much more controlling and cemented." Athena shrugged and shook her head violently, as if to clear it. "Come, we have a High Tribunal to attend."

Love took one unsure step forward. "Wait—a High Tribunal. That sounds important."

"It is the highest 'court of law,' so to speak."

Dite surveyed her flaming red gown, which was charred and ripped and smoke-stained. Her hair was probably a mess, as well. "I think I should clean up."

Ena smiled at her then, and nodded. "Yes—you should. And perhaps some memories will come back to you." Thought's voice took on such a note of hope that Dite almost felt embarrassed by her own insufficient brain. "I'm going back to the Temple to prepare. I'll meet you back here in a while." She quickly planted a kiss on Dite's cheek and left.

As Thought left Love's Palace, Dite could swear she heard her mutter, "May the Moon help us all." And felt tingles of trepidation up and down her spine.

"High Tribunal," she said aloud to herself, and shivered in the sudden cold of Love's Palace. "Rose, Rose!" Dite quickly took off up the stairs, almost wondering if there was some escape from this High Tribunal business.

"Mistress?" Rose was waiting for her in Love's Boudoir when she came rushing through the door.

"Rose, a High Tribunal has been called and I need to get cleaned up before I go." Her voice came out in a quick, breathless rush as she was pulling off her slippers and struggling with her gown.

But Rose, who had always seemed so capable and full of energy, stood and stared at her, still as petrified wood. "A High Tribunal?"

"Yes!—Rose? Would you please help me?" Dite had managed to get herself tangled up in the gown she was trying to pull up over her head.

"Of course, Mistress." Rose finally stepped forward and took over the task, strangely silent.

"Something wrong?" This Dite mumbled around a mouthful of fabric as Rose stripped her.

"You know the last High Tribunal was called over three hundred years ago," was all Rose would say.

That thought gave Dite pause. If the High Tribunals were called so infrequently, it could only mean that they were called only in dire emergencies—was this one? "Why was it called last time, Rose?"

"The Revolutions," she answered, unpinning Love's long hair. "The English, French, and American Revolution all occurred pretty close together," she said. "But back then, it was because of one of the Fathergod's schemes."

That sparked a vague memory in the back of Dite's mind. "I keep wanting to say Hate."

"Oh, yes." Rose was buried in the wardrobe now, and she had to raise her voice for Dite to hear her. "Your brother played a big part in the Revolutions, all of them."

Dite nodded. "Yes, I almost remember it now. And isn't the High Tribunal reserved for only Firsts and Elementals?"

"That is correct, Mistress. The High Tribunal is the oldest of all the other Tribunals." Rose returned, holding up the gown for Dite's approval.

It was more chaste than the other two she'd worn, this one designed in a slightly later style—and it looked French, too—than the Medieval gowns she'd worn. It was white with the same bell sleeves, only these were gathered up with pink ribbons and consisted of different layers of fragile lace. Rose buds made from silk decorated the bodice (which was rather high this time) and waistline. Down the front, panels of delicate lace decorated the skirt part of the gown, which had a slight pink sheen.

"It's lovely, Rose." Love smiled her approval and held her arms out wide for Rose to slip the gown on her.

"Now, Mistress, have a seat and I'll dress your hair. You'll have to dress appropriately to your office, Mistress."

"What do you mean?"

"Well, Mars will carry his red sword of war. Artemis will bring her bow and arrows, the signs of the huntress. Athena will probably bring her owl with her, a symbol of wisdom. You see?" Rose's nimble fingers were pulling and pushing at Dite's blonde locks now, and Love kept biting her tongue to keep from crying out.

"I see. So I must have symbol of Love, yes? What should I take—a heart-shaped box of chocolates?"

"You, ah, generally wear Love's Rose, Mistress."

"Aren't *you* Love's Rose?"

The redhead giggled. "Quit pulling my stem, Mistress! You know Love's Rose is the eternal flower."

The words sparked a strong memory in her mind, and she felt a tugging at her insides. "It's a big white rose blossom, isn't it?"

"Of course." Tug, tug at the hair.

Love's heart was pounding. "What does it mean, exactly, Rose?"

Twist, pull, curl the hair. "Love's Rose holds all your powers as a Goddess, so to speak. As long as Love's Rose lives and flourishes, Earth realm is fine. You once told me that Love's Rose is a meter. By looking at it, you can judge the state of love on Earth realm."

Love was so excited, she nearly jumped out of her seat. The only thing that stopped her was Rose yanking at her hair right above her. "Where is it, Rose? Have you seen it?"

"Of course, Milady, I always keep it for you. You usually don't wear it except for special occasions."

"May I see it?"

Rose giggled. "'Tis your Rose, Milady, you may look at it any moment you wish. I was just going to get it for your hair, anyway." She moved off into another part of the room.

Loki. It was all Love could think of. As long as she knew the Rose was safe, then Earth realm would be safe. But now that she really concentrated on it, she thought of Loki and all the times he'd schemed and plotted against her. Loki would like nothing better than to see an end to Love, both in Immortality and Earth realm. In fact, yes, as though a light had just come on, she remembered.

Loki hated her. Deeply, deeply hated Love. Hundreds and hundreds of years ago, Loki had fancied himself to be in love with Artemis, the virgin huntress. Of course, Temis spurned his advances and Loki had blamed Love herself ever since.

Wouldn't that snake love to catch me at my weakest and get rid of me then, Dite thought bitterly.

"Here it is, Milady." Rose returned, dropping a fragrant white rose into Love's lap.

Dite carefully picked up the blossom, which was much larger than average American roses, and inhaled the scent deeply. Its smell was much stronger than that of the roses on Earth realm she'd been familiar with, but it was beautiful nonetheless.

As Rose primped and pressed and played with her hair and gown, Dite examined the blossom carefully. It was large, open, and there wasn't even the smallest sign of wilting. "This looks okay, right?" She double-checked with Rose.

The serving girl took the blossom, tucking it up into Love's hair after she looked at it closely. "You like for it to be a bit more open than this, but it looks wonderful. And, it sets off your gown," she added with a giggle close to Dite's ear. "I'm all done."

Love rose to her feet and, after inspecting her reflection in the mirror and finding everything to be presentable enough, made her way back into the Great Hall of Love's Palace. She found Cupid pacing back and forth by the fireplace.

"You'll wear a hole in the stones if you keep that up."

"Mistress!" Cupid's eyes lit up when he spotted her standing on the staircase, and he rushed forward to kiss the back of her left hand. "This one has returned from Earth realm with all tasks completed." Proudly, he punctuated his announcement with a courtly bow.

"Thank you, Q." She bent to drop a kiss on his forehead. "How do I look?"

"Just like the way the Goddess of Love should, Mistress," Cupid nodded emphatically.

Dite laughed. "Good, I suppose. There's a High Tribunal just been called."

The boy's eyes went wide as he looked up at her. "High Tribunal, Mistress? Oh, no."

"Nothing to worry about, Q, it's hardly worth a thought." She fluffed his curls and gave him a reassuring smile.

"Are you sure, Mistress?"

"I'm not worried." She presented much more confidence than she felt. The truth was, she was feeling even less like a Goddess than before, and she was still unsure about everything she'd learned so far. It was all just so strange and incredible, she still felt—most of the time—like she was waiting to wake up from a strange dream.

"Why don't you run on upstairs and see what Rose is up to." She gave him a smile and a friendly pat to send Cupid on his way, and for a few moments she just enjoyed the silent time to be alone with her own muddled thoughts.

Love walked around the Great Hall a moment, touching the beautiful tapestries and the delicate china and crystal. She kept expecting to touch something and have all sorts of wonderful memories, but the things she saw were just that—things. They meant nothing.

Athena found her sitting still as a statue in a big armchair in front of the fireplace. Love was curled up into a little ball, her knees pulled all the way up to her chin, and staring unseeingly ahead of her.

"Love?"

"I'm fine." The words were simple and empty, a little rough coming from Love's throat. "I'm just confused. Let's go." She unfolded herself from the chair slowly, creaking like an old rocking chair when she finally found her feet. Strange, even Goddesses could creak.

Thought tucked her arm through Love's and gave her the best smile Wisdom can manage. "Don't worry." It was the only encouragement she could manage to give Dite, because truthfully Athena felt a little queasy about the whole thing, herself.

Before the two women could cross the hall to get to the back entrance of Love's Tunnel, there was a knock on the front doors. Surprised, they looked at each other, and Dite shrugged. "Open."

Athena let out an audible gasp when the doors opened to reveal the visitor, and Dite thought she could feel her friend tensing up. "Ena?" she murmured, too quietly for the visitor to hear.

"Love, Thought." The visitor smiled widely. "You both look lovely." He stepped right into Love's Palace without being asked, moving so quickly and so fluidly it looked almost as though he stepped on air.

Love was on the verge of asking him who he was when Ena pinched her arm. Love took the hint and kept her lips glued together, even as Athena stood next to her silent as marble, staring at the man with the strangest expression on her face.

Finally, Athena nodded at the man and stepped forward. "I had thought we would see you soon enough at the High Tribunal, Lord God."

Dite felt as though she had been physically hit in the face. The man standing before her was the Fathergod, the Christian God, as Athena said. He looked nothing like the expected descriptions of him said he would. He was not an old man by appearance, and his dark hair had only a few signs of white. There was no long beard, no long robes. No, there seemed to be nothing remarkable about him at all. He wore plain clothing, some long one-piece shirt that he wore belted at the waist. His feet were encased in thick leather boots.

"I came to see Love, I did not expect to find you here, First of Nine." The Fathergod's voice was strained, and Love sensed a long history between the two that made it hard for either to be friendly.

Dite, hearing her name, stepped forward. "Welcome to Love's Palace, Lord God." She kept her tone cool and formal. "Is there something I can do for you?"

"Nooo… No, I just wanted to see how you were doing, Love." He smiled and dipped his head in recognition of her.

She gave him a very slight nod back, lowering her eyes just to his shoulders and then raising them to meet his. They were a very placid gray-blue, and there was a certain soft benevolence to his smile. "Never been better, Lord God," she lied crisply.

He smiled, and she sensed a certain undercurrent beneath the kind expression in his eyes that made her skin jump slightly. "Then I will be seeing you both at the High Tribunal, hmm? It is to begin in three Earth hours, so do not stray far." He directed his words to both Aphrodite and Athena, but his eyes remained glued on Love the entire time.

"We will be there." Athena's tone carried a warning with it.

"I look forward to it, Wisdom." The Fathergod smiled coolly at her, bowed to both women, and left without another word.

"He wasn't what I expected."

Wisdom nodded slowly. "He has…changed, somewhat. The problem with Creations of Belief is that we often must change with the beliefs, and humans are fickle creatures. Their tastes and their faith ebbs and flows like the tide, so there is no telling what they will think next. But the Fathergod…nay, the Fathergod was corrupted by his own greed."

"Deities have greed? I mean—"

"No, I know what you mean." Athena smiled reassuringly as Love got tangled up trying to explain her thoughts. "You are not perfect, I am not perfect, and the Fathergod is not perfect. He is no different from you or I, Dite. He is no different from Mars or Hades, or Loki even. He is only a

Creation of Belief, and as such he is subject to changing when those beliefs change. But yes, deities can be greedy—you know Loki is a selfish, greedy creature. The nature of Christianity…well, it was a corrupt religion even in its very early beginnings."

Love nodded. There had been some problems with Christianity's corruptness. "I think that makes sense." She started to pace. "We have three Earth realm hours."

Athena watched her closely. "Did you have something in mind?"

"Actually." Love turned and bathed her friend in a brilliant smile. "I do." With that, she picked up her skirts carefully and ran off towards the back of the palace.

Wisdom watched her go, wanting to laugh but unable to express the sound. "I'll see you there!" With that, Athena went back out of Love's Palace to summon the East Wind. She had some preparations at the Temple that needed to be seen to.

Love, on the other hand, had different ideas. Without a word to anyone, she slipped into Love's Tunnel and was riding away on the underground waterway before Athena even thought to ask herself where Dite could possibly be going.

CHAPTER ELEVEN

Remember

Traveling through the dark, silent tunnel gave her a feeling of trepidation, and she began to mentally plan ways to make the passages brighter, cleaner and less frightening. She felt ridiculous, a Goddess that had apparently been living for thousands and thousands of years, feeling afraid of the dark, but she just couldn't help it. The tunnels were much more fearsome-looking now that she was alone than when she had rode with Cupid through the very same tunnels.

Reminding herself how silly she was being, she sat quietly and waited as the boat wound along the narrow waterways, automatically following some unseen directions. It was a welcome relief when the swan boat finally stopped and she was able to climb back out into the sunshine.

Soon enough, she was standing inside her destination, patiently waiting for audience with the Elemental she'd come to visit. Currently, he was preoccupied talking to one of his consorts and two of his children, though he did pause to give her a soft smile when she first entered the dwelling.

Finally, the meeting broke up, and Love gave Loki a warning glance as he walked past her with a smug smile on his face. Thor gave her a little wink and a pinch on her thigh, with a whispered "Good luck at the Tribunal" before he, too, left.

"My Love." Finally, Fire was able to turn his attentions to her. He stepped forward and took both her hands in his own, dark eyes dancing. "What can I do for you? I thought you would be preparing for the Tribunal. Sometimes, these things go on for weeks and weeks in Earth realm time."

Love laughed. "If the world can live without me for twenty-six years, a few weeks won't hurt. I came for help, but if you're too busy then I understand."

Fire shook his head slowly, grinning. "I am never too busy for you, my Love. What do you need help with?"

"I have an uneasy feeling about the upcoming Tribunal, sweet Passion. I want to be prepared. I want my memories back. I need to be myself." The desperation in her plea made his eyes turn soft with sorrow.

"What can I do that you have not already tried?"

Dite grinned ruefully. "The fact is that you probably know me better than I do anymore."

Passion laughed richly, pulling her close into an embrace. "I knew you better than you knew yourself long ago, my dearest Love. But you are right to be wary, and I caution you that my son and the Fathergod both have reasons to see Love abolished for good." Fire drew back and looked deep into her eyes. "But I will stand next to you, and many of the other First will, too. All the Elementals and most of the First will be on your side, but you do need to be prepared for what Loki and the Fathergod might do."

Love nodded; she had expected as much.

"Come." Fire finally tore himself out of their embrace completely, decisively placing her arm through his. "We will take a short journey together and unlock some of your mind." He bent to place a sweet kiss on her cheek before telling her to "Hang on."

And suddenly, she was on Earth realm. No blackness and disorientation this time, she was suddenly transported to Earth realm within the blink of an eye. Amazed, she stood squinting in the bright sunshine, then looked up at Fire with wonder written all over her face.

Passion laughed and patted her hand. "It comes from experience, don't worry." Fire gave her a wink and they started to walk. "Where are we?"

"…Earth realm, right?"

He smiled patiently, raising his eyebrows in silent question."Oh." Love glanced around, quickly taking in the beach, the tropical scenery, the busy people in shorts and tank tops rushing from here to there, and the glittering lanes of traffic clogging up the busy streets. "Los Angeles?"

"Close enough; Miami." Fire nodded approvingly.

"Why are we in Miami?" She'd been expecting to go somewhere a bit more exotic, though Miami wasn't exactly the most boring place in the entire world, either.

"Walk with me." Fire again pulled her arm through his, and arm in arm they walked down the busy streets together. Their pace was much slower and more casual than the rollerbladers and businesspeople who were whizzing past them, and every so often they couldn't move in time before one of them just stepped right through the two Otherworldly beings.

Love listened intently to Fire as he explained. They walked and they walked and they walked, and Dite was surprised when they walked so much her feet began to hurt, but still they kept walking. Eventually, they had walked the entire beach boardwalk and then Fire actually led her out into the water and they walked around the waves. The whole time, Love barely spoke.

"I can't tell you much; I don't know every single detail of the story. But I can tell you more than any other being in Immortality can, except of course the Mother. That's because, for so long, my own existence did not matter to me the way you did." Passion lowered his eyes, and Love knew that if he were capable of it, he would blush. After a quiet moment, Fire pulled himself back together and when he began again his voice was flat and his face remained expressionless.

"In the beginning, Immortality was a big and empty place. I mean, think about it. There was only the Mother, the Elementals, and those beings that you will never see no matter how long the world needs Love. The same beings were the same then as they are now, and they were never around when the rest of us were. The Mother, mostly, was away as well.

"So us Elementals had little more than each other in the early, early times. Our greatest pleasure came from watching the happenings on Earth realm. Our own existences were empty without Earth realm. So, we watched. We watched and the time went by so, so slowly. There was much less to see in those days; you'd be amazed if I told you. There were no people then, only animals and big monsters roamed the Earth that could not think or feel, only follow their own ingrained instincts. It was a scary, solitary time.

"Then came human beings, and these were the most fascinating creatures of all. The Elementals were able to develop our other aspects, such as thoughts and feelings. We soon discovered how versatile and how capable the new species was, and watching Earth realm became increasingly pleasurable.

"Then the weavings started. Air wanted to create an embodiment for Thought; Water wanted to create Love; Earth wanted to create the Goddess of Hearth and Home; everyone was doing something. So, I sat back and watched it all go on.

"And then, came Love." He paused long enough to grace her with the most tender smile she'd ever imagined. "There was feasting all over Immortality for days and days and days while the First Creations were being weaved. See, many of the weavings took place far too early. Air was finished weaving all nine Muses before they were needed on Earth realm.

"Water had weaved Love, the new emotion for Earth realm, but you could

127

not be until there was Love on Earth realm. It's all very hard to explain, so you're going to have to be satisfied with that.

"Finally, someone felt the emotion that would be called Love. Then, you appeared in Immortality, filled out your weavings, and became the Creation you are today. I did not actually become acquainted with you until fifty Earth years or so had passed, but you remember that."

Love nodded, breathless as she listened to his story.

"You were always a little too interested in the humans, but so was I, so I always understood. You had this desire to live life as one of them, to visit Earth realm and make yourself visible in front of them. In fact, my Love, you upset a lot of people for many years because you were just too attracted to the humans.

"But it was the nature of what you are that made you that way. You *are* Love. You are everything that Love is and will ever be; and your problem is that you fell in love with Earth realm. You loved the people on Earth realm so much, and you always wanted to help them and make them happy. And, my sweet, you have always firmly believed that Love is the key to happiness.

"'If you find something that you can love unconditionally, you will be truly happy,' you always say, and you spent all your time creating and fostering love on Earth realm.

"In fact." Passion sighed like the wind, and Love saw a wave crash in the ocean in the distance. "Because of the love you created and all the wonderful things you did, you created a need for another of Water's children: Hate."

Love gasped. It was her fault there was Hate in the world?

"Now, don't upset yourself, for the truth is that without Hate there can be no Love, either. We must—always—maintain the balance. You had some bad situations with your brother, though. In fact," Fire laughed, "you're very good at upsetting beings in Immortality. Loki and Hades both hold grudges against you because they blame you for their love lives, though Hades has a more tender spirit and he has since tried to forgive you.

"Freya, Thor's wife, has always had a vendetta against you. You probably don't remember now, but there was a time when she tried to wage a war against you. She even came to me. Freya is another of Eurynome's names— you've met her, yes?"

"The sloe-eyed beauty that walks like part of her is on fire?"

Passion laughed. "That's her. You see, Love, that is one of the many secrets you and I share."

Love turned her eyes up to smile at him. "Oh?"

"We—you, and I—created Eury. In the human sense, she is our child."

"*What?*"

"Let me explain." Fire held up a hand. "I am not a good storyteller, and I tend to forget the order in which all these things happened." He took a deep breath to collect his thoughts, and continued on.

"It wasn't until after the Ice Age that you came to speak to me. You look the same now as you did, then, but your eyes. Your eyes then were so wide and innocent, and you came to Castle Flame all smiles and optimism and excitement. That was, of course, thousands and thousands of years ago."

"I almost remember. Didn't my father create the Ice Age out of frustration?"

Passion nodded. "Yes, very good! When you came to me, you told me that you'd had the most wonderful idea. You are actually more well-rounded than Athena would have you believe, because when Water wove you he borrowed weavings from both Earth and Air, to help balance you."

"I...see."

"Weavings are the most difficult thing to explain; don't worry overmuch about it."

"What was my idea, when I came to you that first time?"

"Oh...oh, yes." Fire smiled apologetically and continued. "You looked at me and you told me that you thought Passion and Love should work together, and wouldn't it be wonderful for us to create a romance that had both? Well, I was intrigued by the idea, because in those days First Creations and Elementals almost never worked together. Then, it was rare for even First Creations to work together, much less an Elemental and a First. It was unheard of, but you were brave and full of excitement back then. Nothing could stop you from trying.

"And I loved you, my darling, oh how I loved you even then. It wasn't strange for me to love you, of course, because there are very few Gods in Immortality that can look at the face of Love without falling for you. Most of the Gods have tender hearts for the Goddess of Love; it is to be expected.

"But I was an Elemental. None of my weavings were used in your making, so I was not attached to you in any way; but I knew that I should have more control over myself than the Gods had and that I should not love you. But I loved you still, and I agreed to your plan.

"Our first attempt was not as wonderful as what our later attempts would be, but even in those early days we discovered that you were right after all. The most perfect romances had to have both Love and Passion. We had discovered something new and wonderful, and it was a thrilling time."

Love shivered slightly, half-remembering things that happened long, long ago.

"We went on to create the most beautiful romances ever. You know some fairy tales?"

"Sleeping Beauty?"

"That was us. And Cinderella. And many of the others. But then...something happened."

"Something?" Hearing the tale from Fire's own lips, she no longer found it to be totally unbelievable that the fairy tales she'd heard were based on long-ago realities.

"We discovered that we—I mean, you and I, Love and Passion—would never, could never, be together. I could tell you the long, awful details, but to retell them is to relive them. Suffice it to say that I searched the realms of Earth and Immortality for a solution, for some...way for us, but there is none.

"Things changed, then. You were angry and bitter and lost your wide-eyed belief in the wonders of love. Love could no longer bring you happiness, and you saw an end to all the romances we crafted. Out of this came what is now known as the tragic love story.

"For the longest time, you made a game out of bringing so much love to two people and then finding a way to rip them apart. You could not be consoled, and you spent all your time on Earth realm making love into something that comes with heartbreak.

"Well...love on Earth realm was never the same again after that, and soon enough people began to realize that love is both pleasure and pain. It was a balance, a better balance than what we had before, and so the rest of Immortality was appeased with everything. In fact, it was only because of your change that Water was able to make Hate into a much lesser deity than he would otherwise have achieved. So in a way, by turning Love into a two-sided coin, you reduced Hate."

Dite felt a sad, sharp stinging in her body. She was almost hazily remembering it: the pain, the heartbreak, the longing for Fire. Oh, how she had longed and yearned for him, only to discover it could never be! The pain was so great, then, that she could not stand for anyone else to have love, either. If Love and Passion could not be together in Immortality, then they would not be together on Earth realm, either. And so she had destroyed all the wonderful romances, and she had created more perfect romances and seen bitter, horrifying ends to them as well. She was crazed. "And that's when Eury came along," she murmured suddenly, almost remembering it.

Fire nodded. "That's right. You and I felt something no being had felt before: Desire. You manifested it accidentally on Earth, just through your own feelings, and Eury had to be woven and appeared in Earth realm. She almost instantly became your rival, but that is a long tale."

"So we created Desire. It is only because of you and I that it exists."

"I am sure it would have manifested someday. But she is special in that two Otherworld beings manifested her, instead of humans. But…Love?"

"Yes?"

"You and I are the only two that know that secret."

Love was shocked. "What?"

"Everyone believes that it manifested itself naturally on Earth realm, the same as the other lesser creations. You and I kept it as our secret. Even Eury doesn't know—unless someone found out and told her."

Love's head was aching. "I don't feel that this is helping me remember who I am."

"But it is, and that's why you have to trust me. You need to know your own personal history to begin to remember anything, darling Love."

"I don't want to hear it!" Dite cried, putting her hands over her ears. "You don't know how strange it is for me! I don't know if I am honestly remembering these things you speak of, or just imagining I remember to fill the holes in my brain. How do I know you speak the truth about all this? I don't know what to think anymore!" she wailed pathetically.

Fire pulled her close for a hug, patting her hair comfortingly. "Do you remember ever not trusting me? Do you recall me hurting you in any way?"

Love sniffed and shook her head.

"Then trust me, my Love. Trust me because you know that I am more in love with you than any being could ever be."

"Shhhh," she whispered. "We are not supposed to speak on such things."

"We are in Earth realm, and we can speak however we wish here." He looked down at her. "If you had your memory, I might even try kissing you."

"Don't." She had to pull out of his arms. "You know what could happen."

"I do—do you?"

Love shook her head. "I'm not…exactly sure…but I know it's bad."

Fire sighed. "We don't really know, but we think it is bad, yes. I guess we shall never find out."

Love looked at him with sad, sad eyes. "I guess we shall not."

Passion shrugged, turning his eyes to gaze out over the water. "I suppose

I could spend the rest of our time telling you amusing stories or trying to coach you into remembering." He turned to look deeply into her eyes a moment, looking pained. "I would do anything to help you get your memories back, my Love, but I don't think I can help."

Love shrugged. "I remembered things when I looked at the tower room, and I remembered before I came to Earth realm the first time, and I'm starting to remember even now a little." She turned away, frustrated. "But my head seems to be full of holes. All the memories start leaking out of it, and I forget all over again."

Fire nodded, expelling a long, tired sigh. "That is the nature of the Affliction, unfortunately, my Love."

She grimaced and stared out over the water. The swells in the distance seemed to be crashing more viciously and climbing to higher peaks. Love shivered. "What can I expect, at the High Tribunal?"

The Elemental snapped his fingers long enough to create a spark, forming a small fire ball in the air and drawing Love close to keep her warm. She was rather impressed by the display, but couldn't bring herself to admit it. "The High Tribunal is always unexpected. There is almost never agreement between any parties, and it usually turns into a barely-organized debate between the Firsts and Elementals. It's almost as bad as the Lower Tribunal and the Consort Trib."

Love sighed, and the noise seemed to fly from her lips off into Earth realm. "The High Trib is meeting because of me, isn't it?"

Passion shrugged, dropping an arm around her shoulders and pulling her against his side. "Probably, but only because the Fathergod called the High Trib. Knowing him, he has some devious new plan to take over Immortality."

"What do you mean, take over Immortality?"

Fire quirked an eyebrow at her. "That is what the Fathergod has been trying to do since the very first Christian." The Elemental shook his head, sadly. "It's a pity he practically destroyed humanity doing it."

"And you think that's what he's trying to do now?"

"I can't imagine he's calling a High Trib to think up a cure." After seeing the concern and fear in love's eyes, Fire quickly changed to a lighter tone. "But I'm so pessimistic, anyway, always looking for the bad things. Even if that is the Fathergod's intention, he can't pass a vote without consent from three of four Elementals and three First Creations." Reassuringly, he squeezed her shoulders and offered her a smile. "And he'll never get that many to agree with him."

Dite felt worry eating at her, though, and she frowned as she looked out over the ocean. "Does he understand that abolishing Love would also destroy the love that mortals have for him? Without Love, there can be no Creations of Belief."

Her companion squeezed her against him comfortingly. "I know, my Love, believe me I know. But we have gone on this way for so many millennia, many have grown complacent and forget the fundamentals that hold our existence together." He scowled darkly, eyes turning black with anger. "And the Fathergod has, for quite some time now, been trying to organize Immortality into a scheme more like the Bible's. He thinks Immortality should have a 'Heaven' and 'Hell,' as Christian belief dictates." He smiled slightly and shrugged. "But our ways are very, very slow to change and it is the whim of mortals—not deities—that dictates our existence."

"There but for the grace of mortals, go I," she quipped humourlessly, tilting her head back to look up into the sky. "I would like to return now, Fire, and have a few words with Wisdom before the High Trib."

"As you wish." He gave her a smile, cupped her chin in his hand, and leaned close to whisper, "Immortality."

And after it all, Dite stood once again in Love's Palace, still no closer to discovering her own identity.

CHAPTER TWELVE

Tribunal

Rose and Cupid were waiting for her when she returned from Immortality, each wearing wan faces of fear and concern. Love, realizing that she could not ignore their problems, gave each a look that said "Make it quick" before announcing that she would soon depart for the Temple of Thought, and then on to the High Tribunal.

Q glanced at his friend before quickly rushing forward, kneeling by Love's skirts, head bowed low. "Mistress—we worry."

Dite, trying to hold onto her patience, reached down to pat Cupid's head affectionately. "Tell me then, dear ones, what is the matter?"

Rose's voice was shaky, and Love could swear her eyes looked tearful when she finally looked up. "Milady, Q and Rose are afraid that perhaps you will not return from the High Trib."

"Don't be ridiculous! Of course I will be returning. It took Athena and Mars more than twenty years to effectively finish off old Rome—even Love can't be abolished in one day." She thought her response was simple and logical, and as honest as she could be.

Both her listeners were horrified at her frank words. "Oh, Mistress!" Cupid almost sobbed. "How can you say such things?"

"I'm only stating a fact, Cupid, and get up off the floor, for pity's sake! Now, I truly have matters to attend to."

"Mistress?" Rose took a step forward. "Have you instructions for us?"

Dite paused mid-step, already on her way to Love's Tunnel. "Oh…right." She turned to both and bathed them in Love's sweetest smile. "Cupid, if the Trib carries on too long you must go to Thor. He was once a dear friend of mine—I think—and you must tell him to look for Loki in Earth realm. Ask him, as a favor to Love, if he will help protect new love against Loki's interference. Watch it closely for me, and go to Thor at the first sign of trouble."

"Mistress, forgive Cupid, but Thor cannot travel to Earth realm on his own, and neither can Q."

Love quirked an eyebrow, hands flying to her hips. "You think I don't know that, don't you? Believe me, if he has to, Thor will find a way to get to Earth Realm. Go to Hades, if you absolutely must." Cupid's lower lip quivered at the suggestion, but he nodded stiffly.

"And Rose," she smiled at the little serving girl, "if the Trib lasts for more than one Earth week, I'll want you to move into TROM for a little while."

Rose's face fell. "Move into TROM! Mistress, have I not served you well?"

Love laughed and cupped her cheek. "That is not the problem at all, dear one, no. I just want you to go on a little spy mission for me. In TROM, you will be closer to both Sorrow and Hate. My brother and sister have tried for years to undo all my work, and I know they will be up to no good while the Trib meets and there are no First Creations to keep them from mischief. You know how to summon me quickly, even while a High Trib carries on, so I need you to keep an eye on them for me."

The girl's eyes were wide with fear, but she nodded. "As you wish, Milady." She sketched a shaky little curtsy and then ran off through the palace, not even sparing a backwards glance for Cupid.

Love patted her consort's blonde girls and gave him a wink. "Don't worry, Q, I will return eventually."

And finally, Love was on her way.

The Temple of Thought was once a temple of worship in Athens, Greece. Athena, patron deity of the city, had taken the temple as her own right before the Peloppensic wars that ripped ancient Greece apart. Now the Temple was Athena's residence while she was in the realm of Immortality, and the ancient structure made an impressive sight as Love's swan boat floated right out from inside the Tunnel into a lake behind the temple.

The Temple was all white marble, round with a high, domed ceiling. Wide white columns surrounded the circumference of the Temple, each elaborately carved at the top and base. Long steps led up to the inside of the temple, and Love was content to look around the Temple, hardly remembering ever being there before.

"Love," she told the door, which was beautifully carved with flowing lines and twirling decoration.

"Dite!" The First Muse was curled up on a long cushioned bench inside the temple, carefully studying a rolled parchment. "What are you doing here?"

"I wanted to speak with you before the Tribunal." Love bent to drop a kiss on her friend's cheek, sitting back on her heels on the marble floor. "I like what you've done with the place." She gestured vaguely around her, still glancing around at all sides of herself to see the Temple's interior.

The high ceiling was painted in one of the most beautiful murals Love had ever seen, a beautiful painting depicting the gods and goddess in Mount Olympus, where the ancient Greeks believed the deities dwelled. Squinting her eyes, Love could even pick out the Greek concept of herself, Aphrodite, mixed in with the other Grecian Creations in the painting. Thought, who had very little use for ornamentation or material things, had only a few pieces of scattered furniture. Most guests and visitors had to sit on the floor, and so the Muse had thrown a few rugs haphazardly across the thick flooring. The rooms were hardly separated, because Wisdom had no use for walls, either. Instead, there was an indistinct division of the sections of the house with tall pillars and beams in the ceiling.

Dite finally decided she like the open, airy feel of the Temple and grinned at Athena with genuine appreciation.

"I've barely changed anything here for seven hundred years," Athena replied quickly, dark eyebrows drawn together. "What about the Tribunal?"

Love finally turned her attention away from the Temple's décor to look squarely at Wisdom. "If anyone knows what to expect, it's you. And I want to feel prepared for this."

"Me?" Athena raised an eyebrow. "Why would it be me?"

Dite smirked, reaching forward to playfully tug at the Muse's long white tunic. "You're Wisdom, remember?"

"It doesn't make me an expert on greed," Thought replied waspishly. At Love's glower, she immediately looked sorry. "I'm sorry," she apologized. "But even I cannot tell you what to expect. I'm very worried that we have not yet been able to find the Mother."

"We can't have a High Trib without her, can we?"

Ena shook her head, brown curls wagging furiously. "No; we cannot. The Mother is always the highest word in a High Trib. It's very audacious of the Fathergod to even suggest it." She sighed. "But one has been called, and we are obliged to attend, being First Creations."

"He's going to try and abolish me, isn't he?"

Golden eyes went wide. "Surely even he would not be so presumptuous! No, the Fathergod would not be so bold. Whatever he suggests, or says, it will be very clever. That's why I worry."

Love smiled at her friend softly. "But isn't it the nature of Thought to second guess nearly every idea and notion?" She reached out and clasped Ena's hand. "You will not be able to debate him if you are afraid."

The Muse opened her mouth as if to deny Love's words, then nodded quietly. "I know. What about you? Have your memories been returning? How do you feel?"

"I remember some, but there are big pieces still missing. I cannot tell you the names of the other Firsts, or most of the Lesser Creations. I cannot even tell you the things I have done on Earth realm."

Athena's owl-like eyes bored into Dite's for a few long heartbeats. "Do you believe yourself to be the one true Goddess of Love, the carnation of the emotion itself, the deity created by man and fleshed out by the Elementals and the Mother?"

It was the most important question of all: Did she believe herself to be what they said she was? Was she the Goddess that she was believed to be? Love swallowed hard and had to look away from Thought's intense gaze. "No. I still feel human. I don't have the memories to make this a reality for me. I still feel like some weird mistake has occurred."

Wisdom closed her eyes and nodded slowly. "Very well, then, that is what we have to deal with." She squeezed Love's fingers tightly with her own. "I wish you luck at the High Tribunal."

Dite stood, struggling to keep her eyes dry. It seemed she was so much more emotional than she'd been in life. "Forgive me, Athena."

"There is nothing to forgive, fair friend." The Goddess managed a tremulous smile. "I will do whatever I can to protect you from the Fathergod's plan, but you will be required to speak for yourself in the presence of the High Tribunal."

"I know."Athena found her feet and stood before Love, eyes shining. "Remember this: Do not speak for them, speak for you. Do not say the words that you think you must say, say the words that you find in your own heart. And, Love?"

"Yes?"

Ena leaned forward to clasp Dite in a tight hug. "Don't be afraid."

"I won't." The words were spoken to thin air, though, as Athena suddenly vanished from the Temple.

Love took a deep breath. The High Tribunal was about to commence.

Dite wrapped her fingers around each other, took a deep breath, and had to wait only a moment before she, too, was suddenly transported to the sacred meeting place that could be reached through no other means.

Love appeared seated in her chair around the long oaken table. Each chair was high-back and carved elaborately for the specific deity who would sit there. Athena's chair was covered in scrolls, random letters from ancient civilizations, and other small symbols of her office. Dite gave her a stiff nod down the table, squirming uncomfortably in her chair carved with hearts, flowers, and abstract images of mothers with children and lovers holding each other.

As she looked around the table, each seat began to fill up slowly. The four Elementals appeared in their chairs, which were higher than those of the First Creations, each chair stationed in a straight line on a high platform across the table. Fire gave Love a little smile from his flame-decorated chair, while Water looked at her with unhappy eyes.

Finally War, Hades, and Artemis appeared in their seats next to Love and Thought, each nodding at the other gathered deities. Love wondered why there were five First Creations, if there were only four Elementals, but could not ask the question now.

The room filled with light and suddenly the Fathergod was seated at his spot at one end of the table, his eyes alight with certain happiness. Love shivered.

He nodded to each Elemental and First Creation slowly, then brought his hand down on the table in a sharp slap. "This High Tribunal now commences."

"Be damned!" Fire suddenly roared. "The Mother is not here; there can be no High Tribunal without the One's presence!"

A slight murmur accompanied the Elemental's words, but Love was too busy noticing the look of intense anger that came over the Fathergod's face. "I have called this High Tribunal and therefore, there is no need to await Her arrival. You act as though She is unaware this Tribunal has been called, but you know She is not."

Fire's eyes were still sparking with rage, but he said no more as the Fathergod began.

"There has come to my attention a problem." His words were slow and without emotion, perfectly enunciated. "It seems one of our First Creations has suffered the greatest of all malaise, the Affliction." His eyes rested squarely on Love, and it was all the Goddess could do not to look away or start fidgeting under his powerful eyes. Instead, she held her chin up and met his gaze without hesitation.

"This Afflicted First Creation is thinking with a human mind, and because of this is totally unable to cope with her own powers and emotions. This liability imposes grave danger to Earth realm, for what is a deity that cannot control their own gifts?"

The other members of the Tribunal were silent as a grave, each holding his or her own breath as the Fathergod continued on.

"Even after being given a 'tour' of Immortality, even after spending time with each Elemental, even after being reminded repeatedly of who she is, this First Creation still thinks with her human mind and still suffers this horrifying illness." His words had grown more impassioned now, but Love was not impressed by his eloquent speech.

"Because of the actions of this Afflicted First Creation, Earth realm suffered a great trauma that has still not been completely taken care of. The human thoughts of this First could be the undoing of Immortality as we know it."

After this grand finish, he seemed almost drained, giving the others the opportunity to share their opinions.

Following the rules of the High Tribunal, the Elementals were allowed to speak first. Earth nodded politely to his brothers and began in his quiet, simple way. "There is no proof that the Affliction will be a permanent condition, and Love has made some significant progress since her return here."

"Ah, but there is no proof that the Affliction will ever be completely cured, either. No other First Creation has been struck with this before. None of us know exactly what to expect," the Fathergod reminded them.

"Love also fixed the wrongs she committed in Earth realm, and traveled bravely through Chaos to do so. Human thoughts or no, only a deity can travel through Chaos." This from Air, who looked as calm and patient as one talking to a surly child.

"She traveled through Chaos with the aid of Wisdom itself, which can be the only true weapon within Chaos. Love was, in fact, embraced by Thought and taken through Chaos completely by the will of Thought." Smoothly, the Fathergod offered his rebuttal against Air's intelligent words.

"She is not the Goddess of Thought; she is the Goddess of Love, and therefore, her thoughts play the least significant role in her place as a deity. Her emotions are still that of a First Daughter of Water, and that is what makes her a Goddess, not the thoughts she carries in her mind." Emotion bravely kept his voice level, keeping his eyes fixed firmly on his daughter.

139

The Fathergod rose his shoulders in a small shrug, as if to bat away Water's words completely. "How can she perform her role as deity, without the knowledge? How, in fact, can she perform her duties without even the memories to aid her? It took her thousands of years to learn her craft, do we have another thousand so she may learn it again?"

Fire's eyes were blazing when he finally had his turn to speak, his words directed as bitter darts against the Fathergod. "Love has performed many of her duties with my own aid, and I am readily available to aid her more. Cupid is one of the most competent consorts in the whole of Immortality, and she has the added advantage of the written texts to help jog her memories. More mortal writings have come from Love's work than any other First Creation. She will not be alone in this endeavor, no matter."

"With all due respect to him, Cupid is not Love; only she is. He cannot even travel to Earth realm without her say-so, and you are an Elemental who should not be at all involved with the workings of the First." The Fathergod's eyes blazed almost as brightly as Fire's.

Artemis cleared her throat softly, reminding the two hotheads that it was finally the First Creation's turns to speak. She waited silently until the Fathergod and Fire had both turned their eyes to her, and then she dipped her head slightly. "I was born a mortal woman, and did not become a deity until after my death. I was not created by humanity, as were the other Firsts, and I had only a few weavings added to me. I have a human mind, and a mortal heart. Yet I perform my duties as they should be, and I have survived." Bright green eyes settled on Love, and Artemis offered her a small smile. "Having once been a mortal does not make me any less a First Creation, nor does it make me less of a Goddess." She turned to Fathergod, her eyes taking on a hard look. "To say that Love can no longer be Love simply because of a slight obstacle is foolishness, for then you must do something about me, as well." The Huntress's rigid frame took on a challenging air with her last words, as though she would spring into battle that very moment.

"You have had thousands and thousands of years to overcome your mortal shortcomings. Love may not have that much time." With a flick of his wrist, the Fathergod turned toward the next seated First Creation, as if dismissing her.

The God of the Underworld gave Artemis a look of pride before turning to face the rest of the Tribunal, casting a quick look at Love before beginning slowly. "Though there have been times that I have doubted the choices of the Goddess of Love, by and by I began to see the wisdom in what she has done.

Without her, there could be no Immortality. There could be no High Tribunals, and there could be no Earth Realm." Hades smiled softly at the subject of his speech, silently forgiving her a grudge he'd held since the fall of the Roman Empire. "And I can tell you now, just by being here with her now, she is no less the Goddess that she was twenty-six Earth years ago."

"Forgiving Love does not suddenly mean that she is still competent." The Fathergod's words were cold, and he had never had very pleasant feelings towards Hades, whose power and control over the Underworld the Fathergod had always envied.

War, next to Love, nodded at his father before beginning. "There is an expression on Earth realm." He smiled at the Goddess next to him, the one whose name everyone had spoken thus far. "It says that 'All is fair in Love and War.' I had to think for a while on what that expression meant, and eventually I had to track down the original author and ask the Muse that inspired the man to write such a thing." War's dark eyes glittered with private amusement, and it was a well-known fact that he had the most complicated weavings of any of the other First Creations. "Why should Love and War even be considered in the same breath? I'll tell you why." He leaned forward as if to impart with some sage insight. "Because each is an intense experience, and any human that experiences either will be forever changed." Mars sat back and nodded wisely. "Love is a First Creation, and no matter what happens, there is nothing that can change who she is."

The Fathergod looked as though he wanted to smirk at War's words, but Love saw a deeper emotion shining in his eyes that looked almost like pride. "Even mortals do not know what is best for themselves, most of the time."

Athena met Love's eyes for a long moment before turning the golden orbs onto the Fathergod. "I am Wisdom." She seemed to straighten in her chair. "And I *think* that Love is more than capable of handling her duties. In fact, I am convinced that she is quite able to take care of all the things she must take care of. I *know*, as only knowledge can know, that she is ready to assume her full duties as the Goddess of Love." It was a short, simple speech, but Thought's conviction was so great it seemed to fill the room.

Love saw the Fathergod's lips quirk, as though he was fighting off a smile, before he spoke directly to Athena. "And had we based all our other great decisions on your thoughts alone, Wisdom, many things would be different now."

And then, Dite grew hot all over as every eye rested on her. She felt the terror welling up inside of her. It was her turn to speak for herself.

Love took a slow, deep breath, closing her eyes to collect her poise. She drew her shoulders back and met each pair of eyes around the table, looking from Elemental to Elemental to First Creation to First Creation to Fathergod slowly. "You each, in your own ways, have spoken words that are true for you. Perhaps there were some things you said that were true for others assembled here. And yet, no matter how eloquently you speak or how pretty your words sound, there is no one here—*no one*—that may speak truly for anyone else here. And none of you are capable of speaking what is absolutely true for me." Love stood up, towering over those seated at the table.

"There is not one face here that does not spark some small memory for me. I look at each of you and I know, somewhere in my heart, that I should be able to recite a complete history for each one of you. I should be able to recall all the times we worked together or spent time together, I should know hundreds of little anecdotes, and I should be able to call you by all the various names you've had over the years. Yet I can do none of these things, and this shortcoming gives me a deeply defeated feeling.

"I do not know if I am capable of becoming, or being, what you all seem to think I should be. But I do know that I shall try. If it is true that I am what you say I am, I want nothing more than to remember every small moment of that existence. I want to be able to close my eyes and call up different memories at will, always discovering some hidden truth within my heart.

"But I cannot promise, to myself or to any of you, that it will happen. I know that I feel much different than I did after my death, but I cannot say if it means anything truly significant." She felt her eyes tearing up and knew she had to sit down quickly. "I am so terribly sorry." She sat heavily and struggled to keep her eyes dry.

War reached out to hold her hand tightly under the table, and Fire looked at her with reassurance in his eyes.

The Fathergod rose one eyebrow, as though surprised at Love's honesty. "Well," he said, and his eyes were already glowing with victory, "as I said before, we cannot continue with a Goddess of Love who feels so very human. The nature of the office is that it must be controlled by a deity. I have a proposal that I think we can all agree on."

Love heard Athena mutter something negative and shot her a warning glance.

"It is my opinion that Love will not regain her memories of being a deity. The strongest memories in her mind now are those of being a human, and it is this problem that must be taken care of. There is only one way to rid Love of this terrible problem, though it is a little extreme."

Love saw Fire's eyes narrow as the Fathergod continued.

"We must re-weave the Aspects that make up the Goddess of Love."

A collective gasp went around the table, and suddenly everyone started talking at once. Fire had jumped to his feet and was shouting so furiously, Love was sure he was about to jump across the table at the Fathergod. Water, too, was hotly challenging the suggestion.

The Fathergod rose his hands in the air, his face still clothed in that grave, concerned expression. "The arguments have already been heard. Let your voting reflect what decision you have made."

Passion murmured something angrily to Water, who nodded. The Fathergod shot them both a sharp look of anger, and they stilled.

"Elementals," the Fathergod boomed, and with that, the voting began.

"Against!" Fire slammed his fist down on the table to emphasize his anger. "I vote against the re-weaving."

"As do I." Water's voice quivered with rage, and Love could see the inner struggle that Emotion was going through.

Air was staring across the table at Love, his clear eyes dark and shadowed. "Forgive me, Love, but I must agree with the Fathergod's plan. Logic would point out that his argument is correct. Perhaps a re-weaving would be better than trying to teach what cannot be taught."

As if struck by a physical blow, Dite felt the breath rush out of her. Intelligence had agreed with the Fathergod! Passion and Emotion both sided with her, but Intelligence itself seemed to think that she was a lost cause. Shocked, she looked to Water, whose face reflected the same pain she felt.

Earth was slower to respond, looking from the Fathergod to Love and back again for so long that the Fathergod finally gave the Elemental a prompting look. "I, too, must agree with Air. The changes in Love are notable and remarkable, and she was originally weaved to be something different. Her weavings were completed thus for a reason, and now her inner balance is not right for her office. I agree to re-weave her."

Fire cast a look at his brother Elemental that Dite was sure caused some catastrophe on Earth realm. She felt hot and worried and wanted to squirm in her seat, but across the table her father held her eyes and made her feel more secure.

"The Elemental vote is tied," the Fathergod announced, and Love saw his eyes practically dancing with joy. "First Creations?"

"I vote *against*!" Hades announced loudly, unable to wait for Artemis to go first. "The Goddess is made up of her experiences as well as her weavings, and re-weaving Love would take us back thousands of years. It isn't worth the trouble just because she's having problems now." He winked down the table at Dite, who managed to give him a tremulous grin in return.

"I'm with you, Hades." Mars slapped the sword at his thigh as if to make a point. "All's fair in Love and War." He reached out to squeeze Dite's knee comfortingly.

"I, however, am forced to vote for the re-weaving." Dite was shocked at Artemis' choice to agree with the Fathergod. She had only moments before spoken eloquently for Love. "But only because I think you're going to discover, *Fathergod*," she spit the word out almost contemptuously, "that it cannot be done. Who are you, to tell the Elementals they must begin a re-weaving? Only they can decide that amongst themselves, and even us Firsts have no place to share our opinions in this."

"Water cannot refuse the decision of the High Tribunal," the Fathergod snapped, shooting a pointed glance at the Elemental in question. "Athena?"

Thought looked at the Fathergod, then at her father Air, before speaking. "Love and I are both First Daughters. I have known Love since right after her weaving, and I have been close with her over the long years." The Muse looked at Love with wet eyes, and Dite was shocked. Everyone knew that Wisdom knows no emotion. "I was the first one to discover her Affliction, I was the one to take her around Immortality, I was the one who traveled through Chaos with her, and I was the one who took her back to Earth realm. If I thought that there was any way to help Love, I would have found it." Athena drew a long, shaky breath. "My father is right. Logic and wisdom would dictate that there is no other way." Ena's golden eyes met Love's. "I'm so sorry, darling, but I must vote for a re-weaving." Thought's voice broke and she bowed her head.

Dite felt as though her feet had just been ripped out from under her, and a clamp went around her heart. "Oh, Athena," she whispered, feeling her heart sink.

The vote was tied.

"We-ell," the Fathergod drawled, eyes alight with pleasure. "The First Creation vote is also, tied. In the event of an even tie—"

"Wait just one minute," Water stopped him. "There is one First who has not yet voted."

"But there's only—" Fire looked at his brother Elemental. "You can't be serious."

"It's her Aspects, her memories. Love should get a vote." Water slammed his hand flat on the table. "She is a First, after all, and everyone at the High Tribunal gets a vote—do they not?"

"Yes, allow Love to vote!"

Other voices added their opinions, and the issue of Love's vote began to turn into a heated debate. The Fathergod slammed his fist on the table and called for silence. "Elemental, you are correct. Love cannot be excluded from the vote, even if the matter at issue is one that determines her competence." He smiled benignly at Dite. "Love? Do you care to speak?"

Once again at the center of attention, Love stood up, clasping her hands together to hide the trembling. "I did not want my vote to be the deciding vote of this Tribunal," she began slowly, keeping her eyes away from the others gathered around her. "But it is, and I must follow my instincts and do what I think is best."

She smiled around the table, trying to comfort those that would be upset at her next words. "But you are right, and I have never been one to argue with Intelligence. I do not feel or think like a Goddess, and I truly do not believe I am. Perhaps the best thing for me is that I be re-weaved."

"Love—*nooo*!" Fire jumped to his feet and Love had to step back, terrified he was going to lunge across the table at her.

The Fathergod, losing no time, slapped his hand on the table. "The decision is final—the Goddess of Love will have her Aspects re-weaved!"

Once again the room erupted into arguments. Everyone started shouting and slamming things at once, hotly challenging each other and the Fathergod and Love in some cases, and hotly agreeing with self-righteous flair in the others. Completely divided amongst themselves, the First and Elementals screamed back and forth at each other.

Love, looking at the Fathergod, saw him observing the scene with glee, and she knew that he'd planned the whole thing to cause tension amongst the ranks of the highest powers.

"The re-weaving will commence immediately," he finally continued after a slight lull in the heated debates that were arising between them all. "Water, you may begin and proceed as you wish." This last statement he announced with a benevolent, generous tone of voice. Almost as though he were a benefactor.

Fire was standing in front of Love as though he could protect her from the re-weaving, his face contorted and red. "I will not have it! I am an Elemental, and I say no!"

"Your Aspects were never used for the Goddess of Love, Passion," Air reminded him gently. "Your blessing is not needed to complete this work."

Passion's face was twisted as he struggled to find some way to stop what was happening. "Love, no," he whispered to her.

"Sweet Passion, there is nothing to worry about. I will still be me."

"That's what you don't understand! How can you be yourself with no memories at all? Experience makes you who you are." His voice broke, and Dite's heart went out to him.

"Come, child," Water sniffed, holding out his hand. "I cannot believe you are agreeing to this, daughter, but now it is what must be done."

Love slipped her hand inside Water's and patted his shoulder softly. "It won't be that bad, Emotion."

Athena had grabbed Love's arm and was trying to find the words to apologize when Hermes suddenly burst into the Meeting Place, the most sacred of all areas of Immortality.

And, as the popular saying goes, all hell broke loose.

CHAPTER THIRTEEN

Mother

"Forgive me, most respected First Creations, Elementals, Lord God." Hermes was gasping, leaning over his knees and panting for breath. "But I have important news."

"You, as a consort, are not allowed in this place!" the Fathergod roared, his face turning blood-red. "No matter what news you have to impart!"

"As Messenger to the Gods, Hermes is allowed to travel wherever his message must be carried," Air snapped at the Fathergod, moving between deities to get to Hermes. "Tell us your news, lad."

Hermes, still gasping, rose his head and gave Air a warm smile. "Coming…through…the…into the…High Trib…" he sputtered, struggling for each breath.

"Hermes, who is coming?" Ena prompted gently, placing a staying hand on his shoulder.

"Mother." He finally drew in a deep breath, managed a short salute, and vanished. His message was delivered, and he had to be driven out from the sacred place.

In the place where Hermes had stood, a circle of white light appeared in thin air and started to spin. It glowed brighter and brighter until it filled up the entire place where Hermes had stood and suddenly, it was gone.

Where the light was before stood the Mother.

At her appearance, everyone in the room either dropped to their knees or bowed their heads. Athena grabbed Dite's arm and yanked her down on the ground. Faithfully, the First Children all bowed low on their knees, while the Elementals dropped their heads and bent down at the waist. Only the Fathergod failed to show her any respect, smirking a bit at her arrival.

"You've only just missed the voting, Demeter." It was the Fathergod's way to call the Mother in Her ancient names, though it was often said in Immortality that to speak Her name was to slander Her.

"Children, arise and do not be so formal. We are all equal in this, the High Tribunal." She stepped forward and placed a warm hand on Dite's shoulder, meeting the blue eyes with her colorless ones. "Love, you do look lovely in spite of it all."

"Mother," was all Dite could whisper, suddenly remembering the woman and who She was. "Oh, Mother." Love sobbed and fell forward into Her embrace.

"There now, it is not as bad as all that, is it? I have been very busy, and I did not mean to neglect my Love so." She pulled back to wipe at Love's tears, her eyes soft with concern. "Chin up, child, you know how tears pain me so." The Mother smiled at her sweetly, turning to look at the others gathered for the High Tribunal. "It looks as though much has been taking place without me."

If a mortal were to see the Mother, She would appear to be nothing extraordinary. She was short, somewhat plump, and had graying chestnut hair that She always wore pulled into a bun at Her nape. Her eyes had no color, but to look into the eyes of the Mother was to see all the knowledge, all the love, all the Aspects of every human thought or feeling or sense, contained in those small pools. She wore a green-gray shawl that was a bit frayed at the ends around Her shoulders, a one-piece dress that was so simple it could almost belong to any period of history, and a pair of bifocals pushed up on top of Her head. Yet the aura of love and power were all around Her and through Her, and looking at Her any Immortal creature would know exactly who She was.

"You will have to cast your vote," the Fathergod replied smoothly. "Arguments have already been heard, but I am sure everyone will speak again if you so desire." His voice sounded tight and restrained as he spoke to Her, and Love knew it was difficult for the Christian God to admit that the Mother was the deity that had been worshipped first and the longest of all. Though Lord God's popularity eventually excelled the Mother's, he was sore that Immortality had not been reformed to follow Christian beliefs.

"It will not be necessary." She swept through the room to take Her seat at the head of the table, gesturing for everyone else to sit, as well. "I know what you all said." Her eyes twinkled. "I am sure you decided we should re-weave Love, yes?" She nodded at the Fathergod without waiting for his reply. "And Fire, you and Water both disagreed—right? Why should Love be re-weaved if it was done so correctly in the very first place?"

She smiled and looked at Air. "I am sure that Intelligence states that it makes sense to re-weave her, yes? And Earth could not fault the logic, so you agreed to the plan as well." She giggled almost girlishly. "Hades and War, I am sure you both hated the idea of doing such, though I know Hades did not expect such an opinion from himself." The Mother seemed to be enjoying herself, and everyone was loathe to interrupt Her very accurate re-telling of the events.

"Athena, as Wisdom you could not go against your father's Intelligence, and Artemis my dear, I am sure you agreed with the plan because you wanted to see what would happen. Always causing dissention in the ranks." The Mother gave the Huntress a little wink and a smile with these words. "Which left a tie up to Love, yes? Tell me that I am right."

Laughing, everyone nodded agreement that yes, She knew them far too well and had guessed everything exactly right.

Dark eyebrows drew together slightly, and the Mother looked at Love. "Only you, child, make an interesting challenge for me. You are not truly yourself, and so it is much harder for me to decide what you must have done in the face of all this. Were you still yourself, I would say that you disagreed with the plan—but if that were the case, there would be no High Tribunal at all, yes?" She smiled softly at Love. "But I do not think you disagreed. I think you are frightened, and I think you wish to forget some things. You cast the deciding vote to re-weave yourself, didn't you, Love?" Her voice was so soft and quiet, Her eyes so intense, Dite almost felt as though they were in the room alone.

"Yes," she whispered in return, feeling almost like a young child being chastised. Disappointment shone in the Mother's eyes.

The Mother nodded stiffly, sitting back in Her seat which sat above all the others. "Yes, that is something my Love would do. But, I must be the one to disappoint you debating children." Love could have sworn the Mother's chin rose a notch, and She looked to the Fathergod. "You see, a re-weaving cannot commence without my say-so. You wouldn't know that, of course, because I have conducted all the other re-weavings. The reason for that, however, is because only *I* can re-weave." She smiled sweetly at the Fathergod. "So, you have wasted precious time at this Tribunal. Time that could have been spent helping Love. Because I shall not re-weave her, and my decision is quite final."

At Her words, the room was still. No one breathed or moved or spoke in the face of Her decree, and She stood up slowly. "I call this High Tribunal to a close, for there is little more to discuss here and you must all see to the party that is occurring even as we speak in TROM." The Mother reached a hand out towards the table, gesturing for Love to stand as well. "Come, my child, you and I have things we must speak of."

Quickly, Dite scrambled to her feet and placed her hand within the Mother's, heart thumping.

The Mother looked around the table. "What are we all looking at? Off you go, now, surely Earth realm can't all be sleeping and content, can they?" She laced Her arm through Love's and whispered, "Hold tight to me, child, it could take absolutely years to find you in the mess I'm going to take you through."

Love saw Fire's eyes, filled with unspoken emotions, before everything around her suddenly went black and she was no longer in the Immortal realm.

It seemed that the fabric of the Universe was ripping her apart, but Love continued to hold tight to the Mother's arm, and she felt herself moving through time and space. It whirled around her darkly, with a heavy presence she knew she'd never be able to wade through alone. The darkness was absolute and thick around her as she was unexplainably pulled across the universe.Finally, they were standing at an entrance to a dark cave. A stream cut across the ground crookedly behind them. "This is the site of your birth." The Mother was next to her, still holding firmly to her arm. "We are almost one hundred thousand years in the past in Earth realm time. In Immortality, the Elementals are having a high time weaving the Aspects and watching the current goings-on." She turned to smile tenderly at her. "Come, child, and we will witness the very first love on Earth realm."

Scared to speak, even scared to breathe, Love followed next to the Mother as they entered inside the low-lying cave. Still disoriented from her trip, Love stumbled blindly behind the Mother. It was dark and damp within the small cave, but as they traveled deeper Dite began to see the soft glow of light up ahead.

The cave opened up to reveal a wide-open area. Here it was dryer and warmer. A shallow hole in the middle of the room supported a small fire, circled around with large gray stones. A barrel-chested woman with stooped shoulders and dark hair lay in a long trench near the cave wall. She was curled up on a thin straw pallet, face covered with perspiration.

Another, older woman hovered above her. The two seemed to be communicating in short grunts and barks, strange words and sounds that Love was sure she would not even be able to reproduce if she tried.

The younger woman flipped on her back, then, hands cupped around her inflated belly. Her entire midsection seemed to be writhing, and Love caught her breath. "She's having a baby," she whispered.

"I know." The Mother smiled at Love and told her again, softly, to continue watching.

On the straw pallet, the woman began to make higher pitched noises that sounded like short, cut-off screams. The older woman was crouched low over her, still issuing her orders at a fast clip, comforting the younger woman by smoothing back her hair and whispering gently in her ear.

Finally, the younger woman was able to offer a mighty push, and the infant slipped out as though by magic. The older woman grunted out a few more indistinguishable words, holding up the liquid-covered baby proudly.

The new mother said a few words, trying to pull herself up, and the older woman placed the baby in her hands. Love felt a tug at her heart as she watched the young mother's face and eyes as she held the tiny thing close to her breast.

"Oh," Love whispered involuntarily, touched to the point where she could think of nothing more to say.

"It was at this moment that you were 'born' into Immortality. You filled out your weavings and suddenly, the Goddess of Love." The Mother smiled at her softly.

"But how could they weave me before they knew what Love was?"

The Mother shook her head gently, signaling that Love did not understand. "I have felt love far longer than you have been around, sweet child. Love existed in Immortality, but it had not yet been given to Earth realm, had not yet been discovered. The Elementals are a bright, wonderful bunch, and they are the ones that discovered that eventually Earth realm would need far more than just myself and the four.

"The Elementals knew that Earth realm would create love, and thought, and all the other Aspects they created. So the Elementals took the raw weavings of the Aspects and put them together in a balance, in a carnation, to create the gods and goddesses. But it was not until Earth realm created these things, that the deities were born.

"There were times when you—when *we*—were worshipped and revered. That was all stopped with the advent of monotheism, the belief in one God, the Godhead, the Fathergod that dwells with us in Immortality even now. But we discovered we did not need to be worshipped to be needed, and Love, you are very needed. Immortality felt love before your 'birth,' Earth realm created you by discovering love, and the mortals put you on a pedestal and worshipped you as a Goddess.

"But in truth, you possess powers that are not all that earth-shatteringly special. We are not omnipotent, we do not see and know everything that occurs on Earth realm. What you are is a creation, a carnate and solid form of a human emotion. You exist to help balance Earth realm and to foster love, the emotion that makes so much difference to mortals."

"So, Water wove me from the raw Aspects, but I was not sentient until I was created from the beliefs of Earth realm, right?"

She smiled warmly. "Indeed, child, that is it exactly. We are all, all of us, creations of the beliefs of man. So, yes, love existed for me and for others in Immortality before it was felt on Earth realm, but love could not become a carnation until love was believed in by mortals."

It was still a strange, confusing idea to grasp for Dite. She was struggling to find some earthly equivalent to link all this to. "It's almost like a pregnant woman, isn't it?"

"Hmm?" The Mother frowned.

Love stepped away, pacing excitedly with her thoughts. Forgotten, the scene in the cave behind them faded back into blackness. The memories were not needed right now. "The baby inside the woman is forming traits that will be lifelong while he is in the womb. Certain things, like hair color and eye color and even certain personality traits, are already being set for good within the child. But the baby never takes a breath, and is not truly considered to be a person, until the mother delivers the baby into the world. Then it is 'born' and its life is truly begun."

"What a wonderfully human way to think of it!" The Mother, glowing in Her excitement, hugged Dite to Her tightly. "That's perfect—that's exactly what it's like!"

Love grinned with pride. Finally, she felt as though she was starting to truly understand the workings of Immortality and how everything was tied together with Earth.

The Mother held tight to Love's hand once again. "Time to go, now, we cannot linger here." And they were swallowed by the blackness.

"What is this?" Love finally asked once the cosmos stopped spinning around them. They stood before the tallest, most ornate, most glorious castle she'd ever imagined. The gardens and fountains were larger than life and so perfectly maintained and kept that she could only assume two dozen or more people had committed themselves to the task of making the grounds beautiful.

"Camelot." The Mother started forward with Love in tow.

THE CREATIONS OF BELIEF

But the First Daughter wanted to drag her feet upon hearing the word. "You mean—*the* Camelot? King Arthur's Camelot? But that's just a story—it's not real."

"If it had never been real, we would not be here now, would we?" The Mother grinned at Love and pulled her along. "Come on, now, child, even time travel takes more time to accomplish than you might think, and I have other matters to attend to during this century!"

Dite quickly picked up her feet to keep pace with the Mother, who led her around behind the castle to a walled courtyard. Here the gardens were split off by small stone walkways, and flowering trees sailed above their heads. Love breathed in the scents and smells. Unlike Immortality's gardens, here there were birds and bugs and bees and ants and all the other wonderful creatures that made the outdoors such a wonderful, almost bittersweet experience. How she loved Earth realm, she thought to herself.

A truly beautiful woman was seated serenely on one of the small benches in the courtyard. Her dark hair spilled all the way down her back past her waist, held in place by a small gold circlet on the crown of her head. She was dressed in a medieval gown much like what Love often wore, only hers was even more expensive-looking and beautiful, covered in intricate embroidery and delicate French lace and silken ribbons.

"Who's that?"

"The Queen, of course," the Mother replied as if it were the most obvious thing in all the world.

"That's...that's Geunevere, isn't it?"

"Indeed 'tis."

"Wait—" Love was getting confused again. "But I thought that—"

"That you were Geunevere? You were. As a mortal, of course. You came to Earth realm to live the span of a normal mortal life. You were born Geunevere, Lady of Lioness. Your second cousin, once removed, King Arthur, asked for your hand in marriage when you were fifteen. At this moment, you are almost seventeen."

"But it doesn't look a thing like me."

"That is how Geunevere always looked to others. When you looked in a mirror as Geunevere, you would see something closer to your true reflection. That is a funny thing, perspective."

The Mother's words sat with Love for a long time, and later she wondered if there wasn't some meaning to them, some depth, she should have figured out.

"She's beautiful."

The Mother laughed. "Aye, as are you, child. 'Twould be hard for the Goddess of Love to be an unattractive creature. Love is pure, beautiful, and untainted. Aye, 'tis beautiful." She smiled at Love then.

Geunevere was not alone in the courtyard, but that fact did not become obvious for a few moments. As she sat there, a man slipped out from behind the trees and began to sneak up behind her. He wore chain mail armour, but his helmet he'd left at the stand of trees. He still wore a sword at his hip and Love could see the top of his dagger poking out from his boot.

Love, not used to being such a passive viewer, took a hasty step forward. "No!"

The Mother held her back calmly, and Love watched with a beating heart.

"He's going to harm the Queen!" she cried. "Probably for political gain!"

But the Knight was not there to harm Guenevere. That fact became obvious when he quickly sat next to her, drawing her into his arms with a passion Love could feel from across the courtyard.

Then it hit her, and Dite suddenly realized exactly who the young Knight was holding the Queen of Camelot in a secret courtyard on the castle grounds. "That's Lancelot," she whispered to the Mother, "and it's Fire—isn't it?"

"I am going to tell you, now, that I have always had my concerns regarding the feelings between you and Fire. But, aye, that is him. Though the Elementals are never, ever supposed to go to Earth realm for any reason, especially to live the life span of a mortal, the man there is that which is Passion."

"Love and Passion," Dite whispered, watching the couple with an ache in her heart. Oh, she remembered it now. She remembered living here in Camelot, with King Arthur, while her heart burned for Lancelot the whole time. She even remembered Arthur's strange ideas about equality and fairness. What a great King he'd been. What a shame that the only stories about him that lived on revolved around her, his wife who was caught with one of those famous Knights of the round table.

The Mother held her hand tightly. "Try not to let the pain overwhelm you, child, for it can only mean more pain to those you love the most."

"I know," Love whispered, reigning in the pain she felt in her heart. "Must we stay here?"

"Not at all." The Mother drew close to her, and the universe melted around them.

Her eyes were hazy and out of focus when the world finally stopped spinning. It took a few moments of disorientation before Love could finally look around to take in her surroundings.

Strangely, everything she saw carried a hint of familiarity. The white roses in the glass vase on the windowsill, the window that looked out over a lake and a stand of trees in the distance, the white walls with the green vines painted on them, the bookshelves stuffed to overflowing with paperbacks and various papers and knickknacks. Holding her breath, she took in the flowers covering all the tabletops, and even the greeting cards taped to the door and pinned on the walls.

"Wait a minute—where are we? *When* are we?" she added. Haltingly, she stepped forward to touch the edge of the bed. A large, misshapen lump was stretched down the center of the narrow bed, and Dite wanted to know what it was that was hiding under the covers. She bent closer, trying to peek.

The Mother, always so quick to supply information before, remained strangely silent, watching Love without speaking a word.

Dite was peeling back the covers on the bed when the door to the bedroom opened, and she had to quickly move to get out of the way. A woman entered the room, carrying a small wicker tray with a steaming bowl and a glass of juice on it.

"Lunchtime, sweetheart. Feeling any better yet?" She wasn't an old woman, but the lines around her eyes advanced her age and made her look worn.

Love frowned, staring at the older woman's face. Something so familiar...

Without warning, the lump on the bed stirred, and with a gasp Dite realized that it was the form of a sleeping person. "Not at all," the lump mumbled, and the covers were thrown back.

Dite's shrill scream was enough to wake the dead, an expression Hades was always saying.

"It's me!" Love, feeling the tears building up against her eyes, rushed forward to the young woman on the bed. "Listen to me, listen to me! Something is about to happen to you, but you must not lose hope or faith. Some very strange things are going to occur." Love was desperately trying to get ahold of the girl's hand, feeling strange and lost as she saw the person she'd once been.

"Love!" The Mother quickly pulled her up to her feet. "Neither of them can hear you—you are on a different plane of being. You are not made of the same energies or materials as they are. And child." With a soft sigh, she pulled Dite against her breast. "Yes, that is one of the people you became while you lived the span of a human life—but you can not go back. You are the Goddess of Love, not a mortal. I am so sorry this has been hard for you, Love, but you must accept the reality of your existence."

"But it's me! It's me!"

The Mother held her close, stroking her hair. "It wasn't meant to be, Love. You were meant to be exactly what you are. You could not continue to live that life. You are not a human being. You are a Creation of Belief, and it is forever your duty to serve those beings that are most important of all. It is forever your duty to serve humanity, darling child."

Love leaned against Her, feeling weakened by the power of her own emotions. The only thing that seemed truly real to her was the life she'd led. The cancer, the pain, all the emotions and experiences. But those memories were fading, fading, and she longed to hold onto them forever. Yet she could not—it was the nature of the deity life. She could always remember bits and pieces of the lives she led as a human, but nothing substantial and lasting. It was why, no matter how hard she tried, she could not remember with clarity the lives she'd lived so many years ago and so many other times. She'd concentrated so hard on remembering those mortal lives that she had pushed away the memories she had of being what she was—a deity, a Goddess…an emotion.

"Oh, I've been so wrong," she sobbed brokenly. "I kept wanting to think of mortal things, and be mortal. But I'm not. And they kept telling me that I wasn't, but I wouldn't listen."

The Mother held her close. "I know," she cooed, "I know, child, I know."

As Love cried, everything went dark again and the Mother was sweeping her away, off to some other place and time, perhaps. Love no longer cared or concerned herself with wondering where they were going. She knew that she had been wrong all this time, and she'd hurt most of humanity and many other beings in Immortality, and she felt terribly for it all. All this time, she'd wanted to be mortal. She had wasted everyone's time with her own weaknesses and disbelief.

But guilt was another negative emotion, and she'd learned that her feelings held great sway over the rest of humanity. She had to keep her feelings in check, and she had to be careful or she would hurt those in Earth realm she was supposed to help.

When she was finally able to see around her and regain her orientation, she found herself standing up on a mountaintop. The view was spectacular; she could see the whole of Immortality stretched out below her. It seemed to Love that she was so high up she could reach out and touch a cloud, if she so desired. A log cabin was nestled into the snow behind her.

Still staunchly by Love's side, the Mother spoke slowly. "This is where I dwell while I am within Immortality, most of the time. What you must understand, Love, is that it is not always a gift to be a being such as what you are. Now, seeing everything with mortal eyes and mortal thoughts, you know the truth. Our existence is lonely, unbalanced, and quite a bit different from human beings. But we are here in a certain capacity, a capacity that must be fulfilled. What sort of place would Earth realm be without Love, after all?"

Dite nodded. "I think I finally understand. Will I get my memories back, though? Will I ever feel the way I am supposed to?"

The Mother smiled knowingly. "The Affliction has never before struck a First Creation, so there is no precedent. But everything, no matter how big or small, occurs for a reason, Love. Perhaps you needed to suffer this, to better understand yourself and your existence. So yes, I do think your memories will return and you will be your 'old self' again in no time. But do not rush back into it quickly. 'Tis a precious thing, your mortal thoughts and feelings, the fresh view you have on things. Hold to it as long as you can, and your memories will restore themselves naturally."

Her voice seemed filled with such great knowledge and power, Love felt comforted just listening to Her. She did seem to be an awesome being, Love decided, and there was no doubt left in her mind that She was, indeed, the Mother of all.

"Thank You." Dite leaned to kiss Her cheek softly, and sank into a low curtsy. "I will be around, should You need me, Mother."

But the Mother's eyes were troubled. "I am afraid there is still more you must know, my child."

The gravity of her tone caused Love to rise from her curtsy slowly. Her heart started to pound anxiously. "Yes?" The itching was back in her hands, and she rubbed them against the sides of her long white gown.

Her eyes were sad as she reached to stroke Love's cheek. "I am not the best one to explain this to you. I will send you to the Temple now, where the others await your presence."

Dite swallowed back the lump that had risen in her throat. She opened her mouth to speak, but the Mother stopped her with a wave of Her hand.

"There is no time for questions, my child. Just go, and know that I believe in you." She smiled beautifully, her expression full of love, before Dite was sucked into blackness.

CHAPTER FOURTEEN

Morgana

It was only after several moments of disorientation that Love became aware of where in Immortality she was. Around her, within the main room of the Temple of Thought, deities and consorts patiently waited for her to get her bearings.

"Love?" It was Athena who spoke first, seated in the center of the room next to Cupid.

"What's going on?" Dite's words came out harsher than she intended as her legs wobbled nervously beneath her. Scanning the room, she saw Passion, Freya, and Hate all gathered along with Cupid and Thought. It seemed an odd assembly for the Temple of Thought. As far as Love knew, Athena had never been inclined to throw a party.

It was the Goddess of Wisdom who stood slowly, walking carefully toward Love. "Did She tell you?"

Love couldn't find her tongue; she shook her head quickly in response.

The others all glanced at each other and Ena sighed. "Very well, then." She started to pace. "It started ten, maybe fifteen Earth years ago. At that time, you were on Earth realm living a mortal life, and we could not locate you to bring you back."

"Your mortal life was still too young at the time," Fire chimed in. "We couldn't find you for almost eight Earth years later."

Love nodded to indicate she understood. Whatever she was about to hear next, she was almost sure she wasn't ready for it.

"So we were forced to fix the problem ourselves; all of us here today." Ena nodded over her shoulder at the others. "And we waited for you to return. You understand why we could not tell you until now and some of us—" here the Muse cast a glance at Passion—"thought perhaps we should continue to wait. But that option is no longer available to us."

Love threw up a hand to indicate Thought should stop. "You aren't making any sense. Slow down. What problem did you have to fix? And why is it still a problem, if it was fixed to begin with?"

Ena shifted her feet uneasily. "Morgana's soul escaped from the Underworld."

Morgana. The name seemed to cause a cold hand to clamp around Dite's heart. *Morgana.* Suddenly the memories rushed back to her, and she was no longer standing in the Temple of Thought.

She was living as a mortal in Medieval Wales, a young common girl named Rhya. The small country had enjoyed peace with both England and Mercia for almost fifty years, the longest peacetime in the history of Wales to date. The country and her people were flourishing, but Rhya had no interest in the history of the politics that surrounded Wales in the past. She was barely sixteen years old, and too wrapped up in her small world to realize that any day could bring Wales back into bloody conflict with her land-hungry neighbors.

War was probably the farthest thought in her mind. Lately, her dreams had all centered around a young man, a knight who served under the powerful Lord of Gwynedd at the time. So caught up in this obsession was she that Rhya failed to notice Morgana for what she was the first time they met, and later it was too late to notice anything at all.

It would be Rhya's fatal mistake.

Morgana came to Gwynedd from the northern land of the Picts, or so she said. A distant cousin of the Lord of Gwynedd, Morgana arrived in the small province with a retinue of soldiers and handmaidens, driving through the village in a gilded carriage even more splendid than the Lord's himself. Rumors of her beauty had swept through the village, even as far as the outer farmlands in the south where Rhya lived, for days before her arrival. It was because of this that Rhya traveled toward the entrance of the Great Tower to watch the noblewoman arrive. Sir Coran lived within the Tower walls, and Rhya thought to size up the competition. After all, everyone in the village had always agreed that she, Rhya, was the unrivaled beauty of the land.

But the carriage passed through the tower walls without offering even a brief glimpse of Morgana, though Rhya had managed to elbow her way to the front of the crowd.

She would see her rival soon enough, though, and purely by chance during the noon market two days later. Eager merchants had all set up their wares in the hopes of tempting Morgana's party into buying some of their more expensive products, and for hours they set out bolts of silk and jewels to catch the Lady's eyes.

Rhya had gone to the market in her older brother's stead to peddle her family's eggs and milk. She was trading for spices and candles when she saw a buzz in the crowd near her. The commoners were parting quickly, some falling over themselves to get out of the way, as Morgana herself approached Rhya's stall.

To say that Morgana was beautiful would do no justice to the word. "Beautiful" as a word lost all meaning when applied to the stunning Morgana. She walked with so much confidence that it seemed she carried with her the greatest secrets, but in truth it was only her own glory that inspired such high self-esteem. As she moved, everyone stopped to stare at her as though caught in a spell.

Her raven black hair fell in inky waves past her waist, and it shimmered like oil as it caressed her hips with every movement. Morgana's eyes were such a startling green that they seemed to pierce the very air, and Rhya could see their color far before Morgana was close to her.

The Lady's face seemed carved from porcelain, her skin was so fine and her features so perfectly formed. Even without the rich emerald green gown and the silver jewelry she wore, Morgana would have easily been the most beautiful creature walking.

"Good day." Morgana's red lips were curved into a perfect smile, displaying dazzling white teeth. Her smile was beautiful, but Rhya saw that it was also cold. In fact, Morgana's whole demeanor seemed to set her apart from the rest of those around her. It was as though she were encased in ice, so cold and untouchable she seemed.

Rhya found her tongue and quickly mumbled back a reply. "Do you care for something in this stall, Milady?" Rhya couldn't begin to imagine what would bring a Lady of Morgana's standing to her own poor stall.

Morgana's eyes glittered in her perfect, pale skin. When the icy emeralds that were her eyes rested on Rhya's, the young girl felt a shiver that traveled all the way up her spine. "I have heard so many good things about your homemade bread cakes that I had to try one for myself. I do hope you have not sold them all today already?" Her voice was the smooth, cultured sort of nobility, but there was an undercurrent of something more that Rhya couldn't quite place.

Bread cakes. Surely Morgana, a Lady of such nobility, didn't travel all the way to the common market for bread cakes. "Ah, nay, Milady...I have four of them left." Rhya quickly bent to pick up her basket, removing the linen covering for the Lady to see. "Shall I select one for you? "

Morgana smiled in her icy way. "Nay, Rhya, for I shall purchase them all." Casually, she flipped a golden coin at her and plucked the basket from her hands. "Good day."

It wasn't until the end of the day that Rhya realized Morgana had called her by name.

"Morgana." Love was looking at Thought again, shaken loose from her eight-hundred-year-old memories. "It isn't possible. Where is Hades? Surely he was not left out of this at the beginning."

"Morgana didn't escape without help; that much we know. When Morgana was sent to the Underworld, she was sent to stay," Passion declared. "Hades was questioned."

Love felt her patience wearing thin. "And?"

Thought cleared her throat gently to gather attention once more to herself. She continued. "Morgana apparently escaped during a period where Satan was in control of the Underworld."

Dite groaned. The carnation of the being Satan was a very tricky one. Made up of both Hades and Loki, Satan existed only on those occasions when the two beings merged into one. Hades often had scattered, incomplete memories of what happened while Satan was in charge of the Underworld. No one was really sure about what Loki remembered; it was not Loki's nature to reveal such information. "Loki," she spat.

Thought nodded her confirmation. "We can only assume that Loki, as Satan, released Morgana."

"And I was unavailable." Love spit out a human expletive that some of the beings present had never heard before and started pacing, whirling to face Ena. "And? How did the rest of you correct this? Did you find her and return her to the Underworld?"

Thought spread her hands. "We could not, Love, you know that. Morgana was released completely. She was born again somewhere on Earth realm."

Love's eyes shot fire as she glared at the Muse. "What do you mean, 'somewhere'? You still have not found her?"

"She is cloaked by Loki's trickery. We did the only thing we could." At this, the Muse bowed her head.

Dite felt herself go numb. "What do you mean? Athena—what have you done?"

Cupid looked up at her finally, his eyes apologetic. "We had to place a bind on Earth realm, Mistress. It was all we could do."

Suddenly the assemblage made sense. Freya, the Goddess of Desire. Hate. Passion. Love's consort. And Wisdom. "You neutralized love in every human soul born at the time, didn't you? Not just love, but Desire, Hate, and Passion. All that which Morgana may evoke." Her rage was complete now as she stared at them. "I have an entire generation of the emotionless to deal with. Damn you all! What about the balance, that precious balance you are all here to maintain?"

"Love, it was the only thing we knew to do." Cupid's voice pleaded with her to understand.

"How many?" she screamed. No one could look at her. "Damn you, how many?"

"We narrowed it down to a specific month in Earth's time—" Athena began gently.

Love spun to face her, her eyes ablaze with anger. "*How many*?"

"One thousand, four hundred and three."

Dite's legs went weak beneath her and she sat down on the marble floor with a thud. Impossibly, she felt sick to her stomach, though the body of a deity is not composed of flesh. "Loki could create an army with that number."

"They are not old enough yet, but will be soon. It is why we could wait no longer." Thought's voice had grown weaker.

"Fools!" Love spat at them all. "Of course Loki knew you would do that. Of course he knew I was in Earth realm. Of course that was his intention all along. Now he has an army's worth of soulless to help him in whatever scheme he's planning."

"You don't know that for sure." Fire's eyes betrayed his own horror at her words, however. None of them had thought of that possibility, that Loki knew what they would do. That in fact, he had orchestrated Morgana's escape for just such a purpose.

"We had to neutralize those souls to neutralize Morgana's as well," Athena spoke again.

"You played right into his hands," Love was boiling now. "Of course the God of Mischief knows where she is, and he has at his disposal the means with which to get around such neutralization. The other thousand souls will be his, a horde that can feel no remorse or conscience." In her rage, her eyes found Fire's. "How could you allow this?"

Sad stares greeted her question. Very well, she decided. She didn't expect an answer anyway. "They must be harvested and sent to the Underworld immediately; and there is no question about it. If these creatures on Earth realm even have a soul, we must do our best to save them. Call Death here now." Love snatched Cupid's hand as she walked toward the entrance of the Temple to leave. "I am going to the Underworld."

"Love!" Athena took a step toward her. "What are you going to do?"

The Goddess's eyes burned. "I am going to find Morgana. Call Death and harvest those thousand now, before Loki gets to them. He surely has them already, and was hiding Morgana while we were busy in the High Trib. Damnation! The Fathergod is probably his staunchest ally in this."

"I think you are overreacting, Dite. You are talking as though this is some grand scheme." Fire's voice was gentle, as though he were speaking to a crazed woman.

"The Lord of Lies is involved, Passion. How could you think otherwise? Besides, if I am right, then best to fix things now. If you are right, all we have done is harvest a thousand of the unlucky. A thousand who do not belong on Earth realm at any rate. That number alone is enough to swing the balance." At that, Love spun on her heel and left the Temple, still dragging Cupid behind her.

"M-mistress? Are you traveling to the Underworld now?" Cupid's voice shook with fear.

Love eyed him coolly. "Think of it as an adventure, Q. How many consorts have seen the Underworld? Surely, you will have a fabulous story to tell to TROM." She drew a doorway in the air and shoved him into Love's Tunnel before he could protest further.

Morgana returned to Rhya's stall the next week, many hours earlier this time. This day, her gown was fine, thick velvet red. It complemented her thick, dark hair beautifully and Rhya's heart lurched, wondering how any Knight in the tower could resist such a Lady.

"Good morning, Rhya." Morgana addressed her as though they were old friends.

"Lady Morgana." She quickly curtsied, lowering her eyes as the rules of her station dictated. "What has brought you back to my family's humble wares?" It had taken the better part of an hour to convince her brother to let her sit at the stall again this week, and even longer to wrangle out of him a promise that he would not tell their father.

That icy smile again. "Your bread cakes are, indeed, the finest I have sampled. They melt in my mouth as though made from air. I must purchase more. Surely you will tell your secrets to my house staff, so I may enjoy such a delicacy even after I travel back to my land." Charm and poise oozed off her.

Rhya's own mouth felt like ice as she returned the Lady's smile. "Ah, it is our family's most guarded secret. But I did make extra cakes, in hopes you would return." She brought forth a basket, woven only a day before by her own hand, filled with the sweet-smelling cakes.

"Of course you cannot part with such knowledge, then. More's the pity." Morgana's gaze never wavered, and Rhya felt an uncomfortable sensation under her penetrating gaze.

They exchanged money for the cakes. Rhya didn't breathe again until Morgana had vanished down the path, out of sight.

The Underworld could only be reached by one of two ways. Mortals who died on Earth realm traveled to the Underworld down the Path of the Damned, an ominous name for the narrow channel of water that led deep into the heart of Hades' domain. Tended by Hades' skeleton guards, narrow boats filled with the dead wound along to the center of what Christians once called Hell.

Immortal beings, however, could float directly into the same lake. Love's Tunnel ended where Hades' waterways began, and here the air was thick with grief and mortal death. Cupid was balled into the bottom of Love's swan boat, shaking pitifully.

Dite, unaffected by Cupid's display, docked her majestic boat at the edge of the lake and pulled Cupid with her onto the landing that was guarded by one of Hades' most trusted consorts, Merlyn.

"Hello, Merlyn." Love smiled at the aged being, who still held the form he'd known in life. As one of the world's most powerful wizards, the name *Merlyn* once struck fear into the hearts of the English in the Middle Ages. For centuries he had served as Hades' chief consultant.

"Ah, Venus. You have not been this way for five hundred years. It is good to see such beauty in this place of darkness and despair." The wizened old man smiled at her affectionately. "This must be the Cupid I've heard so much about."

"Indeed, this is my darling consort." She planted a soft kiss on his weathered cheek. Merlyn was one of the only humans who, while alive, had been able to see her in invisible Goddess form on Earth realm. "Is your Lord in?"

"Aye, Goddess, Hades is in his chambers. If you go on to his reception room, I'll send word that you are here for him."

"Thank you muchly, Merlyn, but he will receive me in his chambers." Without waiting for a reply, Love gathered up her skirts and stepped across the wooden planks into the main body of the Underworld.

Making her way through the dark abyss, Love found her way unerringly into Hades' private domicile. She remembered now that she had only been to the Underworld three times in the past, and the first time her and Hades had something of a...disagreement.

"Hades?" The word and one sharp knock on his door was the only warning she allowed him before she stepped boldly into his private chambers. Here it was lighter and less oppressive than the rest of the Underworld.

The Tender of the Dead was staring into a fireplace when she entered, and he quickly sprang to his feet. Unlike what many believe, the Underworld was not filled with heat and fire. It was, in fact, rather cold and damp down there. But Hades' inner rooms were warmer and dryer. Love watched the flames crackle in the fireplace as she waited for Hades to speak.

"Love." His voice was a soft sigh. "So you have heard about Morgana."

She nodded and took a seat across from him without being asked, gesturing for Cupid to sit by her feet. "I understand Satan made her release possible."

The God of the Underworld sighed. "I see the accusation in your eyes, Love, and I am not fooled into thinking this is a social visit. As hard as it may be for you to believe, I as Hades have very little control or knowledge when I am part of that particular carnation."

Love waved a hand dismissively. "I am not here to grill you or rack your brain for your memories, Hades. I accept that what is done is done, and even if you remembered how she was released it would be of little help now."

His eyebrows shot up in surprise. "Then what do you want?"

"You are aware of what the others did?"

Hades swallowed and slowly nodded. "I was told afterwards, yes."

Dite leaned forward. "I have ordered those souls to be harvested; if they even have souls. Please, Hades...please reform them, so that they might still have a chance."

For once, the God of the Underworld looked surprised. "You came all the way to Hell to ask me to do that?"

"This is not Hell right now." But her eyes betrayed her light tone. "Those souls should not have to live out their destined lives, feeling none of that which makes them human. Yes, Hades, please do what you can for them. I know you have made it your mission to reform and help as many as possible." Lovingly, she reached out to touch his cheek softly. "The stories about the devil never did you justice, assuming that the Tender of the Dead only tortures and punishes. I know you will help them, but I had to come and ask you as a personal favor to me, to try and give them a real soul."

Hades reached out to grip her hand warmly. "Though you are Love itself, your compassion for mortals has never stopped surprising me. Of course I will do what I can for them, Love. I'll be looking for each of them to arrive and I'll construct a special ring of the Underworld just for them, those poor soulless creatures."

"Thank you, Hades." She stood to hug him. "I would love to have a longer visit with you, but I have a demon to find." Love pulled back to smile at him. "To help you give those poor creatures a real soul and a real chance on Earth realm, Cupid will serve you here for a time. I want these thousand to have more capability to Love than most mortals, and he will show you the way. Cupid knows Love better than any being in Immortality."

"Mistress, nay!" Terrified, he lunged for her skirts and held on like an infant. "Do not punish me this way!"

"Q, stop being ridiculous. It is only for a short time, and the Underworld is not so horrible." She winked at Hades. "I'm sure Hades will keep your torture down to a minimum."

Cupid sobbed pathetically. "I am sorry I went along with them, my Lady! Do not banish me to the Underworld!"

Love lifted him gently from her skirts and patted his blonde curls. "You are not being banished. Loki will be looking for you above all else, knowing you are my consort. Remember the time he imprisoned you on Earth realm? I must hide you away until this situation with Morgana clears. And Hades will take care of you, that I promise you." She kissed his cheek and gave him a squeeze. "It will do you some good to learn more of humans in this way. You have grown too much like a deity in Immortality, and forget that you must love humanity above all else." With that, she left Hades' chambers and went off to search for the most powerful human soul ever born into Earth realm.

Rhya fretted the whole long day, standing in the sweltering heat during the market. She'd not seen her Knight in the whole three long weeks since Morgana first came, and Rhya worried about that. The only thing to give her a smile was the knowledge that Morgana was supposed to leave the very next day, back to the Pict lands and her manor home up there.

Yet Morgana had failed to return to the stall, though Rhya had baked two baskets of her bread cakes very early that morning in anticipation of the Lady's visit.

The more time slipped by, the more Rhya relaxed. She would not see

Morgana again. For reasons she couldn't put words to, Morgana frightened her.

Just as she was closing her stall for the day, Morgana appeared. As usual, she traveled with several of her servants and as usual, they hung back as Morgana approached. Today she wore dark blue silk, and in the twilight Morgana looked as though she were a part of the night itself.

"My Lady!" Rhya couldn't hide her surprise. "I had thought you would not arrive this day."

The Lady smiled in return, reaching to grab one of Rhya's hands. It was such a surprising move, Rhya could only stare without speaking. "Dear child Rhya. I have developed such a fondness for your sweet treats. I came to make you an offer."

Morgana's eyes were magnetic as they bored into Rhya. "I know about you, Rhya. I know that your father is a poor farmer on the southside of Gwynedd and your mother died birthing you. I know you have labored your whole life there. I even know the young Knight you have eyes for, but he will never marry you, Rhya. This I know for a fact. One of his line would never marry a simple farmer's daughter. You must know that."

Rhya felt horrified that Morgana knew so much about her but at the same time, she was captivated. Morgana's voice was soft, soothing, and her eyes never broke their hold over Rhya's. "How—" she whispered.

"How does not matter, dear child. My offer is this: you will come with me to my manor house and serve as my personal maid. I will travel with you and keep you with me always. You will be under my protection."

"Me? But I have never served before. Why would you—"

Morgana cut her off. "Your questions are unimportant. Only my questions matter now. Would you like to come and live in my fine home, Rhya? Would you like to wear fine gowns and have your own chambers next to mine? Surely you are anxious to shake the dust of Gwynedd off your feet. My lands are beautiful. The Picts are a powerful people."

It seemed too good to be true. Without ever really pausing to consider it, Rhya found herself agreeing. It was only when the power of Morgana's eyes were away from her that she questioned her own agreement with the woman.

Leaving turned out to be a simple enough manner. Once Rhya's father met Morgana, he was willing to give her anything she wished, even his only daughter. Why, he even helped Rhya pack her meager belongings that very same night. She would depart with Morgana very early in the morning.

Groggy and sleepy, Rhya had only a few moments to say her last good-

bye to her father before Morgana came. Before Rhya could even catch her breath, she was seated in Morgana's glorious gilded carriage and being whisked away to the Pict lands.

Morgana's manor house was indeed spectacular, and Rhya was quickly made at home there. Her own room was small, but still larger than the tiny space she'd occupied in her father's modest home, and Rhya was immensely pleased with the fine materials Morgana brought her to make gowns with. Though her gowns would never be half as rich as the Lady's, it was still more wealth than Rhya had ever owned before, and she was glad to have it.

Serving Morgana was pleasurable for her. Though the Lady's demands were often and sometimes ridiculous, Morgana was free with her praise and Rhya found herself drinking down Morgana's sweet words hungrily. Truly, just being around Morgana made her feel...weak. As though she became less herself and more what Morgana wanted her to be. But those thoughts came to her less frequently the more time she spent in Morgana's company. Rhya could think of little else than pleasing her.

Rhya lived in Morgana's glorious home a full year before they traveled anywhere. Though Morgana had promised that she traveled often and Rhya would always accompany her, the Lady had left the manor only twice since Rhya came back from Gwynedd with her. Surprisingly, Rhya had never dwelled on this before the day Morgana announced she should pack their things. But the thought of leaving the house, even for a short while, filled Rhya with joy. She was used to being free, to wandering about the countryside. Seeing new faces would make her giddy with joy.

Practically the entire household staff was packed up to travel with Morgana. The woman apparently never went anywhere without most all of them with her. Rhya never thought to wonder about the oddity of this, she was too overjoyed at the prospect of seeing a new place.

They traveled in high style all the way into London. It was a glorious, affluent city, and Rhya watched everything around them in wonder from her cushy seat in Morgana's rich carriage. They would be staying for three weeks in the home of the Duke of Windsor, another of Morgana's distant cousins. Rhya learned that Morgana's line was mingled in with powerful nobles in almost every major country around them. It did not seem so strange to her, then, that she never met any of Morgana's immediate family, and never did she question how Morgana had attained her own manor house without having ever been married.

The Duke's castle was splendid, however, and Morgana was sure to acquire for Rhya a beautiful room just down the hall from Morgana's own glorious chambers within the castle. Rhya thought then that she was happy, that she could hope for nothing more.

She also never questioned what happened to the woman who served as Morgana's personal maid before she took the duty on as her own.

During their stay in England, Morgana declined dining in the Great Hall most nights and chose instead to dine in her chambers with Rhya. The handmaiden felt pleased that Morgana would choose to share her meals with her, when so many others desired Morgana's company.

It was during one of these nights that Morgana started questioning Rhya, and why Love would never forget every detail of this particular mortal life.

The two women were feasting on roast lamb in Morgana's opulent chambers, while the rest of the castle's inhabitants were gathered in the Great Hall below them. Morgana's eyes, as usual, were observing Rhya quietly. Over time, Rhya had learned not to feel frightened when her Lady looked at her that way, but the penetrating green stare always made her nervous nonetheless.

"Do you have strange dreams, child Rhya?"

The question took her by surprise. "Why do you ask, Milady?"

Morgana shrugged off-handedly, but her piercing green eyes never left Rhya's face. "I hear you at night sometimes, whimpering in your sleep. I walked in there a few times to awaken you, and you talk in your sleep, saying strange things I don't recognize. It sounds like another language."

Rhya was surprised. "I know no other languages, Milady."

Morgana smiled. Even when her smile tried to be sweet, her mouth was still icy-looking. "You did not answer my question, Rhya."

Satisfied with Morgana's response to her previous question, and feeling strange under that green gaze, Rhya answered her. "Yes, I do. I see strange things."

A perfectly shaped black eyebrow rose into a question mark. "Such as? Do not be afraid to tell me, darling Rhya. You should know that I am your Lady, and you may tell me anything."

"I see...cities. Old cities, built of stone and marble. People dressed in long, flowing white gowns. Different places and people all the time, and I am always one of them, part of them. The place I see most often is filled with huge buildings, buildings so large they make even this castle look small. Buildings constructed entirely of fire, and one of water. Strange people in odd clothing, leather and animals skins and gowns. They all speak to me as

if they know me, but I am not me in these dreams. I am never me when I dream."

Morgana was nodding throughout this, encouraging more. "Do you know who you are in these dreams?"

"No." Rhya shivered. She felt a strange sensation, as though she should never speak of these things again. She had never spoken of them before.

Morgana nodded; she was satisfied with Rhya's answers. The pleasure of Morgana's approval washed away her doubts about telling Morgana her secrets. Why shouldn't she tell Morgana? Morgana was her Lady; she lived to serve her.

"These dreams are important, Rhya. You must tell me when you have them."

"I shall, Milady. The next morning after every dream when I bring your breakfast, we shall eat together and I will tell you."

"No!" Morgana's voice shook slightly, and she quickly softened her tone at Rhya's start. "You must awaken me when you have them. You remember them better directly afterward." At Rhya's questioning look, she smiled. "I just want to help you, my dear one."

And strangely, Rhya accepted Morgana's reasons.

Another year passed swiftly, with no more variation in the routine. The days blended together so seemlessly, in fact, that Rhya was shocked when thinking back, she realized she was now eighteen years old. Dutifully, she continued to serve Morgana, often sharing with her the dreams she had that seemed to grow stranger with each passing week. Morgana listened with full attention, never commenting. It gave Rhya a strange peace to share her dreams with Morgana, who always listened so well to what Rhya had to say.

It was toward the end of this second year that Rhya awoke one night from the strangest dream yet. She went immediately to Morgana's chamber, just next to her own, but the Lady was not there. Rhya remembered that sometimes Morgana went to the caves near the lake, just behind the manor house. Had her dream not been so disturbing, she would never have thought to disrupt the Lady's privacy, but she felt only Morgana would help her decipher this strange dream. Slipping into her cloak, Rhya quickly stole from the house and made her way to the caves to find Morgana.

A woman had appeared in her dream. It was the same woman she'd seen in a few of her other dreams. She had short, curly brown hair and soft, golden-brown eyes. The woman had identified herself as "Ena" and told Rhya that she was in extreme danger. Then Ena had told Rhya to kill herself, to kill herself this very night before she placed the entire world in danger.

Rhya would not rest easily until she shared this with Morgana, whom she had grown to love and trust above all else.

The girl found the cave without much trouble, and a faint glow of light coming from deep within the cave led her inside the small, dark space. The light could only mean that Morgana was inside.

Find Morgana she did, but thankfully Morgana never saw Rhya. Entering silently, Rhya was led deeper into the cave, where she saw her Lady kneeling before a fire dug in a shallow hole in the center of the cave.

Morgana's face was covered in ash from the fire. Her hands were raised and sticky with dried blood. Her body moved back and forth, and she was locked in some strange ritual.

It was then that Rhya saw Morgana's eyes as they stared into the flames and Rhya realized that all along, Morgana had held some strange power with them. Slowly, Morgana had been changing her.

Rhya needed to see no more. She fled from the caves and from Morgana's manor home for good. Remembering the dream, Rhya obeyed Ena's words and drowned herself that very night.

It wasn't until she awoke in Immortality as Love that all of them began to discover just what Morgana was.

CHAPTER FIFTEEN

Loki

The only way to locate the reincarnated Morgana was to locate all the souls that had been born in the month Athena and the rest narrowed her birth down to. Over one thousand births, and Love had to find them all before she would recognize Morgana's soul.

Even then, she would be hard to locate, protected by Loki as Morgana always had been.

Yet Love had to try. Morgana free on Earth realm could be disastrous.

Ena was waiting at her bedside when Love re-awoke in Immortality.

"Thank goodness." Her old friend squeezed Love's hand. "I was going to send Death after you if you didn't follow my instructions."

"Who is she?" Love was still trying to get oriented. Coming back to herself after eighteen long years of no knowledge was difficult. Coming back was always confusing.

Thought sighed. "Perhaps the most powerful being you can encounter on Earth realm. As usual, you have managed to get yourself into a load of trouble through your foolish exploits."

"Oh, don't scold me, Athena. You know why I do it. You act as though I have some control what I will be born into. You should be thanking me for finding her."

"We found her twelve human years ago, you silly emotion. I've been trying to contact you through your mortal dreams ever since. It wasn't until that witch started to draw them out of you that you actually started to listen."

Love waved an airy hand. "Oh well, I'm here now. So tell me, who is she?"

Wisdom shifted her eyes. "We think she's Loki's daughter."

At that, Love bolted out of her bed. "Loki's daughter? How'd he pull that off?"

"Come on, we have a lot to talk about."

It seemed Love was always catching up on things that happened while she was on Earth realm. That long ago day, the Goddess of Wisdom had presented the evidence. Love learned that Loki had somehow managed to get to Earth realm by living a mortal life. ("That explains why everything's been running so smoothly everywhere for fifty years," Love had said when she found out.) None of them noted Loki's absence, since he was often away creating mischief, it was not unusual for him to be gone from Immortality for long stretches at a time.

Yet Loki had managed to find out who exactly he was while in his fifteenth mortal year on Earth. Athena could never discern how this was done, and they could all only assume one of the other deities had conspired with Loki previously and then come to him in a vision while he was human. Now, centuries later, Love cursed herself for not looking into that more closely. At the time, it was all they could do to undo Loki's mischief, and that fact had seemed unimportant. But now, Love knew the same being was still aiding Loki's evil.

Athena had determined that Loki managed to father a child while living as a mortal. Soon after, he killed himself to return to Immortality in full power.

"He must have then traveled *back* to Earth realm as Loki and given the child some of his weavings," Thought concluded on that far-ago day. "Left there to grow with the mortal after all these years, we cannot take back what he's given. Even if we did know what he gave her to begin with."

And so, they had Morgana. Over the next ten human years, Morgana would be revealed as the most powerful witch ever to walk the Earth. Every being in Immortality was watching her carefully, closely. They all wanted to see just what she was capable of. Unlike the peace-fostering witches that walked Earth realm, Morgana's soul was twisted by evil. She used her power without thought to consequence or care for whom she harmed.

Morgana was capable of mind control. Rhya's mind had been manipulated, yes, but never to the extent that Morgana could practice over normal humans. Though Rhya had been born and lived as a true human being, her essence had always been that of the Goddess of Love. Only because of that had Rhya always been at least partially safe from Morgana, but Athena had never liked the risk of it.

On top of that, Morgana had slowly begun to realize just who Rhya really was. Having Immortal weavings herself, Morgana had a strong intuitive power. She envied the power Rhya had, and envied more that Rhya was never aware of this power. But thankfully, Athena had managed to get to Rhya before Morgana could figure a way to get to her as well.

The more she remembered, the more Love began to worry. It was Athena who eventually commanded Death to harvest Morgana, after they saw what the woman was planning to do.

It soon became obvious that Loki himself regularly communicated with Morgana through her dreams. Love realized that was the reason Morgana was so interested in Rhya's dreams. Loki used his influence to guide his daughter.

They soon found that Morgana and Loki were planning something more horrible than any of them could have imagined.

Morgana was becoming a powerful witch during this time on Earth realm, and using her mind control for anything she wished. Morgana had gained a power greater than that any mortal had ever had: she could neutralize emotion within human souls.

Secretly, Morgana was forming an army of creatures that could feel neither hate nor love, guilt or remorse. These beings had no conscience. They knew only that Morgana controlled them, and they must serve Morgana always.

Her power had only one flaw. She had to be almost constantly near her minions for her mastery over them to keep its effect. Leaving them without her company for too long would cause her magic to fade; they would slowly become full, complete human beings again.

It took ten years for Immortality to realize the full extent of Morgana's powers, and by that time she had gathered more than two hundred people in her control.

Love herself was the one that convinced Death to harvest Morgana's soul from Earth realm, though it was Athena's decree that called him in the first place. For Morgana to die was the only way any of them could figure how to stop her. Many in Immortality were angry at Love, and disagreed with what she'd done.

But it was Love who knew firsthand just what Morgana was like, and it was Love who was forced to take care of those wretched beings that Morgana transformed into soulless, controlled soldiers for her private war on Earth realm.

What Morgana wanted them for, none of them could ever determine.

For many centuries in the Underworld, Morgana refused to speak to anyone. By all accounts of those who watched her, she never uttered a word.

Now Love knew that she had been waiting. Patiently waiting for the day she would be released back into Earth.

Dite knew what she had to do to locate Morgana. While Death was on Earth realm harvesting the souls, she would also travel to Earth realm.

Love knew if she were the one to find Morgana first, she would not call Death to harvest Morgana's soul. No…what Love had in mind for Morgana was far more painful than simple death.

"You're going to do *what*?" Now, back at Love's Palace, Athena paced the floor furiously. Her long white tunic snapped at her ankles as she whipped back and forth across the marbled tiles.

"I'm going to Earth realm to find the witch," Dite repeated herself calmly as she dressed. She pulled a woolen cloak tight about her shoulders, then moved her hands to quickly pin up her long hair.

"I simply cannot allow that!" Thought was angry, a rare enough occasion.

Love turned her face slightly to quirk one amused eyebrow at the Muse. "Do forgive me, Wisdom, I was not aware I was asking your permission."

Athena's eyes blazed for a moment as she met her old friend's gaze. "Sarcasm does not suit you, Love."

"No, nor would I expect it to. Anger does not wear well on you, either." She pulled her hood up around her face, covering the pile of thick blonde curls. "Nevertheless, I'm going. I know Morgana better than you and better than Death, too. If anyone can find her, I can."

"I don't think I need to remind you that you are still not up to full capacity. You're certainly not in shape to deal with this!" Thought barked.

"Well." Heat rising, Dite whirled to face Athena face to face. "Since you and the others have done such a *masterful* job so far, Ena, perhaps I should continue to leave it in your hands, hmm?"

Shocked, the Goddess took a step back. "I will forgive that since I know you are not truly yourself." Her voice was small.

But Love was too angry with all of them to feel sympathy anymore. "Forgive all you want; I neither asked for, nor need, forgiveness from you. My mind is set. I go to Earth realm and I will find Morgana. Only then can I begin to clean up the rest of your mess." She snapped a silver pin through her cloak, near her throat, for emphasis. Pulling the ends together, she pinned her cloak closed and turned away to leave.

"Aphrodite!" Athena sprang forward quickly, placing a quick hand on Love's arm. "Wait. At least take someone with you."

Coldly, Dite shook her arm away. "I'll not expose more beings than necessary to that witch. If I find myself in dire straights, I'll summon Thor to my side." When Athena opened her mouth to speak again, Love cut her off with a wave of her hand. "Enough. I go. Love to Earth realm, Venice, Italy."

And she watched Ena's eyes turn wide with fear as she dematerialized from the room.

Venice was the birthplace of the first soul on the suspect list. Love had finally managed to gain these names from Passion. Fifteen mortal years before, in the warm month of August, at exactly 12:01 in the morning, the first of the Damned was born.

The gondolas wound around the thin, narrow waterways majestically. Love felt the cool breeze off the water as her eyes scanned the crowd. She honed in on her Goddess instincts, reaching out to find a soul among the horde of people…the one soul who could not love.

She was walking along a waterway, her feet gliding over the surface of the water, when the rancid odor of Death assailed her. She felt its darkness moving around her, and she turned with a slight smile to the being she knew so well.

"Death." Love reached out for his hands, gliding smoothly over the water to him. "I had thought you would be moved onto the next location by now."

His eyes, deeper and blacker than anything natural found on Earth realm, bored into her own with long familiarity. "Ah, Love. I was actually waiting for you. I have harvested almost two hundred of them by now. I was on my way out of Europe when Hermes found me."

"Hermes?"

Death squeezed her hands in his own icy, bony fingers. His long, black cloak swirled around him in the soft breeze. "Athena sent word to me that you were traveling here to Earth realm. I thought, perhaps, we should work together to find the witch?"

"Ah, Death. Does no one trust me anymore? One little Affliction, and suddenly everyone wants to keep an eye on me."

The being laughed, a strange, dry sound deep in his throat. "It is more efficient to combine both our powers. You have better senses than I to tract the loveless. What will you do once you find them, anyway?" He rose one shoulder in a shrug. "Much easier if we travel together."

"Have it your way, then, deity." Love stepped off the water to stand next to him, lacing her arm through his. "We shall scour the rest of the continents as a team."

Death grinned…or she thought he grinned. It was hard to determine just what his expression was in his stark white, bone face. "Love and Death traveling together. What strange companions we will make! Come then, Dite, we move east to Asia."

"Damnable hot there this time of year." She offered him a wink and pulled nearer to him, so they would not be separated as they traveled through the cosmos.

Seven hundred fifty-two souls later, Dite and Death were exhausted and out of sorts. Asia, Australia, Africa, and South America had sped by in a blur. Now the two sat close together on a stone bench on the northernmost tip of Prince Edward Island, in Canada. Glorious Spring had come to the island, draping the verdant countryside in rich pinks, greens, and blues.

"Four hundred fifty-eight." Love finally finished her calculations. "One hundred seventy-six here in Canada, leaving two hundred eighty-two in the States." The Goddess sighed. "I knew she'd end up going to America. England, Wales, Scotland...they would have been too obvious. Africa, Asia, and Australia just aren't her style... We should save the States for last. Might as well save these poor souls while we still have the chance."

Death squeezed her fingers with affection. Had she been a human, the contact would have sent a chill through her body. Immortal being that she was, Love only shivered slightly. "Four fifty-eight is not a bad number. She couldn't have more than half of them on her side."

It was a subject they hadn't raised while in the Eastern Hemisphere. These soulless beings were perfect for Morgana to start a small army, but the two beings had yet to encounter any who had knowledge of the woman. Since it was obvious Morgana was now in the States, surely she had already gathered some of the soulless to her side. Loki was still helping his daughter, after all.

Aphrodite sighed wearily. "I did not know that encountering them all would be so blasted difficult."

Death patted her hand in understanding. "I keep forgetting how different it is for you."

"Yes, you are used to it, aren't you?"

The being gave her a sad glance...as sad as his eerily grinning skull face would allow. "Killing, harvesting souls is never pleasant...nor is it something any creature can get 'used to.' I do not relish my purpose here, Love, but I do what I am supposed to do."

Love's cheeks bloomed with color. "You are right, Death, and I am sorry. I am sure no being in Immortality or otherwise could do the service that you do."

He nodded, then stood abruptly. "Well, we have a job to do."

177

"Yes." Love slipped her hand into his long, bony fingers.

Invisibly, the two otherworldy creatures walked down the quaint, tree-lined streets of the island. "There is one here, right?" Death glanced sideways at Dite as they strolled, listening to the lyrical sounds of the native Canadians and enjoying the fragrant smells from flowering trees.

Dite was frowning. "There should be one here in PEI, fifty-three in Toronto, sixty-two in Quebec, leaving sixty in other parts of Canada."

Death caught the strange note to her voice. "What's wrong?"

"I can no longer sense the empty soul on this island."

Death stiffened beside her, and Dite glanced over. "What?"

"How long have we been here?"

"In Canada? Why, not more than—"

"No!" Death's voice was sharp. "Earth realm," he hissed, stopping short suddenly, placing his hands on her shoulders. "How long have we been on Earth realm?"

Love's eyes rolled back into her head as she thought. "I don't rightly know, friend Death...my senses are not what they used to be," she added ruefully.

He glanced around. "I cannot appear here to these mortals without causing quite the stir." Slightly abashed, fathomless black eyes swung her way. "Could you, Love, appear quickly and find out the date?"

"Appear?" she repeated dumbly, then realized. "Oh...appear? In human form? Yes, yes, of course that is what you mean...but why do you need to know the date?"

"To know how old these souls are now...they might be coming of age, so to speak."

It was a horrible thought, and would only make their job harder. "Of...course. I'll appear..." Her voice trailed off. Trouble was, she couldn't quite figure how to do that. She was sure she'd done it before, but...

"You don't remember how, do you?"

No hiding anything from Death. Guiltily, blue eyes turned up to him.

He smiled knowingly. "Focus on a particular individual, hopefully one with a bit more intuition than most, and concentrate on becoming solid. At least long enough to find the date."

Love nodded, her eyes scanning the Canadian crowds on the streets. Finally, she settled on a bright-eyed young girl who was hurrying toward the post office. Summoning her powers together, she stared into the girl's eyes and focused on appearing before her. Side-stepping right into the girl's path, her goddess gaze bored into the girl's as she approached.

"Oh!" The girl bumped smack into the goddess right at the last instant. "Excuse me," she murmured.

Love, so surprised that it had actually worked, almost forgot her question as the girl started hurrying past again. "Oh, miss!"

The girl spun quickly, one black eyebrow raised in curiosity. "Yes?"

Dite managed a friendly smile. "Could you, perhaps, tell me today's date?"

"Today's date?" the girl echoed, eyebrows furrowing. "Why, it's—"

Suddenly, Death stepped forward and grabbed Dite's arm. "Love, no!" He hissed in her ear, and dragged her away from the girl. "Dematerialize, *now.*"

The girl's answer was drowned out under Death's urgent command. Love quickly did as she was told, focusing on her natural form. The girl, shocked, stood staring at the spot Love had occupied only moments before.

"Well." Love spun to face him. "If you think I'm doing it again—"

"Love, hush! Do you not know who that is?" One bony finger pointed at the young woman, who had remembered her purpose and was going back into the post office.

Hearing his urgency, Love's eyes quickly turned back to the retreating figure. All the breath rushed out of her, and if she were a human she was sure she'd have fainted. "Oh, no."

Death nodded, his grip firm on her elbow. "Now I know why you could not sense the soul you needed."

Love, who had spent so many centuries emulating mortals, was white-faced as she nodded. "We found Morgana."

The young woman, of course, never came back out of the post office. By the time Love and Death realized she wasn't going to come out, it was already too late. Morgana was gone, and even Love's power couldn't sense the woman's soul.

Now, after quickly tearing through the rest of Canada and the United States, Love and Death had returned to Prince Edward Island. The two had encountered almost three hundred souls that Morgana had already contacted…three hundred souls that were so utterly under her spell that they would not tell even the face of Death just what, exactly, Morgana was planning.

"Surely she knows by now that we are after her. She *must* know her minions are dead." Love was working her hands nervously, sharp eyes scanning the crowd.

Death's expression was grimmer than usual—a frightening thing, in any case—and nodded gravely. "It would stand to reason that she is trying to create more while we stand here, helpless. You are sure you cannot sense her?"

Dite's heart was beating raggedly in her chest. It had taken longer than expected to harvest those souls left from Athena's meddling in Earth's affairs, and she felt emotionally exhausted. Her lingering mortality still had a firm grasp on her mental functions, it would seem. She felt less like a Goddess than ever. "I cannot."

"Nor can I. Is there anyone in Immortality who might be able to sense her presence, or even where she might have last been?"

Love snorted as her eyes watched the Canadian crowd. "You would know better than I, Death. My memories are not what they used to be."

The cloaked being nodded slowly. "You are right, of course. I keep forgetting."

"Cupid would be no better at sensing emotion than I…Perhaps Passion? Maybe even Hate could sense her…if she has that feeling in her heart, of course. The trouble is, we don't know what's in Morgana's heart…so how could we find the right being? We cannot call them all down to Earth realm." Love sighed and rubbed her eyes, a very mortal gesture of fatigue.

"Love!" Death's voice was suddenly sharp.

She turned, quickly, to see his white face lighting up with excitement. "Death?"

"You and I keep trying to sense Morgana's emotions…but would it not be easier to sense her thoughts? She may not have any emotion to sense, which is why you cannot. But, now, her thoughts—"

"Athena!" Love cried, cutting him off. "Of course, Death, what a marvelous idea!" With renewed enthusiasm, she tilted her head back. "Hermes!" She pulled the golden bell from her belt and rang it furiously. Hermes was known for taking his sweet time when called to Earth realm—he didn't care much for the place.Death took to pacing at her side while they waited for the messenger. Love was grumbling about the pace with which Hermes traveled when the air shimmered and finally, Hermes arrived.

"Just the messen—" He stopped short when he saw who had summoned him, and took an involuntary step backwards. "Uhhh…hello Death, Love."

"Hermes!" Love jumped forward suddenly, and Hermes jumped back so quickly he almost fell over. "We need Athena here—*now*."

The curly-headed youth was nervously whetting his lips with his tongue, staring from Death's face to Love's expression and back again. "A-A-Athena?" he repeated dumbly.

"Hermes, if you don't get your silly self in action this very second—" Love, losing patience, took a menacing step forward, but Hermes was already disappearing.

Death was giving her a look that was as close to a smirk as he could manage. "You are quite a bit more entertaining since your Affliction, dear Love."

She managed a sheepish grin. "Love is never a very patient emotion, remember."

He laughed—which, coming from him, was a terrifying sound. "True enough, Goddess…true enough."

A rendering in the air silenced them both, and finally Athena stood in their midst. "I hear laughter. Have I been summoned to celebrate something?"

Thought's bland expression ceased the amicable mood the two other beings had been sharing between them.

Love recovered her composure first, and quickly cleared her throat. "We, ah, need your help."

Athena did not look surprised. It was not in her nature, of course. She raised one eyebrow and crossed her arms over her chest. "To locate the souls?"

"No, we've done that," Death quickly interjected.

The Muse looked impressed. "Two years, nine months, and twenty days. You two make quite a team."

Love took a shocked step back, the breath rushing out of her. "Two *years*?" They had been on Earth realm far longer than she realized.

"And nine months, and twenty days." Thought supplied the information.

"Never mind that." Death waved his hand dismissively. "We cannot locate Morgana. We were thinking, perhaps, you would be able to sense her thoughts?"

"She has no emotion that we can sense," Love explained quickly.

Athena nodded. "I suspected as much. She is here, then? On this island?"

"Last we saw," Death muttered.

But Thought, with her scathing logic, missed nothing. "You *saw* her? And did nothing?"

"Athena, now is hardly the time for that." Death's tone was sharp.

The Goddess of Wisdom pursed her lips in annoyance. "Very well." She tilted her head back, eyes closing. Soon, her form began to tremble as she was washed over with the thoughts of every creature on the island. "There are none here whose thoughts are especially dark...though there is one individual who seems quite disturbed working in the post office, it is not her..." Athena opened her eyes. "She's no longer in this part of the country."

Love let forth a long, low sigh.

The search for evil would have to continue.

CHAPTER SIXTEEN

Search

Now that their party had increased to three, Love felt even more exhausted with it all than she had before. A new search of the rest of Canada and then the States had turned up no Morgana, but it seemed the number of her minions was increasing.

They were obviously hot on her trail, but somehow the witch managed to move faster than even the powers of Love, Thought, and Death combined. Morgana had moved quickly across Canada and down through the Midwestern United States, leaving in her wake almost a hundred new souls that had to be harvested and sent to the Underworld. Her powers had grown since her last mortal life, and now it seemed she needed to spend only a few moments with a person before stripping them of all emotion and rational thought.

Yet she had no interest of taking these minions with her as she traveled. From what Athena could tell by tapping into their thoughts, she left them with no purpose or instruction, which didn't seem to make any sense, either.

"Then what does she want them for?" Love demanded now. The three deities, exhausted with the endless search, were now stationed in England. They were sitting on benches in Hyde Park. Athena, who was not very good at remembering the names the countries had in these modern days, was studying a map.

"It doesn't add up, does it?" Death agreed. "Why would she create these minions, if she gave them no other purpose than to simply wait for us?"

"They were hardly waiting for us."

"But Morgana obviously left them for us. The way she's running, I think we can safely say that she knows we are after her," he replied.

Athena had yet to say a word, so absorbed was she in studying an atlas of Europe.

"It's sure she knows something is after her, but I doubt she knows what, exactly, it is," Dite reasoned.

"Does the Keeper of all Knowledge have anything to add to this?" Death poked at Athena with one long, bony finger.

The Muse started slightly, finally looking up from her map. "She's moving in a pattern. I think we can expect her in Ireland next. She'll be moving through England, France, and then back around to Scotland and Wales. If we can catch her in Ireland and stop her, we can save the souls she's touched on the way."

Love was on her feet instantly. "Let's go, then."

Athena nodded, her eyes dark with her own thoughts, and rose to stand by Dite's side. Death joined the small circle and the trio knit their hands together.

"To Ireland," they intoned together, and the cosmos opened up to let them through.

Athena was tuning into the thoughts of the Irish before they had even stopped spinning. Love, frantic now with the exhaustion of this mad quest, paced a close circle around the Muse and Death as they waited.

Ena's eyes went wide, and they met Dite's with a look of worry. "She's here. And she's close."

Love sucked in her breath. They had finally found Morgana.

"This way." Athena started off across the sloping hill they'd landed on at a brisk clip.

Dite picked up her skirts and followed along behind her in a rush, snatching Death's hand to pull him along behind her.

"Her mind is such a tumble of thoughts." Ena's tone was dark and disturbed as she practically sprinted across the hill. "It's very disturbing."

"Of course, we have to be prepared for that, Athena." Death's tone was as soothing as he could manage, half-stumbling as Love pulled him along.

"Yes, but I can sense no pattern of thought at all…just one big jumble— oof!" Suddenly, Athena landed right on her bottom.

Like a stack of dominoes, Love collided into Ena's crumpled form, and Death tripped over Dite's skirts behind her. "What in the name of Immortality—" Love began, but suddenly swallowed her words in her throat when she saw what had obviously happened.

Hades, his face a mask of pure rage, stood towering above the three of them. "And what do the three of you think you are *doing*?" he demanded, voice coming out in a loud boom.

"Hades?" Love frowned up at him. Though her memory was not what it could be, as far as she knew Hades had traveled to Earth realm only once in his long, long existence.

Athena jumped to her feet, brushing off her long tunic with quick, angry brushes. "Hades, I cannot imagine what could possibly bring you here when you should be minding to all the new souls we've sent—"

"Why else would I be here?" he demanded, and his anger was obvious in the hard lines of his face. "Between the efforts of you three addle-brained deities, the balance has been swung quite dramatically off. The Underworld is swelling so fast that the Path of the Damned cannot hold the boats. We actually have a *waiting period*!" he roared. "The new level I created now has almost two *thousand* souls. In three *years*, you three have managed to harvest two thousand souls! Do you know what that means?" He glared down at all three of them in palpable rage.

"Oh, no." Death's sigh shook the trees off in the distance.

Suddenly, Morgana's plan became startlingly clear.

"That's what she's been doing all along," Athena whispered.

"And you left the Underworld unattended!" Death jumped to his feet to stand toe to toe with Hades.

A chill gripped Love's shoulders. "We have to hurry before Morgana gets there."

Stark shock danced across Hades features. His voice was shaky. "Surely not…"

"Why else!" Athena cut in abruptly, giving him a scathing glance as she reached for Love's hand.

The four grabbed at each other's hands with renewed fervor. "To the Underworld!"

Love's first realization was of falling along a dark, cold passageway. She tried to keep her grip on the bone hand she held with her fingers, and Athena's hand on the other side of her, but lost both when she was tossed into the water.

She kicked to the surface of the murky water, sputtering out the substance, and was nearly hit in the face with the prow of one of the Underworld's boats. Quickly dodging out of the way, she waited until the boat had neared enough to reach up and grab onto the side.

Pulling herself up and over the boat, she landed with a thud and stared up at one of Hades' skeleton guards grinning down at her. "I'm Love," she choked miserably. "Can you go any faster?"

A cold hand reached down to drag her to her feet, and the silent guard shook his head and pointed one long arm ahead of them. Love let out a horrified shriek. It was amazing she'd landed in water at all, she now saw. The Path of the Damned was so packed with boats that they touched each other as they skimmed across the water. In each, including the one she'd managed to climb into, human souls were practically piled on top of each other. There were just too many of them.

"Thought!" she cried out into the murky air. "Death!" Hades, she assumed, would be transported immediately upon arrival into his private chambers or the room he held audience in.

There was no answer from either of her companions. Love, exhausted with it all, sank to her knees on the bottom of the boat. She looked up into a pair of soulless eyes that watched her and dissolved into tears.

If only they'd realized sooner.

After what seemed an endlessly long time, the boat she rode in finally docked at the platform. Love had jumped out and was brushing off her skirts when she noticed what was missing.

"Where is Merlyn?" Her question was answered by silence, but Love could not ignore the chills of trepidation that traveled up her spine. After so many centuries, Merlyn remained one of Hades' most loyal servants. He wouldn't leave his post unless something was horribly wrong.

Feeling urgency now, Love grabbed two fistfuls of her skirts in her hands and took off running across the platform to Hades' reception room. "Hades!" she called dramatically as she ran, tripping and bumping over souls as she jogged through the Underworld.

Dite came skidding to a dead halt when she finally entered the room. Shocked, she actually fell down on her backside.

"*You.*"

The figure seated on the throne smiled coldly, rising up to face the Goddess of Love. "Once again, dearest Goddess of Love, you are too late." Her beauty was as cold and as perfect as ever, her face seemingly carved from porcelain. Ebony hair rippled past her shoulders in perfect waves. Her eyes, hard and gemlike, reflected malice as they took in Love's form.

Dite scrambled to her feet, kicking her skirts off her feet quickly. "Where is Hades?"

Morgana raised her hand and snapped two fingers quickly. Behind her, to her right, a panel in the wall slipped away to reveal the God of the Underworld. He was chained to the wall with golden shackles. The Tender of the Dead's expression was one of grave remorse.

"Hades!" Love started forward to go to him, but Morgana held up one hand to stop her.

"You take one step in his direction and I promise you, the Goddess of Thought will never find her way out of Christian Hell."

"You monster!" Love cried. "You trapped Athena in Christian Hell?"

Morgana shrugged, her eyes harsh against her white skin. "It's where she landed. I figure, why stand in the way of Fate? You know she won't find her way out of that fiery pit alone, Goddess, and I can see to it that she never gets out."

Dite's eyes narrowed as she stared at the woman. "Loki was here, wasn't he, keeping an eye on the Underworld and waiting for Hades to leave? Then he sent word to you that the Underworld was unprotected and you ended your mortal life to arrive here."

"You are so much more clever when you aren't living the wrong life!" Morgana's laugh was brittle. "But of course, I knew you would figure it out." She leaned forward, taking a few steps toward Love to bend close to her ear. "But I knew you would never figure it out in time to stop me."

Dite felt the un-Goddesslike urge to rip those ebony strands right from Morgana's head...but of course, Morgana's body was no more real than Love's own was. "So, you came immediately to the Underworld to take it over...but how did you manage to trap Hades?"

"Impressed, are you?" Coyly, Morgana glanced over her shoulder at Love as she went to seat herself again on Hades' throne. "You already know the answer to that question, though, m'dear, so let's stop wasting our time."

Love closed her eyes in pure horror. "Loki." As the word rushed out of her, she received a sharp kick to the back of one of her knees from behind. Dite crumpled immediately to the floor as the God of Mischeif stepped forward.

"So good to see you again, Aphrodite."

Love, feeling too out of sorts to control herself, reared back and spit on him as he passed.

But Loki, who knew how to bide his time much more cleverly than Love, simply laughed as he joined his daughter on the raised dias that was the center of the reception room. "Still acting like a human, then, sweet emotion? Such a pity."

Dite felt her own anger bubbling up inside her. "You are a blasted fool if you think the Mother will allow any of this. She knows Morgana's danger more than most."

Loki laughed with sheer amusement. "And we would love to receive Her for a visit!" he boomed, throwing his arms out wide. His face changed, his eyes dancing with joy. "Unfortunately, however, the Mother has been quite detained."

"Yes, she's terrible busy contending with Death." Morgana's smile, seemingly carved from ice as always, curved upward in malicious joy. "Right now, he is sending a message to Her that Love and Thought have both been lost on Earth realm, and he is extremely busy harvesting the souls I wrecked. She will be busy among the humans for quite some time, searching for Her two most beloved First Daughters."

All the pieces of the puzzle finally came together, and Love could have sworn she felt sick to her stomach if she were capable of such a thing. "Death was your accomplice all along." She wanted to beat her head against the floor in pure frustration. That unknown helper to Loki, the one who had helped Loki while the God was living as a mortal, the one who had helped Loki commit suicide during that mortal life so the God of Mischief could return to Immortality with a new and bold plan…of course, none other than Death could have helped the God of Mischief without ever raising suspicion. The lesser deity was so often overlooked by the other inhabitants of Immortality, it only stood to reason that he would seek his own revenge eventually.

"Death travels between the Underworld and Earth realm more freely than even Hades himself." Loki shrugged easily. "He wanted to help."

Love's blood was pounding in her head. "What are you going to do? You've taken over the Underworld, I give you that, but what…" Then, it all became clear. She jumped to her feet again, ready to rush forward and choke Loki out of rage. "What are you going to do with these souls!"

Morgana's smile glittered as she replied, "Why, nothing Hades wouldn't do himself, of course. We'll simply reform them, and release them into Earth realm. Is that not the usual process?"

Immortal or human, Love thought, she was going to be sick. "You've given up taking over Immortality, Loki. Now you will try to take over Earth realm."

"Try?" The God smiled at her. "My dear, the 'taking over' has already begun."

Love struggled to speak, to find some words to combat Loki, but it was useless.

"Now, my dear, as you can see we are simply too busy to contend with you now. Off to Christian Hell with you, now." Morgana airily waved a hand in the air and before Love could protest, the room vanished.

And suddenly, she was stuck in Hell.

Hades had always taken great pride in that he was Tender to the Dead. He had used the Underworld as sort of a "reform" for souls for what the humans on Earth realm called "reincarnation." He would reform those souls sent to the Underworld and then send them back out into the world again.

But with the rise in the belief of Christianity on Earth realm, Hades had been forced to give those souls their beliefs, as well, and dedicated a huge section of the vast realm that is the Underworld to the Christian concept of Hell. It was not by his own choice that he sent souls to this place, but some souls were brought to the Underworld that somehow truly believed they belonged in Hell, and the Tender had no choice. For what, to them, felt like fifty years, he sent those extremely devout Christians who felt they deserved it into Hell. It had long since caused a great debate between the Fathergod and Hades, since there was no section of Immortality set aside for Christian Heaven. It seemed the powers that be were always arguing over what to do with human souls. Hades alone had held this awesome responsibility, and now Love lamented herself for not paying more attention to his job.

Now Love, bedraggled and sobbing from her confused human feelings, sat surrounded by a circle of flames. Around her, she could hear the shrieking of the Damned. She could feel the heat of the place and knew it must be unbearable for those souls who still clung to their human forms.

Nothing had ever escaped from Christian Hell before Hades released them and Love knew, without question, that Hades was not going to release anyone any time soon.

Love's gown caught fire the moment she stepped through the ring of flames. Her clothing, of course, had all originally come from Earth realm, so it would burn even though her skin would not. With an aggravated sound, she ripped the charred material from her body and resigned herself to walking through Christian Hell naked. At least her skirts would no longer get in her way, she reasoned.

She had hope, though. Athena was stuck somewhere in this wide expanse of Christian belief, and Love had to find her.

The Goddess soon found that even she could not walk effortlessly through Christian Hell. The flames, hot coals, pools of lava, and flying sparks did afford her some comfort as she tried to struggle through Hell. Souls still wearing the images they'd carried on Earth realm reached up to claw at her arms and legs as she walked through the vast space, trying to drag her down onto the flaming floor with them. Love pitied these poor creatures even as she shook them off her, calling out Athena's name.

Her instincts, ingrained in her being as they were, were not at full power in this horrible place, either. She was having trouble tuning in her powers to pick up Athena's almost nonexistent emotional pattern.

Shrieks and screams and wails assailed her ears as her bare feet picked a path across glowing embers and hot coals. Love finally covered her ears and eyes, giving into the terror of the souls she felt and running, running to try and escape this horrible place.

Human-like tears streamed down her cheeks as her feet half-floated across the uneven ground, her own throaty cries rising to join the cacophony of agony all around her.

When finally a pair of hands clasped around her shoulders, she could not stop screaming long enough to shake the wretched creature off. Blinded by tears, she lashed out with her small fists. "Off, you miserable being! I am a Goddess!" The thing started shaking her back and forth, and she screamed louder in terror.

One of the thing's hands cracked a sharp slap across her cheek and she stopped screaming, stopped by shock. "Dite, it's me!"

Finally, Love's eyes focused. "Oh, Athena!" She drew her longtime friend into her embrace. The Goddess of Thought was soot-streaked, her usually neat brown curls a frizzy mass, her long tunic hanging in charred and burnt tatters around her body.

"Did you land here, too?" Though not usually given to emotion, Thought clung tightly to Dite even as she spoke.

"No, Ena…oh, it's so much worse than we thought." Love finally pulled back from her friend, and began briskly wiping soot off Ena's cheeks as she told her friend of all that had happened since their return from Earth realm.

When she was finished, Athena's bright, owl-like eyes were stark with terror. "So we're stuck here…we're stuck here while Earth realm is overrun by those souls. The balance will be lost while we're wandering around in Christian Hell!"

The terror all around them was getting to even the strong, stoic Goddess of Wisdom. Love shook her head emphatically. "Ena, listen to me! We have to find a way out of here. We have to stop Loki and Morgana."

Athena laughed dryly and sunk down on her legs, sitting on a hot bed of coals beneath them. "Oh, Love. Dear, optimistic Love. Did you think I was doing nothing all this time? There is no way out of Christian Hell. I can't even figure how these poor souls got here. Hades must have some special means of transporting them."

"Can we not just send ourselves to Earth realm?" Love was desperate to think of some way out of this place.

But Wisdom shook her head. "My powers are considerably dampened...are yours?"

Love sighed. "I haven't tried transporting myself, but I can tell my power isn't what it should be, at any rate."

Athena nodded wordlessly. "Hades' power is greater here, in his own realm. I'm sure he never meant for an Immortal to travel here."

Love, feeling defeated by this new revelation, sank down next to Wisdom. "Then we really are lost."

"I'm sure even Hermes can't travel here. I don't have my bell, anyway." Athena's voice was shaky.

"Hermes wouldn't—" Love jumped up suddenly. "Athena, forget everything bad I ever said about you! You really *are* wise!"

The Muse stared at her friend as though she'd lost her mind. "What am I missing?"

Love laughed happily. "Cupid! I forgot about Cupid!"

Athena was shaking her head. "No, Love. Good try, but it won't work. Cupid couldn't travel here unless he was in the Underworld to begin with."

Love grinned and bent to kiss Ena's cheek. "I stashed Cupid in the Underworld before I left for Earth realm. That darling boy, he must have hidden himself away somewhere. Surely Morgana or Loki would have mentioned if they'd noticed him!"

Now, Athena found her feet as well. "What are you waiting for? Call him. If he comes, I swear, I'm changing my mind about having a consort!"

"Cupid, Cupid...*CUPID*!" Love closed her eyes, waiting.

An interminable minute passed while the two Goddesses waited.

"Oh, I should have known it was useless." Athena threw her hands up in frustration. "No one can find us here, Love, we should—"

"Only for Love." Cupid jumped four feet in the air the instant he appeared, yelping out in surprise. Apparently he wasn't as immune to the hot coals and heat as both Goddesses were.

"Cupid!" Love's tears this time came from joy. She quickly moved forward to catch the boy in her arms and stumbled as his weight came down on her. Athena rushed forward, and the two Goddesses managed to support his slight weight between them.

"Milady, this one is so glad to see you…where is this one, Milady?"

Love laughed and brushed the tears off her cheeks. "Cupid, you have never looked better!" She managed, awkwardly, to plant a kiss on his cheek. "It's a very long story, Cupid, and we must hurry. You have to get to Passion, the Mother, Hermes…anyone."

Cupid's skin was turning pink in the heat of the place. "And do what?"

"Thought and I are trapped in Christian Hell, and—"

"Christian Hell!" Cupid screamed, then started to cry. "Then this one is trapped here, too!"

"Cupid, shush! You know as well as I that if you are harmed in any way, you are immediately transported back to your place of origin. In this case—"

"Love's Palace!" New hope filled his eyes. "Then this one isn't trapped at all!" He smiled with relief. "What do you mean, by injured?" Suspicion filled his eyes as he realized all of Love's words.

"Athena and I are going to toss you into the flames."

"Mistress!" he screamed with new terror.

"Cupid, stop! You will be returned to the palace as hale and healthy as always, and well you know it. Now, calm down, and listen to me. At all costs, you must avoid both Death and Loki, without question. Summon Hermes the moment you awaken in Love's palace, tell him to gather Thor and Passion and tell them that Thought and Love are stuck in Christian Hell. You must tell them to come and get us out first, and we will explain later. Do you understand, Q?"

He sniffled pathetically. "Aye, Mistress, this one understands."

And, without further ado, Love and Thought as a unit tossed the poor boy right into the flames of Christian Hell.

Love, with a sob, sagged against Thought weakly as she listened to his screams. Then, as suddenly as they had started, they stopped again. Cupid had been transported to Love's Palace. "Oh, Athena," she whispered.

Wisdom understood. Gently, she laid a hand on Love's shoulder. "Q will forgive you." She sighed and sat on the coals again, patting the spot next to her invitingly. "I must admit, I'm ashamed I didn't think of that plan myself. You put Thought to shame."

Love managed a halfhearted grin and plopped down next to her dearest friend. "You would have come up with it, if you'd known I put Cupid in the Underworld before leaving."

"How do you feel?" Thought's eyes scanned her face. "Your Affliction?"

Love shrugged. "I know how to use my powers, if that's what you mean. My memories…my memories are not complete. And I do not have my thoughts or emotions under control. I still feel very much a mortal. Like a mortal with too much power."

She sighed and nodded. "Your memory will return. Already, you are remembering things about Morgana and the rules of Immortality. Even I hadn't remembered the consort rule."

Love perked up happily. "Really?"

Athena nodded. "Yes, really. It's really a good plan, Love. I just hope it works," she muttered, leaning back.

Dite understood. She leaned back, as well, and the two lapsed into silence. There was nothing else to do but wait.

CHAPTER SEVENTEEN

Rescue

"Why aren't you wearing any clothes?" It was Thor's gruff voice that broke both the Goddesses out of their thoughts.

"Thor!" Athena's cry was gleeful as she jumped up.

Love threw herself into Passion's embrace and immediately started babbling about everything that had happened. Fire held her gently as she half-sobbed, half-wailed everything that had gone on since their last encounter. He simply stroked her hair, rocking her back and forth, and let her talk.

"Oh, Fire," she finally finished and let herself wind down, comforted by the strength of his arms around her.

"Shh…my Love, it's all right. Thor and I are here to rescue you, and you should know by now that Thor never turns his back on demoiselles in distress." He tilted her chin up to look into her eyes. "Where's my strong emotion that I know so well?" he whispered gently.

Dite sniffed back the tears that threatened and offered a smile.

He planted a soft kiss on her forehead. "There now, that's better. We'll all get out of this."

Love nodded and stood back, trying to calm the pounding of her heart. She finally realized that her and Passion were not the only ones there, and stepped back farther to look at Thor and Athena.

"Thor." She smiled and floated into his arms for a warm embrace, as well. She remembered, now, that she and Thor had always been close, though much more so since his affair with Eurynome had begun.

He kissed her cheek and gave her a scowl after she'd stepped back. "You are not attired in the manner befitting a Goddess." Thor had always been fatherly toward her, which was ridiculous since she was several millennia older than he.

Love giggled girlishly. "My gown caught fire and became useless."

He snorted.

Fire stepped forward, dragging his own short tunic off, and handed it to Love. "Nevertheless, you should put this on. Your beautiful skin is already marked from the sparks in the air." His hand gently caressed hers as he passed the tunic to her.

Athena, sighing because it was impossible to believe that even in the middle of Hell Passion and Love could see only each other, stepped between them. "And getting out of Christian Hell?"

Fire laughed and offered Wisdom a wink. "Moving too slowly for you, are we, Thought?"

She snorted in reply.

"Very well, take my hands." He reached out. Love quickly rushed forward to take hold of both him and Thor, and Athena latched on to both men as well.

"Hold tight and stay close," Passion told them. "Being separated at this point would be disastrous." He winked. "Elementals can leave Christian Hell whenever we want, but I might have trouble finding you two ladies again if you let go."

There was a rendering in the air around them, and Love felt some invisible force that seemed to be trying to rip them apart. She could hear her own scream in her ears as her grip on Passion's hand tightened.

Until finally, they were in Love's Palace in Immortality. Dite's eyes opened to see Passion's dark gaze, Athena's white face, and Thor's impossible scowl. Giddy with laughter, she fell over onto the floor. She rolled right over and kissed the marble floor, which had never before been so beautiful.

"We made it!" Athena fell on the ground with relief and exhaustion as well, and soon she and Dite were embracing.

Passion's smile was soft. "Now, I suggest you two ladies rest while I locate the Mother and go to the Underworld to stop Morgana."

At that, both Goddesses quickly found their feet. Heated protests sprang up from both of them, and Passion had to throw up his hands. "Enough! Neither of you is in any condition to face Morgana again, and well you know it."

But the two Goddesses were adamant they would see to the end of their fight against Morgana. While Passion summoned Hermes, Love and Athena went upstairs to change clothes and wipe the soot from their bodies.

Finally, four Elementals, Love, Thought, and Thor had all gathered in Love's front Hall. They were waiting for word from Hermes that the Mother had been located.

"What about the souls being sent into Earth realm?" Thought wanted to know. The seven of them were debating, arguing, and blaming one another. It was not very productive. No one seemed to hear Thought.

"Stop!" Love, standing on the table, raised her voice to be heard above the others. "Morgana and Loki work together because they agree, and that is how they are defeating us now. If we don't—all of us—settle on a plan of action now, they will continue to defeat us." She stepped down.

Water nodded in approval of his daughter, and placed an arm around her shoulders as she moved to stand next to him. "Love is right."

"What about the souls being sent to Earth realm?" Athena repeated.

This question was met by silence from the group.

"First," Love reasoned, "someone must get to Death. Only he can harvest these souls…but not as he is, working with Loki and Morgana."

All eyes turned to Earth, whose expression was as unchanging as ever. "Aye, I suppose I must go and speak to my son. I will find him on Earth realm, and go with him while he sends those souls back to the Underworld. But before we begin the harvest, we must make sure things are working normally in the Underworld again."

"We will dispatch the messenger to you with the news immediately," Air confirmed. "Travel now to Earth realm, get your son, and await our message there."

Earth nodded, his eyes betraying his true troubled thoughts over the situation, and disappeared.

"So, the rest of us will travel to the Underworld to contend with Morgana and Loki."

At that, the group as a whole lapsed into silence. Love drifted away from them to seek out Passion, who was staring into the fireplace. There was no fire lit.

"Fire?" Love stood at his elbow for a few moments before her voice jarred him from his thoughts.

He looked at her with an expression of pure torment, one hand reaching out to stroke her cheek. "My Love," he whispered, voice made rough with emotion. "Even in your assumed mortality, you are brave and courageous as ever."

Love, knowing that Fire was never one to give compliments lightly, blushed under his gaze. "Dear Passion, you are truly my hero after your rescue in Christian Hell."

He laughed lightly, only his eyes betraying the weight of his words. "I told you before I would go into the pits of Hell for you, my Love."

She smiled back just as lightly, but her throat felt almost too tight to get the words out. "And now you have proven to me that you have never told me a lie."

"And I never will," he vowed, his eyes smoldering on hers.

"Just the messenger." Hermes' voice rang out like a shot, and immediately Love and Passion's attention was drawn away from each other to the youth standing in the middle of the small crowd.

"Did you find Her?"

"What did She say?"

"Is She on Her way?"

At the barrage of questions, Hermes quickly threw up his hands. "One at a time, please. Yes, I found Her. No, She is not on Her way."

"What?!" Air stepped forward. "Then what does She want us to do?"

Hermes pulled a small scroll from his belt, and unfurled it, clearing his throat. "I wrote down Her words so I would not forget." That was strange in itself. Hermes, as the messenger, could remember even the longest speeches verbatim. He cleared his throat once again. "Dear children, I am well aware of what is unfolding. I am sure you know what to do, and will do what you think is best. Hermes has been instructed to come to me again when you have all finished with this business. And to Love, I look forward to seeing you returned to your full self soon. Remember what I told you on the hill."

"That's *it*?" It was Love's incredulous voice that broke the spell of silence in the room.

Hermes only smiled, gave a smart salute, and vanished, leaving the little scroll to tumble to the floor and roll across the marble, where it landed against Dite's foot.

"Hmph." She snorted. "Well then, to the Underworld?"

Air was the first to recover. He reached out his hands and nodded. "To the Underworld."

The group formed a circle, confirmed the destination, and as a unit vanished from Love's Palace.

With the power of three Elementals holding them together, the group as a whole managed to end up in Hades' reception room, where Morgana sat on the throne, waiting.

"You are much more resourceful than I would have thought." She directed her words to Love. "I hadn't expected you to get out of Christian Hell so easily." Morgana's eyes betrayed no surprise or worry, only a mild annoyance at Love's return. Those jewel-like eyes slid past Love to take in Water, Air, Passion, Athena, and Thor. "Greetings, Elementals, Muse, Protector."

"Where is Loki?" Passion stepped forward, angry heat in his eyes.

Morgana smiled at him, the way a woman smiles at a man she is interested in. "You are much more pleasing to look upon than I would have thought. Perhaps you would like to rule Earth realm at my side?"

Passion snorted and returned her smile. His was tight, controlled, and almost as cold as hers...which was a remarkable feat coming from the Elemental Fire. "In human terms I am your grandfather. Now tell me, where is Loki?"

"She doesn't know." Air stepped forward. "Her mind is such a swirled jumble...a black mess...I wonder what that devil did to her to make her patterns so unstable."

Love, whose compassion had never stopped amazing the rest of Immortality, took pity on Morgana then. "The poor thing...she has no way of really knowing the wrong of what she's doing. She's only following the orders he put into her head." She stepped forward, focused solely on Morgana now. "Morgana, we can help you if you let us. I know it must be scary, your own thoughts so terribly out of control, never feeling any emotions in your heart... Please, let me help you, Morgana." Unthinkingly, she stepped forward. Dite stretched her hands out to the woman in her compassion for the witch.

"Love, wait!" But Athena's warning came too late, because Morgana had stepped down from the throne to grab Love's outstretched hands.

Ruthlessly, Morgana yanked Love so that she fell face forward, and pulled Love up roughly against her side. "Now you can all watch while I release the souls into Earth realm. My own pack of demons that will sway the righteous, the pure, and the innocent. I will eventually control them all." She smiled in her evil, glittering way. "I will be their Queen."

Passion growled and stepped forward, but Morgana held up a hand to stop him in his tracks.

"My powers here are great, Elemental, and I would not tempt them if I were you. I can turn her mind into a blackened heap, Air," she added when she saw him moving forward off to her left. She smiled at his look of mild surprise. "And you know I can do it, Thor," she added to the hulking giant, who was trying to move around the crowd to sneak up behind her. She shook Love violently like a rag doll.

Caught in Morgana's touch, Love could not utter a word. The woman's power was too great.

"Will you risk it, Fire?" A perfect black eyebrow arched upward. "Will you sacrifice your Love for the good of humanity?" Hard eyes turned to Water. "And you, Water, will you watch your First Daughter be destroyed?" That icy smile again. "Air, do you think your precious child will let you destroy Love to get to me? And Thor, will you see Love demolished?"

Morgana waited a long moment, scanning each of them. "No? I didn't think so." Still dragging Love, she rose one arm. "And now I will release my minions into your precious Earth."

A loud bang caused the otherworldly beings to jump, and suddenly Loki was in the room. "Morgana!" he barked, striding up to the throne room. "I see you've managed to make a mess of things."

"Father." The smile Morgana reserved for him was no less icy or hate-filled than her normal expression. Her eyes glittered with a strange ruthlessness.

"I'll bet he regrets not giving her any emotion now," Water mumbled to himself as he watched the scene unfold.

Passion stood poised, waiting for an opening that would allow him to snatch Love from Morgana's grasp.

Loki's smile came no less easily, but was no less mean than his daughter's as he stepped forward, though Loki was a being that could ooze charm with every move he made. "I think you are forgetting that I will ultimately be the one to rule Earth realm, daughter."

Morgana scoffed, her grip on Love still tight. "You do not have the knowledge or the power to rule there. Besides, someone must rule here."

"You expected I would stay here while you go on to Earth realm?"

She shrugged lightly. "And whyever not? You are the devil."

"Oh, Morgana." Loki reached out to stroke her ebony locks, smoothing the hair back from her face. "You foolish child." Then, without warning, his hand closed around a fistful of her hair, pulling her head back. "Release Love, Morgana, and accept your punishment for your ways." He shook her.

"Father!" she gasped. As he pulled harder, Morgana finally released Love. The Goddess fell in a heap to Morgana's feet, and Passion was the first to reach her in the group that jumped forward to grab her. Fire scooped Love up into his arms and backed away from the father and daughter who seemed to be fighting over the throne of power they both so craved.

"Poor Morgana," Loki whispered, his grip on her hair still firm. "You didn't think I would really keep you around after I was done using you, did you?" He smiled at her as she began to struggle. "There, there, daughter. I'm sure you will like Christian Hell rightly enough." He rose up his free arm, ready to send Morgana into that dark horror, when Love suddenly cried out.

"NO!" Still weak from the drain Morgana had put on her, she could only reach her arms out feebly. Fire still held her tightly in his embrace. "Loki, please. Give her soul a chance."

Loki turned to look at Love, surprise on his face. "What do you suggest?"

"I'll take her," Love gasped. "She can become one of my consorts."

"You must be *kidding*?" This from Passion, who almost dropped Love in his shock.

"No." Love shook her head, and slipped down to her own feet. "She'll be trapped there, unlike my other consorts, but I think I can help her. Please, Loki, give me the chance to help her."

The gathered deities and Elementals gaped in open-mouthed surprise at her. Loki only stared for a long moment, then nodded slowly. "Very well, Love." He closed his eyes, then, and his hands began to glow. Slowly, carefully, he reached inside Morgana's chest. With utmost gentleness and care, he carefully drew out three silver threads. "I take back those weavings I have bestowed," he intoned, "to be replaced with any of Love's choosing." He wrapped the shimmering threads around his wrist. "For now, for the next one thousand years, a prisoner only to Love, and Love's command." With that, he released her.

Furious, Morgana reached up to attack Loki, but he caught both her wrists with one hand. "There now, daughter, do not be so ungrateful!" With a fierce shove, he pushed her at Love.

"Morgana." Gently, Love gathered the poor misguided soul into her arms. "Off to Love's Palace with you, now, so you can get settled." Love snapped her fingers and Morgana disappeared from the room.

Finally, they had all solved the problem of what to do with Morgana's soul. Athena was still staring at her oldest friend in supreme shock and disbelief.

"Loki." Passion's voice was sharp. "My son."

The God of Mischief gave the Elemental a halfhearted smirk. "I suppose you will stop at nothing to keep me from releasing these souls, then."

"I am already trying to determine what your punishment should be."

Loki laughed. "How lofty we think we are all of a sudden!"

"Why don't you release Hades before I'm of a mind to start taking weavings, myself," Passion replied, his voice thick with controlled fury.

Loki sighed, sitting back on the throne. "It doesn't matter, anyway. I could have let Morgana release the souls and then stopped her." He sighed again, the sound almost forlorn, which was strange coming from the God of Mischief. "But the balance tends to benefit me more often than not, and I could never go through with the plan."

Love gaped at him. "You mean, you never had any intention of seeing this plan to the end?"

He grinned in the devil-may-care, reckless fashion that only Loki could pull off accurately. "Not once."

Dite dissolved into giggles. "You damnable trickster, you just wanted to give us all something to do!"

Loki stood and bowed to her in a gentlemanly fashion. "I could think of no better way to welcome you back, my dear."

Still laughing, though the others in the room seemed to be in a state of shock, Love rushed forward to plant a warm kiss on his cheek. "You old devil! Of course you never wanted to rule the Underworld—you can do that almost any old time!"

"Well." Loki grinned down at her with real affection. She remembered now, a private conversation she'd had with Loki some fifty Earth years ago, where he'd finally forgiven her for a grudge he'd held since 4000 BC. "I did want you to take care of Morgana for me...but I knew you'd never agree if I just asked you outright. I couldn't save her mind, myself, though I did try."

"Poor Loki," Love whispered sadly, "of course, you wouldn't do such a thing to your own child. She got out of the Underworld on her own, didn't she?"

"She managed to trick Merlyn! Can you believe it? That's when I formed my plan to make you all think the whole thing was my doing all along. Death was in league with me, but he knew my real intentions."

"You still threw off the balance of souls in the Underworld." Athena was angry. "And caused the rest of us plenty of years of trouble while you were at it!"

Loki waved a hand to ignore her. "Hades grows bored in his old age. Trust me, he's pleased as can be with all the activity around here."

"Well." Air, lacking emotion, was hardly upset by Loki's actions. "I think I'll be getting on to Cloud Castle now. Loki, as usual, you have managed to out-trick me. I look forward to your next endeavor." He offered Loki a bow, which the God quickly returned. The rivalry between the two of them had not changed. Air was known to lament, time and time again, the many logic weavings he'd given to Passion when the Fire Elemental was weaving his son Loki. "Come along, Athena."

Still in a state of surprised shock, Athena slipped her arm through her father's and the pair vanished.

"I guess I'll be summoning Hermes and writing a small little note to the Mother. You'll be glad to know you never fooled Her for a second, Loki." Water couldn't help but to give the rascal a grin.

Loki shrugged lightly. "You win some, you lose some. I'll get even Her one day," he vowed.

"Sometimes we forget, Loki, that you are not completely evil. You just love discord." Love planted another kiss on his cheek. "You may come and visit with Morgana any time you wish…so long as you send word you will be arriving beforehand!"

Loki laughed and nodded to show his agreement. "I have some talking to do with Hades. Would you like to join me, Thor?"

The old Viking god made a grunting noise of agreement. Loki and Thor went way back history-wise, both being Norse deities.

"Let's go, Passion." Love grinned up at Fire brilliantly. "I think you and I can scare up some more excitement between us."

The Elemental snorted as he took hold of Dite's fingers. "I think I've had enough excitement, for once."

Love's laughter could still be heard a few moments after they disappeared.

"I wonder," Loki turned to Thor, "if I could come up with some trickery to allow those two to be together?" He rose his black eyebrows in question.

Thor thumped a hand on Loki's back companionably. "*That* situation is out of all our hands, old friend."

Together, the pair went off to release Hades from his shackles and put rights to the Underworld once more.

CHAPTER EIGHTEEN

Love

Love was deposited at Love's Palace after her long journeys with a very changed view of Immortality in general. She was starting to see things as a Goddess once again. She had forgotten, in her mortal thinking, that the gods and goddesses of Immortality were often confusing beings whose opinions and feelings of one another changed on an almost constant basis. Loki, of course, simply loved throwing a wrench in the works. If there was anything Loki didn't like, it was when everything ran too smoothly.

Passion had kissed her cheek chastely before disappearing himself, mumbling something about having arrangements to make.

Dite smiled to herself and gave into a very human feeling she was having, letting loose a loud yawn in the front hall of her palace.

"I didn't think Goddesses got tired."

Love turned at the sound and smiled once again. "Morgana." She stepped forward. "No, Goddesses don't ever get tired, but I'm sort of...not a Goddess right now." At Morgana's surprised look, she just waved a hand. "It's a long story, and we'll have plenty of time together over the next few years for you to hear it, I promise."

Morgana eyed her warily. "What are you going to do to me?"

"Well, now, I guess I don't rightly know. I have a personal attendant, already, in Rose. And Cupid takes care of my errands to and from Earth realm for me. You don't seem particularly suited to cleaning things...so I guess I must leave that up to you. What would you like to do here in the palace?"

The woman eyed the Goddess with suspicion. "I don't understand."

"Well, you can't ever leave the palace, not even to travel within Immortality. And I was assuming you would want some sort of duties to perform while you are here."

"Like a punishment." Morgana nodded, feeling as though she finally understood.

Love laughed at Morgana's expression. "No, child, not a punishment at all. I'm trying to help you, Morgana. So that you might, perhaps, form a soul. And learn a few things, too. Is that all right with you?"

Morgana met the Goddess's eyes, so filled with love and compassion, and nodded. "How can you be so kind to me, after all I've done to you? Even while you were living as a human?"

Dite could only grin in reply. "It's my nature...I'm Love."

Morgana shook her head.

"You'll understand, someday." Love threw an arm around her shoulders. "How about getting you settled, hmm? We'll go upstairs and pick out your chamber for you, perhaps send Rose up to the tower to find you some clothes to wear...but all I have are gowns from the Medieval period, would that be acceptable to you?"

Morgana was staring around the palace as they walked up the stairs together. "Oh, I won't need clothes, Goddess...just some fabric. Could you get some fabric?"

"Fabric?" Love was impressed. "Morgana, you know how to make your own clothing?"

The woman smiled proudly. "Of course. Don't you remember those gowns I wore while we were both living on Earth? Those sort of fashions couldn't be bought in those days!"

"You made those glorious gowns with your own hands?" Love looked at her with wide eyes.

Morgana blushed, proud at the admiration in Love's voice.

"Morgana." Love was grinning brightly now. "I think we may have found a duty for you to perform, after all!"

After leaving Rose with specific instructions to get Morgana settled into her new room and to procure several yards of varying fabrics, Love paid a visit to the Underworld once more.

"Love!" Hades came from behind where she stood waiting in the receiving room, his arms outstretched for her to rush inside.

"Hades." Smiling, Love returned his hug with real warmth. "I just wanted to see that things are back to normal with you." She eyed him carefully.

The god of the Underworld, however, was looking better than ever. "Our ranks are swelled to overflowing, Merlyn is serving out a punishment for being swayed, and Loki has been banished from the Underworld for fifty Earth years." He winked. "In other words, things are pretty much the same as ever."

Love's laugh was musical as she squeezed his hand warmly. "I won't keep you busy for too long, then, but let me give you my sincere thanks for looking out for Cupid while I was on Earth realm."

Hades broke up into laughter. "That one! He spent the entire time looking terrified and sobbing. Once I got him out of his funk, however, he proved valuable enough." The Tender of the Dead winked at her. "Filled with the most scandalous stories about his Mistress, that one!"

Love blushed. She could only imagine the things Cupid had said about her.

"Don't worry." Hades winked. "Your secrets are safe with me."

Dite laughed and gave him another quick hug. "Well, just send me a message if you ever need anything, Hades, and thank you again."

"You, too, Love. I am always at your service." He bowed to her as she disappeared, back on her way to Love's Palace.

Rose and Cupid were scurrying around the inside of the palace, setting up the feasting table and pulling out decorations in such a frenzied manner, Dite could only suspect one thing. She took in the scene for a full five minutes before clearing her throat loudly, getting the attention of the two consorts. "Did someone invite some people over?"

"Mistress!" Both chimed at once and ran forward to greet her, Rose carrying a nosegay of roses in one hand and a silver candleholder in the other, and Cupid lugging an armful of pewter goblets.

"We've been waiting for you to arrive for a while now, Milady," Rose gushed. Of course, it took a while for even Immortals to travel to the Underworld and back again. Her face was bright with excitement. "Fire instructed us that we should get the palace ready."

"*Fire* instructed you?" Dite quirked at eyebrow at her two excitable friends. "And what, exactly, is Fire planning?"

"Oh, we don't know, Mistress." Cupid confirmed this with Rose by turning a grin at her, and she nodded happily. "Only that we should prepare for lots of feasting and enjoyment."

Love was quickly losing patience with all of it. "Well, Fire is not the one who runs Love's Palace—I am, and I have okayed no such event." Loftily, she gathered her skirts up in one hand and started up the stairs.

The younger two in the Main Hall looked after her with worry. "Mistress? Should we halt preparations?" Cupid's voice was trembling.

"Carry on until I say differently, and Cupid?" Love turned halfway. "Wait until *I* give you the instructions, okay?" She gave him a little wink on her way up to her chambers to take the bite out of her words.

Pausing to check on Morgana, Love made her way to her chambers. Her memories had started rushing back at a much faster pace now, and she was beginning to remember what it meant to be a Goddess.

Something the Mother had said in that last note had her mind working overtime, though. What was it She said? "Remember what I told you on the hill."

The Mother had told her that she should hold onto the fresh view she had of things. The fresh view…

"Hermes, Hermes, Hermes," she sang upon entering her chambers, already reaching to pull the pins out of her hair.

"Just the messenger." Hermes materialized in the center of the room. He looked around a moment, then glanced at Love somewhat warily. "Uh, afternoon, Aphrodite."

"Don't look so frightened, Hermes, or I'll send you off to the Underworld with a message for Hades," Love chirped, giving him a bright grin. "Can you go to Castle Flame for me today?"

"I'm on my way to TROM just now, but after that I need to head towards the Southern Region, anyway," he offered.

Love was already sitting near the window, writing out a quick message to Fire. She rolled up the note and kissed it. Love's kiss always worked as her personal seal—she was remembering things much faster now, and she knew she had to hurry.

"Please, deliver this in all haste, Hermes." She rushed back over to the curly-haired youth and thrust the scroll at him. "I don't have much time left before my Affliction is completely cured."

Hermes started to break out into a grin when he saw the expression on her face. "I thought that was a good thing."

"It is—but there's one thing I have to do first."

The messenger to the gods shrugged. "Whatever you say, Love." Hermes gave her a smart salute before vanishing.

Dite had to laugh at herself. Poor Hermes; she'd confused him so much recently.

But she had other things to worry about right now. Quickly, Love pulled out a gown from her wardrobe and started getting ready. Before it was too late, before the last vestiges of mortal thought were completely gone, there was one very important thing she had to do.

She had stripped off her old gown and was trying to arrange her hair, sitting in her shift and underclothes, when Hermes re-appeared in the bedroom.

"Message for Love—oh I'm sorry!" He quickly hid his face.

Love snorted. "I'm completely covered, Hermes, I just don't have my overgown on. Don't be so ridiculous and give me my message."

"Well, I'm glad to see your memories haven't all come back—I guess," Hermes mumbled, handing over the scroll. "Will you want to write a quick reply?"

Dite was tearing open the letter, sealed with a little gold flame, and nodded. "Most likely, Hermes, if you don't mind a moment's wait."

The messenger was leaning against one of her bed posters, looking harried and bored. "I just hope you two will be done exchanging sometime today."

"Oh, hush," she muttered, finally finished reading the letter. "Yes." She looked up at Hermes with a wide smile. "I don't have to write anything—will you remember what I'm about to tell you?"

He took on a wounded air. "I am, after all, the messenger to the gods."

"Yes, I'm sorry." She smiled to soothe his rumpled feelings, because everyone knew that Hermes was a sensitive sort. "Just tell Fire that I agree, and that I will be here waiting."

"Aye, aye, Love." He saluted and dematerialized again.

Wearing a grin, Love quickly turned back to dressing herself. Fire was on his way to discuss her plan. She just hoped he would hurry.

Dite was waiting in her rose garden when Fire finally made his appearance. She was nervously pacing back and forth, the pink silk of her gown coming dangerously close to rose thorns in the breeze she created, and muttering to herself when he walked down the path. "Finally!"

"My Love." Fire's eyes were light with amusement. "Why such the hurry?"

"Because, as I mentioned in my letter, we must speak before all my memories come back."

"You're already getting a bit melodramatic." Fire winked. "Now I know my Love is coming back."

Dite took a swat at him in mock rage. "I might just not tell you anything, you keep giving away 'compliments' like that!"

He laughed. "Oh, you know I'm only poking a little fun. Come, let's discuss this 'very important business' you mentioned." Moving with ease, Fire took her hand and steered her towards a small bench in the center of the rose garden.

Dite had thought about this dilemma since she first discovered it, and now she knew the solution came purely from her lingering mortal ideas and thoughts. Once her memories returned, she would either forget the solution completely, or brush it aside. The Mother's words in Her letter had triggered the idea, crazy though it was. But as one last favor to the Goddess in herself, the mortal part of her had to try and set one very big problem to rights.

"Fire." She gathered his hands in hers and met his eyes. "Isn't it true that the only reason Love and Passion—you and I—can't be together is that you are an Elemental and I am a First Creation."

"Yes, you know that, but—"

Love held up a hand to stop him. "Just listen to me." Her fingers were shaking, and she was sure she would never get it all out before the last remains of humanity within her mind were gone. Already she was receiving images and feelings and thoughts so fast she thought she might be sick or dizzy; she just couldn't tell by the churning in her abdomen which it was. "But there is nothing wrong with a First Creation and a First Creation seeing each other, is there?"

Fire's eyes narrowed. "No…"

Dite smiled. "Passion, why did you never use your First Aspects to create a First Child?"

Confused by the shift in conversation, Fire grimaced. "I don't know, Love, can we—"

"Answer me, it's important."

With a sigh, the Elemental shrugged. "I guess I had the notion that I would 'save' my First Aspects. For what, I don't know."

Love could feel the growing excitement, but now her mind was filling up so fast with information from the past eight thousand years that she didn't think she could talk fast enough. "Do you still have them?"

"What?"

"Your First Aspects. The weavings that you received from the Chaos realm—do you still have the First Aspects of the Elemental Fire?"

"I have Passion, Lust, Ambition and maybe some others—why do you ask?"

"I think you should weave your First Child, Fire."

Fire frowned at her. "But I have a First Son—sort of—in Mars, and also in Loki. You know that."

"But you did not weave Mars, the Fathergod did." Love was growing impatient.

"I weaved plenty of carnations, Love, and I don't understand where you're going with all this. Thor, Desire, Greed, they are all Lesser Creations, but the Lesser Creations are needed as much as the First."

He didn't understand. Love grasped his fingers tightly. "Passion," she whispered. "If you used your Aspects to make Passion your First Son...."

"...Then Love and Passion could always be together!" Fire cried. With a whoop, he pulled her to him in a tight embrace. Then the reality dawned and he pulled back. "But it wouldn't be me, Love. It would be an entire new Creation. And I would change, forever and ever, if I took out the First Aspects I have in me. I would become, probably, a lot like the other Elementals who used many of their First Aspects."

"I know." Love sighed. "But it is the only way I could think of, and I wanted to tell you before all my mortality fades and I start thinking too much like a Goddess."

He nodded, jaw tight as he stared straight ahead. "It is something I must think on, Love. I've grown accustomed, after all these thousands of years, to the way I am."

"I know." She squeezed his fingers and stood. "Now, I suppose I should get ready for the party I'm throwing."

He laughed and stood with her. "I know you're angry at me, but you never did have the 'return celebration' when you returned back to Immortality. Now that you are here, I think it's time for Immortality to know you're going to be okay and you're back to business now. Now that everything's been settled and taken care of."

"I know. Once I thought on it, I realized you were right. But," she gave him a wide smile, "I expect you to play the role of host for the celebration. After all, it was your idea."

"I would like nothing better." He threaded her arm through his own and they started back to Love's Palace. "I'll be returning to Castle Flame for a bit, but I will return before too many of the guests arrive. I promise," he vowed.

"You'd better." She winked. "Or else I'll be sure you have to seated 'below the salt,' as they say, instead of at the high table."

He laughed. "You wouldn't dare." Fire dropped a quick kiss on her cheek before he vanished, right outside one of the wide doors leading into the palace.

Dite continued inside and started making preparations for the guests that would arrive shortly. She was finally going to have her welcoming feast, and it was sure to be a trying experience. Most of the deities couldn't gather together without getting into debates and arguments, and Thor and Mars were sure to get into a heated argument about weapons and battles as they always did.

The Palace was turned into a festive place eventually, and soon the long feasting tables were set up and ready for all the deities and Elementals and consorts that would be gathering. Most of Immortality was sure to be in attendance, and Love's Palace would be swelled to the limit with partygoers.

The main bustle, however, was taking place in the kitchens. Love personally oversaw the dishes that were going to be served, and she couldn't help but think how ridiculous it was for them to always have food at such celebrations, when it was never necessary for Immortals to eat a thing.

Rose had placed roses and banners all around the Great Hall, while Cupid was placing fresh rushes across the floors. It was shaping up to be an exciting time, indeed, and Love was quick to get herself ready for the festivities.

Athena, as usual, was the first to arrive. She was quickly followed by the other three First Creations: Hades, Artemis, and War, who brought with him his consorts of Violence, Brutality, and Inhumanity. Artemis came in full companion with twelve Valkyries, and already the feasting was shaping up to be a troublesome affair.

Freya and Thor came together as usual, and Sorrow and Hate arrived one right after the other. Soon Compassion and Purity arrived, and Love had to quickly seat them as far away from War's consorts as possible.

Then it seemed as though the rest of TROM showed up all at once, and suddenly Love had her hands full with Fear, Crisis, Bounty, Harvest, Laughter, Rage, Pity, and countless others. Fate showed up, all three of her, with Hecate the Crone, and Love had never seen a gathering so large in Immortality before.

A very exhausted Hermes arrived, fresh from delivering the invitations all around Immortality, and he proudly bragged to one and all that he'd made sure to take the invitations to Love's Affair to even the farthest reaches of Immortality.

"We can't fit many more!" Dite replied, and twenty-two Immortals laughed. Hate grimaced, and Sorrow sobbed. She thought she saw Inhumanity trying to fight back a giggle, though.

Loki arrived just before the first Elemental, with the promise that he would be up to no mischief on this most special night for Love. Reluctantly, and because Air (along with eight of the Muses) was standing behind him, Love was forced to lower the drawbridge and let him inside the palace.

Water and Earth arrived next, and none of the Immortals could ever remember a time outside major crisis or the High Trib that all four Elementals were gathered in one place—though Fire had yet to arrive.

The party was in full swing now, and many were making pointed remarks about wanting food, but Love would not begin the feasting without Fire. She finally had to be away from the loud, boisterous bunch and waited outside on the drawbridge for him to arrive.

Inside, the deities and their consorts were having a rowdy time, and the noise spilled out from the castle into the front courtyard where Love waited. She couldn't help but to smile, though, for she knew that most of them loved nothing quite as much as goading each other into argument and debate. Strife, especially, was sure to be enjoying himself, for he thrived on such things. And judging from the loud clatters and banging she heard from inside, War and Thor had set up a small contest. Dite knew that they would first compete with one of Thor's Viking weapons, and Thor would probably win, before Mars challenged him to a duel with swords.

Love had seen them going at each other enough times that she was in no hurry to get back inside, and spent a few long moments enjoying the cool air.

"Why aren't you inside? I thought this was your party." The voice came from somewhere behind her, and Love spun around quickly to place it.

"Hello?" Dite squinted against the castle's lights. "Are you there?"

She saw the swish of an Elemental's long robes and laughed. "Father, is that you? Playing tricks on me again, are you?"

Finally the figure stepped out of the shadows near the castle. Definitely Elemental, she decided. The long robes, height, and stature gave that away immediately. "Air? Earth?"

He stepped closer, revealing short-cropped gray hair and a slight smile. His robes were long and red. Dite squinted. "Loki, you promised not to cause any mischief tonight."

"I'm not Loki." He stepped closer to her, and Dite let out an involuntary shriek.

"*Fire*? That can't be you."

He smiled slightly, and the wrinkles at the corners of his eyes and around his mouth deepened. "'Tis I."

"But what—" Dite reached up fleetingly to touch his cheek. Everything about him seemed different. "What happened?"

The Elemental smiled softly. "It was just my time to 'come of age,' dear, sweet Love." He kissed the back of her hand softly.

He was so different...so very, very different. Love felt a wrenching sensation deep in her heart and tried to keep the horror she felt from showing on her face. "But…"

"Do not worry, dearest. There is much we must discuss…but later." Again, he politely kissed the back of her hand. "If you will excuse me, I think I will join the others inside." With a swoosh of red, the Elemental pulled away from her.

Watching him walk away, she felt a hollow, empty feeling in the pit of her stomach. Fire was, for all intents and purposes, gone—at least as far as she was concerned. His eyes no longer seemed to smolder the same way, and he was no longer looking at her with that same restrained hunger. He wasn't the same being…not anymore.

Were I a mortal woman, she though to herself, my heart would surely break. Lost, Love sank down onto the warm grass and wished she could give in to the release of tears.

"Looks like you had the right idea; getting away from that mess in there." Yet another voice from behind.

"Thank you, but I came out here to be *alone*." She no longer cared to deal with strange voices in the middle of nowhere. Love had enough surprises to last her, thank you very much, and that was the way she felt about it—be damned *whoever* was talking to her from the thin air.

A male chuckle greeting her snapped reply, and the stranger seated himself on the grass next to her. Love wouldn't grant him the pleasure of glancing next to her. "Well, I was going to go inside, but I heard you were out here."

She snorted. "I am in no mood to chat with consorts right now, thank you. The feasting will begin shortly, so you had better find your place before the lower table gets filled up." Love finally glanced over her shoulder at him. "Your weavings must be off; your age isn't right for a consort."

"I'm no one's *consort*," he spat, dark eyes gleaming in the shadows. He stood up, angrily. Love noticed his powerful build, which was also all wrong for a consort. Most consorts were smaller in stature, and appeared as young men or woman. This being was closer to the age-appearance of Love, and he was too dark and brooding-looking, she thought, to be a proper consort. "And I had heard you were a sweet, beautiful creature—but you're a mean, waspy little snob."

Love, too, jumped to her feet to stand toe to toe with him. Though she only reached his chest, she was fighting mad enough not to care who or what he was. "What I don't need is one of Loki's minions toying with me when I'm having a difficult enough time." She snapped, "And furthermore—"

"Loki's minion!" He exploded, running an aggravated hand through his dark locks. "How dare you accuse me of such!"

"I've never seen you before! And I know *everyone* in Immortality. So you must have only just been weaved."

His dark eyes narrowed with anger. "I guess you think you're clever for knowing that, but it doesn't mean that I was weaved by Loki! He's not even capable of weaving a being like me."

Love wanted to smirk, for who was this new fledging to be giving himself airs already? "And what sort of being are you?"

"Interested now?" he snapped, teeth gleaming against the darkness when he smirked at her. "I'll just bet you are." He turned to walk away.

But Love was heartbroken and ready to pick a fight with anything that was nearby. "I'm afraid you haven't been invited to my feast!"

The figure stopped walking and turned, very, very slowly. He looked at her over his shoulder, dark brows furrowed. "That is where you are wrong, for I have been invited."

She laughed. "No sir, *you* are wrong. This is my feast, and I know I did not invite you."

He smiled with victory at her. "I wasn't invited by you—I was invited by your co-host, Fire."

"*Fire*? Are you his consort, then?" In spite of herself, Love wanted to know who the stranger was.

He'd turned again, and was walking back towards the palace. "No." He looked over his shoulder at her long enough to give her a slight grin. "His son."

His *son*. For all the effect those two words had on her, Love could have fallen straight back onto the grass. His *son*. He'd done it. Mother save us, she thought, Fire had done it. Now she knew why Fire looked so different. He'd accepted her crazy, mortal plan.

"Passion?" she whispered after him, her voice squeaking.

The figure stopped again, though Love was sure he could not have heard her soft whisper from across the distance between them.

"Do you have his memories? Do you—" But she could think of nothing to say or ask him. Though she nearly bubbled over with curiosity, it was impossible for her to find words. I should have been a Muse, she decided, angry at her own clumsy tongue, at least then I would have eloquence in such situations. Love quickly picked up her skirts and jogged after him. "Please, forgive me for my rude behaviour, but I was upset about Fi—your Father."

He finally turned to face her, crossing his arms across his chest. His eyes were still dark with anger. "I have the memories of Passion," he replied shortly. "It is a very strange thing. They are sporadic, and confusing. I remember…" He shook his head, quickly breaking off.

Love stepped closer, looking at him more carefully. He did look like Fire had once looked, but there were a few marked differences. "What other weavings do you have?" Did he have Water's weavings? In mortal terms, it would make them "related," though such things were largely dismissed in Immortality. There were no true family relationships here.

"I have some anger, because Passion must have such. I have intelligence and knowledge from Air, and a little creativity, too. A little emotion, some compassion, from your father."

"So they all know."

He nodded, then his lips quirked upwards into a small smirk. "It was supposed to be a surprise for you."

She looked up at him and felt lightheaded. How long had she and Fire dreamed of being together? But this wasn't Fire—this was his son. All the passion she had loved in Fire now stood before her, a carnation in his own right. Yet it wasn't the same. "You are not as much like him as I would have expected."

He rose an eyebrow. "What was the first thing you said to him at your first meeting?"

Though that meeting had occurred thousands and thousands of years ago, Love could still remember. She cleared her throat primly. "'It's a pleasure to meet you.'"

"Exactly. And what did you say to me now?"

Sheepishly, she looked down. "I know that I was rude, but you must understand that I loved Fire for thousands of years." She looked up at him pleadingly. "And to see him…in the state he is now. I know you don't understand, because—"

He held up a hand. "But I do understand; I am a part of him. Passion was always the strongest part of him."

"But you are only a small part of his passion, just as I am only a small part of Water's emotion."

"No." The First Son shook his dark head back and forth. "Fire used all his passion to create me. He gave me the memories of Passion and the…feelings." He frowned. "Looking at you now, I, too, can remember that first meeting. You were always the one who brought out the passion in Fire." He laughed.

"Only now, you have truly brought it out—for good."

Love hung her head. "I was not myself when I made the request, you must understand. I never meant for him to change so dramatically."

Passion tilted her chin back up and held it firmly, looking down into her eyes. "I am glad you made the request, and so is he. He is truly like the other Elementals now, and there is something special that happens to them once their First Aspects have been woven away. Without me as a part of him, he can control himself and his element better. It was time for him to have a First Child, my Love, so do not hang your head and feel sorry. Please, don't ever be sorry for this, for it cannot be undone."

She gazed back into his eyes wordlessly for several heartbeats, then nodded slowly. "You are right, I know. I just do not want to cause him—or you—pain of any kind."

He smiled softly, and Dite noticed that he had a nice smile when it wasn't bitter or mocking. "I know. You would do anything to keep from hurting another being." He stood back and offered her his arm. "Would you like to go to the party with me?"

Love beamed up at Passion and slipped her arm through his. "I would like nothing more."

And together, the two First Creations Love and Passion walked inside to join the rest of the party. Nothing would ever be quite the same again in Immortality.

The end of this tale

Printed in the United States
1011200004B